NECESSARY
RISK

John F. Baugh

NECESSARY
RISK

A Novel By
JOHN F. BAYER

BROADMAN
&HOLMAN
PUBLISHERS

Nashville, Tennessee

0-8054-4016-X

Published by Broadman & Holman Publishers, Nashville, Tennessee
Page Design: Anderson Thomas Design, Inc.
Typesetting: PerfecType, Nashville, Tennessee
Acquisitions Editor: Vicki Crumpton

Dewey Decimal Classification: 813.54
Subject Heading: FICTION
Library of Congress Card Catalog Number: 97-43159

Unless otherwise stated all Scripture citation is from the New International
Version, copyright © 1973, 1978, 1984 by International Bible Society.
Also used, KJV, the King James Version.

Library of Congress Cataloging-in-Publication Data
Bayer, John F., 1947–
Necessary risk
    p.   cm.
ISBN 0-8054-4016-X (pb)
I. Title. II.
PS3552.A85869N43   1998
813'.54—dc21

97-43159
CIP

1 2 3 4 5 02 01 00 99 98

DEDICATION

To my wife, Brenda, for being there and never doubting.
For her encouragement, patience, and love.
For waiting while I wrote one more word, one more sentence,
one more paragraph. Thank you. I love you.

ACKNOWLEDGMENTS

Thanks to Vicki Crumpton, who, albeit unknowingly, started me on this particular dream and helped see it through to the end.

Thanks to Sara Fortenberry, who dared to do what I did not want to do, would not have done, and did it successfully.

PROLOGUE

The leather fibers separated, slowly at first.

"More to the right, Billy," Jimmy Michaels said into the mouthpiece of the voice-activated, two-way radio that hung around his neck.

Billy Tippet disengaged the safety brake on the support dolly and relocated it along the rim of the 290-foot tower. He cautiously peered over the concrete rim to see that Jimmy Michaels had not started to pendulum with the move; then he instinctively moved away from the edge. Heights didn't bother some people, but Billy Tippett was not one of them. He kicked himself once again for taking the spotter's job.

"Right there," Jimmy radioed.

Billy set the brake on the support dolly and shook his head. The only thing standing between Jimmy and a gruesome death below were the safety dolly, the ropes attached to the dolly and to Jimmy, and the leather safety harness strapped around him.

Jimmy's rubber-soled climbing shoes bit into the concrete of the reactor cooling tower as he moved gazelle-like over the curved surface. He was one-third of the way down the tower's face, inspecting the concrete for anomalies. And there were plenty to be found.

It's wrong, he thought. It was no longer just a suspicion. Something was not right with the huge twin cooling towers. But that was why he was here, he reminded himself.

The strain tortured the weakened leather. The fibers first held, then stretched, and finally began to part.

"How much longer?" Billy radioed to Jimmy. It was nearly quitting time, and Billy could almost taste the beer he'd stashed in the trunk of his car.

"Not too much longer," Jimmy answered. "Maybe ten minutes." He moved along the tower face with the ease of the experienced rock climber he was.

"How 'bout a beer when we finish?" Billy radioed.

"You know the answer to that," Jimmy responded, as he marked and recorded another worrisome defect in the concrete surface.

"Yeah, I know. But I keep thinking you'll come to your senses one day. Besides, didn't you tell me drinking was legal with that religion of yours?"

Jimmy chuckled to himself. Billy never gave up. He wondered what the young spotter would say if he told him his real occupation. He knew Billy thought he was crazy. Crazy for working hundreds of feet above the ground and crazy because of his deeply-held religious beliefs. It was a tossup as to which Billy considered more insane.

"Everything is permissible . . . ," Jimmy quoted as he examined the concrete, "but it would be a poor testimony."

"Yeah," Billy answered. "You told me. It wouldn't look good. It would uh . . ."

". . . compromise my witness," Jimmy finished. Jimmy ceased his inspection for a moment and shook his head. For a moment things had gone fuzzy. He was slightly disoriented. *The flu,* he thought. For that split second he'd been dizzy, and now he was trying to remember the last grid he'd inspected. He checked the grid chart attached to the kneeboard strapped to his right thigh. It had been a long day. He shook his head once again. Hour after hour of being suspended from a rope two hundred feet above the ground could weary anyone, even someone as physically fit as Jimmy. Normally he had no trouble remembering which of the marked grids he'd finished with, but today he was having trouble recalling even the simplest thing.

"That's it, *witness.* Like on 'Perry Mason.' That's the part I don't understand," Billy radioed back.

"Not exactly like 'Perry Mason,' but I'll explain it to you after work."

"Over a beer?" Billy asked hopefully.

"Over a cup of coffee," Jimmy answered, feeling worse as time progressed. "I'm going to need something to wake me up."

The leather fibers continued to fray. Each separation insured that more fibers would fail because of the additional strain placed on them. There was no sound, no forewarning, only the unrelenting march toward total disintegration.

Jimmy Michaels glanced at the ground below. It shimmered in the distance much like a faraway object in desert heat. He had climbed higher rock outcroppings near his home here in north-central Arkansas, so it wasn't the height that was bothering him. He fondly thought about the upcoming trip with his sons to the tall bluffs towering over a portion of the Red River. He hoped he was up to it. *Has to be the flu,* he reasoned once again. It was going around the community and had taken a considerable toll on the student body of the local high school. He would have to remember to take some aspirin when he got home. Maybe he could head it off. It would be the boys' first rock climb on the three-hundred-foot bluffs.

It was almost over. The weakened strands would fail in seconds.

Jimmy's first reaction was disbelief. It felt like one of the rides he had taken with his sons three months earlier during their trip to Walt Disney World. One moment he was tethered to the funnel-shaped tower by rope and harness; the next he was free-falling through space. His arms flailed, involuntarily seeking a handhold that did not exist. His body struck the flared base of the cooling tower at 120 feet and began cartwheeling, a free-falling object out of control.

Jimmy Michaels did not scream—he knew it was useless as he tumbled through space. His last thoughts were of his wife and two boys, and he said a prayer for their safekeeping just before he slammed into the hard-packed earth.

The leather harness, free of its burden, dangled at the end of the rope. To the men below who had witnessed the terrifying incident, it looked like a giant clock pendulum suddenly stilled.

CHAPTER ONE

1

David Michaels wondered if he possessed a hidden streak of masochism or if he was just crazy. At forty-seven, he was proving to himself that he was too old to be playing war games with the youthful members of a Marine Force Recon company. He lay on his stomach and rolled his 6'2", 200-pound-plus frame to the right, trying in vain to get comfortable. The Panamanian heat was stifling. But the insects, snakes, and the OPFOR, the Opposing Force, which had his Force Recon company pinned down in the miserable, stinking swamp of Fort Sherman, were infinitely worse.

Commander David Michaels's marine company had come to the Jungle Operations Training Center (JOTC) for training in jungle survival. Panama's Fort Sherman, home to the JOTC, provided everything needed to instill survival skills into the thousands of soldiers it processed each year. At this point, however, David Michaels had discovered that survival carried a much different connotation than he had previously ascribed to it.

David peered over the prickly saw grass, searching for Captain Frederick Merrill, C Company's CO. The Panamanian sun was beating down with unabated ferocity; sweat rolled down David's face at the slightest movement. His Kevlar helmet, a state-of-the-art head protection resembling the old German WWII helmets, trapped and focused the heat with amazing precision. The eighty-pound packs worn by the men of C Company added to David's discomfort. David knew the OPFOR was wearing identical gear, but the men of this Opposing Force, the Jungle Operations Training Battalion (JOTB) wore the battle gear every day. The OPFOR based on Fort Sherman lived with the heat, insects, and snakes daily—proof that the human body could adapt to almost any condition. But C Company was a Force Recon company from Camp Pendleton, California, and as hot as it got in Southern California, it could never compare to the misery meted out by the jungles of the Republic of Panama.

Michaels surveyed the immediate area. The men of C Company were spread out on the edge of a swamp, a dense tree line to their left and a sparser one in the distance to the right. David knew the Caribbean waters lapped at the shore less than a mile from where he lay hidden by the thick, tropical foliage. C Company had been caught in the open swamp by the OPFOR when Merrill had miscalculated the speed with which the men from Fort Sherman could negotiate the spongy terrain. Now every man under Merrill's command lay facedown in the muck of decaying foliage and rank swamp water, surrounded on three sides by the OPFOR. It was their third day in the swamps, and David was certain that being captured by the "enemy" was preferable to swilling the bacteria-infested waters of the putrid swamp.

Michaels twisted his head to pick up Merrill's hand signals. A young marine lance corporal lay next to him, his sweat-streaked face reflecting the fatigue of three days with no sleep. His face was covered with the beginning of a blond stubble. David knew the young man, if not for Marine Corps regulations, would shave only every other day. But this was the Corps, so he shaved every day when he was not face-down in swamp water.

Captain Merrill was holding his hand up, directing his two M-60 machine gun crews. The remainder of the company was up and moving, with M-16s at the ready. At Merrill's signal C Company moved rapidly toward the thinner distant tree line to the right. Almost immediately, indicators on the Military Identification Laser Engagement System (MILES) activated as "enemy" snipers selectively recorded hits on the marine company. The marines frantically searched the tree line for the "enemy." Unable to locate the aggressors, the remainder of C Company began running for the far side of the swamp. The MILES continued to record hits on the fleeing marines. The men whose gear indicated they had been shot stopped in their tracks and squatted in the swamp, removed from action by the rules of engagement.

The swamp changed from shallow muck and mud to putrid water and sludge that sucked at the marines' boots like some living animal intent on devouring them. The water was deeper, almost to the men's waists. Half of C Company lay in the shallow swamp, their MILES recording hits. Most were "dead." The remainder of the company slogged through the waist-deep sludge, their goal the far shore and relative safety of the thin tree line. Both of C Company's M-60 gun crews were still in the swamp, the gunners and assistant gunners victims of OPFOR weapons.

David Michaels moved through the water, the effort draining. He was still alive, although he could not figure out why. The OPFOR had been in the tree line to their left and had taken out half the company. The "dead" would be transported to the Fort Sherman barracks. As he fought the fatigue and mud, he almost cursed himself for not letting himself be "shot." But, he reminded himself, curses were not what soldiers expected from their chaplain. It was perfectly acceptable for the men to express themselves in gutter vernacular, but not for the man who wore the three gold stripes of a navy commander and the cross of God.

"How much longer you figure, Commander?" the young, stubble-faced lance corporal asked.

"Don't know, Corporal," David wheezed, struggling for breath. "Captain Merrill's still up front, though. We might make it yet."

The corporal stumbled, and David grabbed for him, preventing him from going under the slimy water. "We was set up, Commander. You know that, don't ya?"

David nodded his head in reply. It was all he could manage. The swamp mud was taking its toll; his remaining strength dwindled rapidly. The rest of C Company—more than forty men—were strung out in a ragged double line abreast, advancing on the far tree line. Most were content to deal with the swamp one foot at a time, their heads hanging on their chests, their eyes fixed and glazed, staring at the green and brown gook that floated on the water's surface.

Michaels looked up in time to catch a frantic signal from the company commander, but it was too late. MILES gear once again began popping all around him, and finally David's gear signaled a hit. The marines stared into muzzles protruding from what they had thought would be their sanctuary. C Company of the Force Recon Marines had just been wiped out in the swamps of the Jungle Operation Training Center, Republic of Panama. To the credit of C Company, it had taken the OPFOR three days to do it. Most newcomers to JOTC lasted less than a day in this first exercise. But David Michaels knew that little piece of information would not placate the C Company CO.

As Commander David Michaels surrendered to the exhaustion of the previous three sleepless nights, he promised himself that he would never volunteer for Marine Corps duty again. His mind was willing, but his middle-aged body, despite its appearance of an Olympic athlete, had long since yielded to the ravages of time. He was too old and finally ready to admit it.

The remains of C Company and the OPFOR were loading onto waiting humvees, the army's replacement vehicle for the venerable Jeep. David struggled from the swamp, thinking of another jungle thousands of miles away and a million years ago.

He wore one gold bar back then. As a new marine second lieutenant, he had been proud of everything the bars and the simple code of the Corps, *Semper Fidelis* (forever faithful), stood for. He had to contend with swamps and snakes and insects, but he had been younger and dedicated. Most importantly, he had possessed the one thing a soldier needed above all else—a sense of purpose.

David had not been a chaplain then; he had been a marine. After the Naval Academy and training in the rugged desert of Camp Pendleton, he had been assigned to the Fleet Marine Force (FMF) as a communications officer. The FMF had been the place to be and David had been elated. His elation lasted as long as it took for two of his fellow officers, platoon leaders both, to get themselves blown away in the jungles of South Vietnam. Rumor was that one had been killed by his own men, "fragged," after an ill-fated attack on a superior force. David had been assigned a platoon and had gone into the jungles in another part of the world; he came out knowing he would never look at life the same way again. He had seen things no man should see, things that had made him retch long after his stomach had emptied. He had listened to the dying sounds of men, women, and children and crawled and cried and screamed through firefights in the mud and dark and torrential rains. After seeing marines too young to vote die from bombs strapped to children they never saw, David Michaels had come away from Vietnam with questions that had no answers—at least not on this earth.

It was at this point in his life that Second Lieutenant David Michaels found God. It had not been in the form of a blinding revelation but an understanding nestled deep in his soul that told him there was an answer, a reason, a purpose. That madness, as it existed at his level, was a product of man, and there had to exist One who knew the answer. It was an answer not to be found within the constraints of time and earth. It was an answer that sounded ridiculously simple on the surface: the answer was Jesus Christ, and David Michaels embraced that answer as he had accepted being a marine, with the fierce confidence of a man who knew he had found the truth. He left the Corps after six years, graduated from seminary, applied for a commission in the United States Navy Chaplain Corps, and started again, this time on the right side.

His work was difficult at times—tough to accept the workings of the military in religious matters. David accepted his fellow chaplains who were of different Protestant faiths, but he stumbled when he encountered his first Muslim chaplain. It seemed that everything he was fighting for was being undermined by the very organization he worked for. He finally recognized that the chaplain corps needed conservative Protestants like him. When he realized that there was as much work to do within the chaplain ranks as without, he was convinced that this was where he belonged. He had found a home.

David stepped into the humvee. "Chow time," he said to the blond corporal.

"I just want to die," the corporal answered, fatigue etched on his youthful features. "I'm going to sleep for twenty-four hours."

"Think about what you just said," David said. "Is it really time to die?"

The young corporal's blue eyes met the chaplain's. He shook his head, then pulled the Kevlar helmet down and went to sleep. His last thought before he dozed off was that all preachers were crazy and chaplains were crazier than most.

David grinned through the mask of dried mud and sweat. The sun was setting, but it was still hot. He could not remember being in a place that was always so hot. Even the Saudi desert cooled off when the sun set. Recently he had heard one chaplain say that if hell existed on earth, Panama must be it. David agreed.

The sun was just disappearing when the humvees rolled into the barracks area of Fort Sherman. The men "killed" earlier were milling around, waiting for their company commander and the rest of C Company. The vehicles pulled to a stop and the weary marines crawled out. David noticed a marked lack of the enthusiasm that normally accompanied the Force Recon unit members. They had been embarrassed by ordinary soldiers—army soldiers—and they did not like it.

David forced his body out of the humvee, thankful that the ride had not been in the rear of a five-ton truck.

"See you Sunday, Commander," one of the marines called as he walked by.

"Sunday," David replied, unable to say more. He moved toward the officers' quarters, shuffling rather than walking. All he wanted was a hot shower and the bed he knew was waiting for him. He had not noticed the uniformed officer waiting at the muster area. As the man approached, David felt his blood run cold. He could just make out the cross that adorned the collar of the uniform. A chaplain. David knew something was wrong. David's thoughts wandered home to Arkansas and his father. *This man is here to tell me my father is dead,* David thought.

The smaller man held out his hand. "Commander Michaels?" he asked, knowing he had the right man.

"David," David replied, shaking the offered hand.

"Sam Bishop," the chaplain said. He wore the markings of an army infantry battalion and the lighter oak leaf of a major. "I've got some bad news for you."

David felt his heart thumping in his chest. He had always wondered what he would do, how he would react when his time came to deal with the death of a close family member. His mother had died when he was too young to know what it meant, and his father and brother were his family. Now he knew he would have to rely on the same source of strength he continually told others about—the strength of his Savior.

"Dad?" David whispered.

Major Sam Bishop saw the resignation in David's eyes. "No. Your brother, Jimmy. He was killed yesterday."

David Michaels felt the pounding in his chest accelerate to fever pitch. His breath was short, and an invisible jackhammer was going wild in his head. He had steeled himself for the possibility of his father's death—someday. But he had never considered that Jimmy would die before him.

Sam Bishop saw David Michaels's face go white beneath the grime and sweat. He grabbed the navy commander just as he was about to hit the ground and gently lowered him the rest of the way. He yelled at the men still congregated around the humvees. "You guys got a corpsman?"

A navy second-class hospital corpsman reacted at once, running to the side of the fallen chaplain. "Let him down gently," he ordered. "Put his Kevlar under his feet and hold on to 'em." His manner was matter-of-fact, and the army major obeyed the enlisted man without hesitation. "He's in shock," the corpsman diagnosed immediately. "What'd you tell him?!"

"That his brother died yesterday," Sam Bishop said, looking away from David's face.

"Great," the corpsman replied sarcastically.

David opened his eyes, embarrassed at the attention he was receiving and doubly embarrassed because it was necessary. "I'm fine," he mumbled, shaking his head side-to-side. "Sort of took me by surprise."

The corpsman was still holding David's right wrist, monitoring his pulse rate that had now returned to normal range. "Yeah," he responded, glancing at Sam Bishop. "I can see where three days with no sleep, no food, and an out-of-the-blue announcement like that would surprise a person." Sam Bishop could not miss the stinging rebuke in the corpsman's voice, but no one challenged a corpsman assigned to an FMF unit in front of the unit's members, not even an army major.

David rose to his feet slowly, the corpsman assisting him. "I'll get my things together," he said, starting for the barracks.

Sam Bishop was beside him. "You'll have to take a commercial flight. Nothing's leaving Howard today," the major said, referring to the U.S. Air Force's only remaining active air base in Panama. "I booked you on Continental to Houston and into Little Rock. That okay?"

"Sounds fine. Thanks."

"There's a car waiting to take you to Tocumen," Bishop added, using the name of the international airport twenty miles west of Panama City. "Plane leaves in about three hours. You'll just make it."

"Thanks, Major . . ."

"Sam."

David nodded. ". . . Sam, for everything."

Major Sam Bishop stopped as David walked on. *It's never easy,* he thought. And with a brother chaplain, it was even harder. He made a mental note to pray for David Michaels during evening prayers.

2

The setting sun glinted off the smoked windows of the Collins Construction International Building in downtown Little Rock, Arkansas. The building was an icon to Arkansas business and firm evidence that the small southern state was making its bid for a share of the northeast industrial exodus. Collins had begun in New Jersey, just across the river from New York, and had moved its corporate head-quarters to the warmer, friendlier South. The fact that Arkansas was cheaper than New Jersey, union-resistant, and government-subsidized had been added incentives offered by the former governor, who was now president of the United States.

Wayne Young, head of security at the international construction firm, stomped across the carpeted floor. "You've got the harness?"

"And the ropes. Settle down Wayne. It's taken care of."

"What about the reports? Emerson asked about those first thing."

Harmon Douglas watched the security head pace to the office win-dow, his hands clasped behind his back, his large, bald head wagging in consternation.

"And the reports. They're in my safe. And someone has already talked to Michaels's safety man, Billy Tippett. He doesn't know a thing. All he was doing was spotting for Michaels. He never saw the harness up close. He doesn't suspect a thing."

"Autopsy?"

"No chance. All Clayton County has is an undertaker acting as coro-ner. An autopsy would have to be done in Little Rock and only if there is a question as to the cause of death. In this case, there is no doubt."

No doubt, Young was reminded, if you don't count the sedative Jimmy Michaels ingested with his coffee earlier that morning. Not much, just enough to produce mild disorientation and induce forget-fulness. Just enough to make him ignore the change in safety har-nesses. It had worked. Only he and one other person knew about that, and he would take steps to see it remained that way.

Wayne Young turned to face Douglas. Harmon Douglas was a bril-liant man when it came to numbers, but he was out of his league in this matter, and Young knew it. He would listen to what the comptrol-ler had to say and then follow up himself. It was up to him to cover his own tracks, and he knew it. Should outside sources get wind of what went on at Collins Construction International, he, Wayne Young, would be covered. That was his bottom line.

"Let's get Graham in here. We need to coordinate this thing. I want it out of the way by the end of this week."

"That's pretty fast. What about the family?"

Young retrieved a folder from the top of his desk and opened it as the sun slipped beneath the horizon just over the westerly bend of the Arkansas River. He read the contents of the folder and looked up at Douglas. "Father alive . . . mother dead . . . one brother in the navy. He has a wife and two sons, both still in high school. Father's a retired pulpwood lumberman, and the brother is a navy chaplain." Young shut the folder and tossed it on the desk. "I don't foresee any problems with them." He then pushed a button on his intercom. "Maggie, get Mr. Graham for me, please."

Carlton Graham entered the office from a side door. As usual, he brought an immediate feeling of unrest with him. His dark charcoal suit and freshly laundered white shirt with a lively silk tie did nothing to disguise the barely controlled rage that lurked just below his urbane appearance. He was a bitter man, and his bitterness tainted everything around him, like a malignant cancer that could not be halted. "Good evening, gentlemen," Graham said.

"Sit down, Carlton," Young ordered. "We've got some things to go over."

"That we do," he agreed. "That we do."

Young cleared his throat. "Harmon tells me we have the reports, the rope, and the safety harness. What I need from you is a report that states the following: Jimmy Michaels died from his own negligence; Jimmy Michaels was ultimately responsible to check the condition of the equipment he was using; and the liability, as far as OSHA is concerned, lies with Jimmy Michaels."

Carlton Graham smiled—he was in his element. "In other words, you want me to say Jimmy Michaels killed himself because of stupidity."

Young grimaced. "I want you to do what you get paid to do," Young ordered, exasperated with the man already. "I want it in writing, and I want it today. Is that clear?"

Graham's smile broadened. He glanced at Harmon Douglas out of the corner of his eye. The company comptroller was fidgeting in his seat. *Don't have the stomach for this, huh Harmon?* he thought. He turned his attention to Wayne Young. "I already have the report written. It states that the safety harness had been inspected within the required length of time, that it was found satisfactory, that the trolley and ropes were within safety limits, and that the death of Jimmy Michaels must rest with the man himself. It also states that OSHA finds CCI free of any liability under the circumstances and that CCI does not owe the Michaels family any compensation for the 'misfortune,' shall we say?"

The security man relaxed. It sounded as if Graham was holding up his end of the bargain. "Get me the report today. Mr. Collins wants to see it. Also, when is the hearing to be held?"

Carlton Graham hesitated for a moment. "Tomorrow, during the funeral."

"But . . ." Harmon Douglas began.

Young waved a hand, silencing the comptroller. "I like that. There won't be any problem with the family attending."

"You know the family of the victim is not allowed in OSHA hearings of this nature. We're there to determine the nature of the death as it relates to worker's safety and nothing else."

"I know all that, but that doesn't stop some families from wanting to attend. And in this case, with the culpability questionable, it could become sticky should family members show up. Yes, I think tomorrow will be excellent. I'll inform Mr. Collins that the matter is well in hand."

The sun had finally set over the river as Young turned to look out his twentieth-story office window. Down the corridor, in the executive suites, he would be able to tell Mr. Emerson Collins that he had personally taken care of the situation and that no further interference in the North Arkansas Nuclear Generating Station construction project would be forthcoming. "You men may go," he said with his back to Graham and Douglas.

Both men rose to leave, the comptroller with a worried look on his face, the OSHA inspector with a small grin.

3

Jean Michaels knelt beside her bed. She could not recall how many times she had been on her knees since she received the news that Jimmy had been killed. Prayer, it seemed, was the only comfort she could find. Both boys seemed to be taking the tragedy as well as could be expected. Both were in high school, and they knew the dangers inherent in their father's occupation. They were athletic and had taken to rock climbing with their father. Terry, the youngest, was the muscular one. Thomas, the older, was the slim, intellectual one. Both worked out in their home gym, and they were stronger than anyone would have suspected. Apparently, they were also stronger mentally and spiritually than Jean had given either boy credit for.

She said a short prayer, feeling guilty that she could not come up with new words to express her anger and frustrations. Then she rose and walked into Jimmy's study. His desk was littered with report forms and notes. She absently rummaged through the mess, her thoughts shifting imperceptibly to something Jimmy had said a few nights earlier. Her rummaging took on a more concentrated, systematic search at the recollection of his remarks. She stacked and sorted the papers, matching sizes and forms. When she had them sorted, she began with the first stack. She had been at it almost an hour and was getting discouraged when she found it! *Here it is! This is what Jimmy had been talking about.* She folded the papers and wondered where to store them. She knew of only one place—her personal safe-deposit box at the bank. She grabbed her keys and headed for the car, feeling slightly foolish that she was playing spy only one day after her husband had died. But she continued, remembering Jimmy's words through the pain and grief: "Jeanie, something is strange on this one. I don't know what it is for sure, but it's something."

To Jean Michaels, the confirmation that something was indeed strange was bolstered by the papers she was carrying—papers she must safeguard at any cost.

CHAPTER TWO

1

The McDonnell-Douglas Super 80 intercepted the outer marker of Little Rock's instrument landing system as it began its final approach into the capital city's Adams Field.

Sunrise touched the eastern sky as David Michaels gazed out his window. The flight from Panama had begun almost twelve hours earlier; it had been a sleepless night for David. He unconsciously ran his hand over his short-cropped gray hair and checked the date on his watch. His brother's funeral was today at two o'clock. His thoughts drifted to Jimmy and the good times they'd had growing up in the mountains of central Arkansas. He smiled at the memories. Neither he nor Jimmy had been saints. Each had had his share of problems, but they had been minor skirmishes compared to the things kids faced today. Cigarettes and beer did not have the same impact as marijuana, crack cocaine, or heroin. Fights, mediated by parents or teachers, not police, had been a matter of fists, not guns.

David felt the plane slow as the nose pitched up just before the wheels touched the concrete runway. He could see the terminal through his window. Even the old Adams Field terminal had been sacrificed in the name of progress; the new one was more fitting the world of modern air travel.

David pulled a worn, tattered New Testament from his coat pocket. He had used the same testament many times, always to console others in their grief. Now *he* needed the words it contained. He thumbed to the back of the thin testament and found the book of Psalms, its worn pages falling open to chapter forty-two. He was lost in the Scripture when the plane stopped at the gate.

The empty feeling persisted. He had always been the one offering comfort, and he could never understand why the people he comforted did not accept the word of God and be done with it. Now he knew the answer. Grief was not something that magically disappeared with the reading of words. His only consolation was the fact he knew Jimmy was a Christian and was in heaven. But even that knowledge did not mitigate the feeling in his gut, nor the guilt he felt stemming from what he recognized as lack of faith.

He retrieved his carry-on bag and followed the other passengers from the plane. James Michaels was waiting behind the restraining barriers as David passed through the gate. He could see his father's red eyes and defeated posture, and he instantly felt empathy for the older man. The old man had retreated into his shabby clothing.

"Dad," David said, as he took his father in his arms.

James was uncomfortable with the open display of affection but finally wrapped his arms around his older son. It was then that the tears came, staining their clothing, as father and son stood among the other passengers.

The morning was bright as David and his father walked from the terminal building. Morning rush hour was just beginning, and the highways around the city would soon be clogged with commuter traffic. David threw the one suitcase he had retrieved from the baggage carousel into the bed of the pickup truck and placed his carry-on in the cab as his father slid behind the steering wheel.

The two men had not spoken as they left the terminal, and David was not sure how to begin. "How did it happen, Dad?" he asked, surprised at his own directness.

James Michaels maneuvered the truck from the parking area. "He was inspecting the surface of that new cooling tower on the nuclear generating job in Clayton. They told us the leather harness he was wearing broke," James told David, his voice almost cracking in the process.

"But . . . ?" David continued the implied thought of his father.

"But I ain't so sure. You know how careful your brother is . . . was. He would always check and recheck his equipment—even when it was his and he *knew* it was in perfect shape. There's just somethin' that don't add up."

David nodded. His father was right about Jimmy. His brother had been climbing the rocks in Arkansas since he was in junior high. He had always been meticulous about his climbing equipment. "How are Jean and the boys?" David asked.

"Seem to be doin' as well as could be expected. Boys seem to be doin' a little better'n Jean."

"Yeah," David agreed, "they're just like Jimmy."

"Funeral's at two," James Michaels interjected.

David checked his watch. They would be in Clayton by eleven. The northern Arkansas town was due north of Little Rock, set back from Highway 65 a couple of miles. Though Clayton was only a few miles from the highway, it might as well have been a million. Clayton existed in a time warp, a throwback to the past. The pressures affecting "outside" towns, as they were known to Claytonites, were slow in coming to the small mountain burg. Drugs had never been a problem. Marijuana growers, relishing the supposed remoteness of the Ozark Mountains, came and went, usually to the Arkansas prison farm. Politics was more a matter of theoretical discussion than a practiced art form, and the politically vogue issue of health care was rendered moot by the town's two resident doctors, each of whom had been in Clayton for more than twenty years. Fees in eggs, chickens, and potatoes were still accepted. It had been a good place to grow up, David reminisced.

They were heading into North Little Rock, the capital city's twin sister across the Arkansas River. The traffic had thinned on the outskirts, and in minutes they were traveling along Interstate 40, heading west.

"All the arrangements made for the funeral?" David asked his father.

"Reverend Shackleford is doing it," James answered, not taking his eyes off the road. "He's Jimmy's pastor at First Community. Good man. Godly man. Says to tell you that you can do part of the service if you want or he will take care of it. It's up to you."

David sat back, his head leaned against the back of the seat. "I'll let him take care of it," he mumbled.

"One more thing, Dave," James Michaels began.

David looked at his father out of the corner of his eye.

"Jean has some papers she wants you to see. Says it's about time your engineering degree paid off."

David sat upright. "What kind of papers?"

"She didn't tell me. Only thing she said was she was sure you could read *governmentese,* you being in the navy."

David's curiosity was piqued. "That's all she said? Nothing about what it might be?"

James shook his head. "Not to me. Got the feeling she thought I might be better off not knowing what it was. She worries about me. Thinks I'm an old man."

David smiled. "You are an old man, Dad."

"I'm seventy-one. Your grandfather was ninety-six when he died. *He* was old. I got twenty-five years yet according to my calculations."

"I guess you're right, Pop," David acquiesced, his thoughts turning to Jean and what she had found. He crossed his arms over his chest and rested his head. He was snoring softly as his father turned north onto Highway 65 and headed for Clayton.

2

Billy Tippett could still see it. It played like an old black-and-white movie segment stuck in a tape player. One second Jimmy was securely tethered to the rope, the next he was free-falling two hundred feet to the ground like a rag doll thrown from a car window. He could even hear the muffled "thud" as Jimmy hit the flared side of the tower, and his body began to cartwheel as it continued its downward flight. Then Jimmy hit, and the sound of his body contacting the hard-packed earth was the signal for the tape to begin again. Billy closed his eyes, trying in vain to stop the ghastly pictures. Had it been a dream, Billy could have handled it better. After all, he had had dreams before—terrifying, dreadful dreams accompanied by the dark and spawned by the crack cocaine and occasional speedball, a combination of cocaine and heroin, he used. But this was not a dream, and he was not asleep. In fact, he had not been able to sleep since the accident. At first the disbelief kept him awake. Now it was the certainty that it had happened that gnawed at his mind. Jimmy had been a friend. Not a beer-drinking, carousing friend like the rest of his buddies, but someone who would listen when Billy needed to talk. Jimmy had taken time with him as a person, not as a source of funds to keep a drinking binge on track. And Jimmy

Michaels had been something else too. In all of Billy Tippett's life, Jimmy was the first person to care enough to tell him about a man named Jesus. He had not understood in the beginning—he was not sure he understood much more right now—but Jimmy had believed and had taken the time to tell him. To Billy, everything Jimmy had told him had sounded like something out of a fairy tale: God becomes man, dies as man, and becomes God again, so that man might have eternal life. Billy remembered his response when Jimmy Michaels had first told him about Jesus: "The last thing I want is an eternal life like the one I got now," he'd said.

"That's the beauty of it," Jimmy had countered. "It's not like this life. You don't have to put up with addictions, problems, troubles, . . . any of it."

But Billy had not been so sure. Jimmy looked rational and acted rational, but rationalism, in Billy Tippett's world, was an elusive commodity. Still, Jimmy's words had the ring of truth, and Billy had enjoyed being around him. In all of Billy Tippet's short life, Jimmy Michaels was the only truly happy person he had known.

Falling!

The black-and-white tape was running again! Billy clamped his hand over his face, but the tape rolled on.

Now Collins Construction International was concerned about adverse publicity. The company did not want any more attention drawn to the construction site of Arkansas Nuclear Three and Four, and had sent a man to talk to Billy. Billy had played the game. The man thought Billy was stupid and that he did not know what had happened or how, and Billy had let the man think that.

But Billy knew. He knew that the harness Jimmy Michaels had worn that day was not the one he normally used. Billy had noticed the stains that Jimmy had uncharacteristically dismissed as sweat or mildew. At the time, Billy was concerned that Jimmy was not his normal, safety-conscious self. But Jimmy had said he was in a hurry, that he had things to do and wanted to be finished earlier than normal. Now nothing was normal.

Billy knew that both the rope and leather harness were nowhere to be found. He had checked, and they were not in their normal place. To Billy that meant that someone had taken them. And to his way of thinking, the only reason to hide the equipment was to cover up an error or . . . what? He wasn't quite sure.

Billy also knew the name of the dark, greasy man who had poured something into Jimmy's coffee cup when he thought no one was watching. That alone might be worth something.

Billy knew plenty—enough, he was convinced, to be worth something to keep it quiet.

CHAPTER
THREE

1

The twentieth floor of the CCI Building in downtown Little Rock overlooked the city to its northern boundary, which was formed by the Arkansas River. The building had once housed the corporate offices of an Arkansas retail corporation which had abandoned the building in favor of larger quarters. The twenty-story brick structure had been perfect for Collins Construction International's corporate offices when the young governor of Arkansas had courted Emerson and Jameson Collins and their burgeoning construction company as a means to provide jobs in the southern state and to help insure his own reelection. CCI paid one dollar in rent for the state-owned building.

The massive office windows of Emerson Collins framed the north and east of Little Rock. The view from the richly appointed sanctum was breathtaking, but Emerson Collins had no interest in the beauty of Arkansas on this day. He stalked across the polished hardwood floors, his hands alternately jammed deep into the pockets of his tailored suit or clasped behind his back.

Emerson Collins was angry. He recognized, however, that his anger was only a tool, a well-honed, highly developed implement to be used when and if necessary. As the yellow light of the morning sun crept across the oak floor, he paused behind the massive walnut desk and met the gaze of his top security man.

Wayne Young fidgeted slightly under the gaze of Collins. He had already informed the head of CCI of the death of Jimmy Michaels on cooling tower number two. The story Young had relayed was the "official" line, the one that would appear in the newspapers, in the records of the Worker's Compensation office in Little Rock, on the books of the Occupational Safety and Health Administration (OSHA) in Washington, D.C., and in the archives of CCI itself. That was the story Emerson Collins wanted, and that was what Young had supplied. There was little left to do now but answer the questions as they were thrown at him.

"When's the OSHA hearing on the accident?" Collins asked.

Young made a gesture of thumbing through the papers in his lap. "Two o'clock today, Mr. Collins," he answered.

"I don't want any problems with this, do you understand, Mr. Young? No problems at all."

Wayne Young rose to leave. He could not wait to get out of the executive suite. "There won't be any problems, sir," Young assured him. "I'll take care of the details personally."

Emerson Collins turned his back to Young as the security chief left the office. He could not stand the man, but he had to admit that he was the best at what he did. And what Wayne Young did was solve problems.

2

Morton Powell's only vice as he saw it was the single cigar he allowed himself at the end of each day. He held the match so that only the heat from the tip of the flame ignited the end of the Corona. The phone rang as he exhaled. He savored a mouthful of smoke through two more rings before answering.

"Mort, it's Rodale," the man on the line said.

Morton Powell sat upright. Warren Rodale was the special agent in charge of the organized crime task force in the Hoover Building in Washington D.C. Powell knew that Rodale would only call on him for one reason. "What is it, Mort?" he asked, his hand suddenly shaking.

"You've been out of touch for the last few days haven't you?" Rodale began.

"Long weekend at the lake. Came off my vacation time."

"I know that," Rodale interjected impatiently. "What I mean is, you don't know about Jimmy Michaels do you?"

Mort Powell felt his blood run cold. He had a meeting with Michaels set for tomorrow afternoon. "I was just about to call to confirm a meeting, Warren. I haven't had time to get with him yet."

"His funeral is today, Mort. He was killed in a fall from one of those cooling towers. Two hundred feet."

Mort Powell drew a quick breath. His head pounded. Jimmy Michaels had been his current major source of information. And he was a friend. Morton Powell didn't particularly care for Jimmy's conservative brand of religion, but he had overlooked that part of the young man's character. Jimmy had been one of the "good guys," and now he was dead.

Powell unconsciously snuffed out the burning cigar with one hand as he held the phone in the other. As troubling as the death of his friend was, it presented him with a far more pressing problem. Jimmy Michaels was the sole source of information in the investigation of Collins Construction International. Preliminary information had been interesting—even more interesting than Powell had reported to Rodale. The first inklings of possible connections to Washington were floating to the surface, and Morton had to admit to himself that the tenuous links to Washington were more fabrications in his mind than actual associations, but even the suggestion of such allegiances was worth investigating.

Rodale continued, "I know your reports have only been cursory, Mort, but I need to know anything else you might have on CCI and the nuclear projects. This may go well beyond what we suspect, or it might be nothing."

"I'll fax you what I have to date," Powell answered. "It's not much. Michaels seemed to think he was onto something. We talked before I left for the lake. Seems he knew more than I suspected."

"He knew enough to get himself killed. You be careful."

Rodale's reference to murder was not lost on Powell. He knew there was no evidence to call Jimmy's death murder or Rodale would have said something about it in the conversation, but for the task force head to hint at it was sufficient cause to tread lightly. "I'll be careful. But if this turns out to be murder, I want these guys. Michaels has two kids still in school."

"Sounds like you liked the man. I thought you told me he was a religious nut."

"That's before I got to know him. He was religious, but it seemed to be a pragmatic type of religion. It actually made sense at times."

"Stay on it and fax me today," Rodale concluded and hung up the phone.

Powell stared into the dead receiver for a moment before replacing it. He reached over the pile of mail that had come while he had been away and retrieved a file folder. Opening the file, the first thing he saw was a eight-by-ten color photograph of Jimmy Michaels. He shook his head and then began collating the material in the file into a report to fax to Washington.

CHAPTER FOUR

1

The remainder of the ride from the airport to Clayton was made in silence; David slept while his father allowed the monotonous drone of the truck to lull him into a conscious stupor. They pulled into Clayton a little after eleven and began the preparations for the funeral. David showered, shaved, and changed into his white dress uniform, the three gold stripes of a full commander shining on both shoulder boards of his jacket. First Community Church was within walking distance, and David told his father he wanted to be at the church early. He left the house and began walking along the tree-lined street leading to the church.

As David approached the white clapboard church, the cold dread of reality struck. He had grown up in this neighborhood. The houses had changed little with the years, reflecting the conservative, hard-working people who lived in them. First Community Church was still the same, the anchor to which the area was grounded. The white-washed church stood on a small, grassy knoll, its towering steeple rising above the homes on either side. David had always considered the steeple to be a homing beacon, calling to all who cared to listen, to see, to accept the message that was proclaimed from its pulpit.

He was lost in his thoughts when he heard a noise. At first it didn't register; it was only the sound of a quiet scraping along the pea-gravel pavement. When the question came, however, he realized he was not alone.

"Hasn't changed much, has it?"

David turned and met the gaze of two of the most beautiful green eyes he had ever seen. The eyes had not changed, he realized, recognizing their luster and their deepness, but not the person behind them. He groped for the name he knew went with the lovely eyes but failed. Beyond the eyes, short brunette hair framed an almost boyish face with just the slightest hint of makeup. It was a face from the past, but the name would not come.

"I'm so sorry about Jimmy," she said.

"Thank you," David replied.

The eyes smiled back at him. "You don't remember me, do you?"

David felt himself blush, hating himself for the admission carried with it. "To tell the truth, I do remember the green eyes. The hair's a little different, I think. It's just the name that goes with them that escapes me for the moment," he admitted.

"Cynthia Faulkner," the stranger supplied.

David searched his memory but came up blank. The answer lurked somewhere in the back of his mind, but for the life of him, he could not come up with the connection.

Cynthia Faulkner smiled. "Try Tolbert instead of Faulkner. Cindy Tolbert," she added.

"Little Cindy! Jimmy's little Cindy?" David exclaimed, finding it hard to believe the attractive woman before him was the same tomboy who used to shoot baskets with his brother on the basketball goal mounted on the side of the Michaels's garage. Looking at her now, he was inclined to believe he'd not paid enough attention to that young girl.

"No, *not* Jimmy's little Cindy," she retorted, mocking him. "Cindy as in, 'the-same-class-with-Jimmy-Cindy.' But not Jimmy's." Cindy Tolbert smiled then, lowering her head for a moment. "You never did pay much attention to me," she said.

David felt his face redden even more at the gentle rebuke. "I'm sorry," he said. "I thought you and Jimmy were, how do you say it? . . . an 'item.' You were always over at our house and I thought . . ."

"I was over at your house because I had a crush on you, and Jimmy was kind enough to put up with me because he knew it. Jimmy and Jean were the 'item' you're talking about."

"I . . . uh . . . ." David stammered, his voice suddenly lost with the confession by this lovely young woman. She had been—what? Three years younger, no, four. She would have been a high school freshman when he was a senior. A child, really. A child all those years ago, but no longer. Not this green-eyed lady who now stood before him.

"Lighten up," she smiled. "That was a long time ago. Red is not very becoming with that starched, white uniform," Cindy laughed. "A lot of years have passed since then. We all grew up. Although, I have to admit, you seem to be in better shape than most of the men your age."

Even at forty-seven, David Michaels showed no signs of the inevitable "middle-age spread" that affected most men his age. FMF duty had kept him trim and firm. The only evidence that age had any hold on him was his nearly steel-gray hair—cut so short his tanned scalp showed through—and the weathered lines at the corner of his eyes. Even the lines could be mistaken for laugh lines when he smiled, further belying his age.

"We all grew up," David repeated, embarrassed yet again. "It's just . . . well . . . I never knew. This comes as kind of a shock is all," David finally managed to say.

"I was thirteen and you were getting ready to leave for the Naval Academy. I thought I was in love with you then. When you got that appointment to the academy, I had visions of sailing off into the sunset with you. Childish, I know, but that's the way it was. Don't let it worry you. Besides, I got married and everything, just like a big, grown-up girl."

"You said Faulkner, right? Your husband, of course." David could not remember a Faulkner.

Cindy nodded. "We met at the University of Arkansas in Fayetteville. He was an engineering student from Little Rock and I was a business major. After graduation he went to work for the Arkansas Highway Department. We started out in the northwest, around Fort Smith. A few years later the department moved us to Clayton."

To his surprise, David felt a sudden, inexplicable pang of jealousy. How could he have ignored a girl as lovely as Cindy Tolbert? Certainly, age would have been a deciding factor. No senior would consciously admit to interest in a thirteen-year-old girl. But he would have had to have been blind to ignore the possibilities lurking beneath the tomboy exterior, no matter how remote they may have been at the time. Maybe, he thought, he had not. Something in the back of his mind had prevented him from becoming interested in other women. Maybe he had subconsciously remembered a girl from Clayton named Cynthia Tolbert who used to shoot baskets with his little brother.

"How is he?" David stumbled, realizing he did not know the first name of Cindy's husband.

"Robert was working on a bridge project in a neighboring county. Something went wrong, and he . . . Robert was killed," she said, not bothering nor wanting to expand on the simplistic explanation.

"I'm sorry, Cindy."

"It was a long time ago. More than four years. I've worked through it."

"Children?"

Cindy shook her head. "We never had any. We wanted children, but it just never worked out." There was a note of sadness in her voice, bordering on the melancholy, that carried even through the unsuccessful effort to keep her voice light.

"And Cindy Faulkner? How is she?" asked David softly, almost tenderly, warming to the presence of Cindy.

"Tolbert," Cindy corrected. "I've been using my maiden name for a couple of years."

David looked at her with surprise. She recognized the look.

"No, *not* women's lib or the independent thinking of the socially enlightened," she smiled. "My dad owned some property when he died. He left it to me. During probate, I started using my maiden name to eliminate confusion. The property was in the Tolbert name, and you know our local judges. The judge just couldn't understand why I would want to put the property in the name of Faulkner. He started calling me Tolbert and I guess it stuck because I've been using Tolbert since then. No secret."

"So you're now a member of the landed gentry," David joked.

Cindy smiled and nodded. "I suppose that's one way to put it." She nodded toward First Community. "You doing part of the service for Jimmy?" she asked.

"I don't think so. Dad told me Pastor Shackleford said I could, but I think I'll feel better letting him do the service. There's too much running through my head right now."

Cindy nodded in understanding as she began walking toward the church. "I was just coming over early to check on things. Making sure everything was in the right place and all that."

David found himself following the petite woman as they headed for the church. Her earlier admission was only now beginning to dawn on him. "That's kind of you," he said. "I'm sure Jimmy would appreciate it." Even the mention of Jimmy's name within this context was difficult. He had not seen his brother in years, but there was no denying the emotion that welled up in him at this moment. Just the act of entering the building where his funeral service would be conducted seemed an impossible task. Somehow Cindy's presence made it easier.

"He would," she said, as they both mounted the rock steps leading to the sanctuary. "That's the way he was. Always had something good to say about people. Never anything bad. Jean's the same way. They were a match made in heaven, no doubt about that." Cindy stopped on the top step and turned to David. This time her green eyes had a piercing quality about them, as if they were accusing David of some forgotten responsibility. "Have you seen Jean yet?" she asked.

Despite the accusatory eyes, there was no reproach in her voice. David shook his head. "Not yet. Dad told her I would see her here in about an hour. You and Jean good friends?"

"Special would describe it better. After all, we were both in love with the Michaels brothers at one time," she added as she slipped into the dark coolness of First Community's sanctuary, leaving David on the rock steps.

David felt the flush returning once again at the forthright admission by the attractive brunette with the green eyes. An inexplicable feeling seemed to blanket him in a warmth he seldom experienced. He grabbed the handle and entered the building, wondering if there might not be more to his return than he had thought.

The altar was smothered with a vast array of flowers, living plants, and candles. David had never seen such a display of affection demonstrated at any funeral. He was more accustomed to the unadorned atmosphere of military funerals. He could feel tears coming to his eyes, and he brushed them away before he advanced into the large room.

Cindy was already at the altar working her way through the enormous arrangements, checking the cards and notes attached. She wrote notes in a small notebook David had not noticed on their walk to the church. She concentrated so thoroughly on the task that she did not notice David's approach.

"For Jean?" David asked, indicating the notebook.

Cindy did not look up from the notebook. "I told her I would take care of all the details," she said, continuing to write. "She doesn't have the time or the frame of mind to do it. I'm going to send out the notes and cards for the flowers and memorials. It's the least I can do for her right now."

"I'm beginning to think I really missed out on someone special when I missed you," he said and instantly regretted the display of emotion.

Cindy stopped what she was doing for a moment and looked in David's direction. "You should have said that years ago," she said and returned to the flowers. Her tone of voice was noticeably cooler than it had been earlier. Then, as if she regretted the comment she had just made, she said, "Some things can always be rectified."

David ascended the altar. He made his way among the flowers and memorials, reading some of the cards and caressing the petals of the fresh flowers. For a moment, his thoughts were torn between the memorials and Cindy Tolbert. He forced his thoughts back to the point at hand. "Looks like folks thought a lot of my brother."

"They did," Cindy agreed. "Jimmy was special. Always ready to help someone. Always out for justice too. I'm talking real justice," Cindy said, stopping once again. "He believed that problems could be solved if you just followed the directions given in the Bible. He really practiced what he preached. He was like your dad in that respect. Your dad's faith has a sensible side to it. Jimmy was like that too."

"I know that side of both of them. I used to think it was a rather shortsighted, iconoclastic view. Jimmy and I had some good arguments about the literal and symbolic portions of the Bible. Used to keep Dad up nights."

Cindy grinned. "He told me about big brother and his grown-up, seminary beliefs," she said. "But I could tell he was proud of you. 'If David said it,' he used to say, 'there must be something to it.'"

"I'm not so sure anymore," David acknowledged, moving from the altar.

"You mean there's room for discussion?"

"There's always room for discussion," David answered.

"Maybe big brother has seen the light, after all," she said.

"Big brother has seen a lot of things. I look around here," he said with a sweep of his hand, "and think this is really where I should be. A nice, quiet country church in the middle of the mountains. It certainly looks like heaven after what I've been through."

"War's tough, huh?"

"War is more than tough. It's obscene, and the fact that it's even necessary makes it all the more so. But, to tell the truth, I was thinking about my current assignment."

"Which is?"

"FMF. Fleet Marine Force. I'm stationed at Camp Pendleton in Southern California."

"Southern California doesn't sound so bad."

"Don't let the location fool you," David laughed easily. "FMF could make heaven seem like . . ."

". . . a different place," she finished before David could continue.

He laughed easily. "Yeah, a different place. But it's not the assignment so much as it is the thought of being unable to make a significant change. Sometimes I think I could have done more in a church like this one."

"So quit."

David gazed at Cindy Tolbert. That was the solution his brother or his father would have come up with too. Always the direct, the simple. Cindy seemed to possess those same traits, and he found himself warming to this woman. "You make it sound so easy. Don't think I haven't thought about it, either. Slogging through swamps and desert wasteland can make a man think, especially at my age. If I could get a church like First Community here, I just might resign my commission."

"That's a possibility," she said, stopping what she was doing and turning to David.

David met her gaze. *There it was again,* he thought. He could see it in her green eyes. The practicality, the simple answer. "What?" he asked.

Cindy Tolbert stuck the pencil in the notebook and explained. "Pastor Shackleford is ready to retire. He's been here almost thirty years. Says it's time to catch up on some fishing. Anyway, the church is getting a committee together to find a new pastor. I don't see why it can't be you, do you? Seems like the perfect solution to me. Your home is here. You have enough time in the military to retire if you want. This church is a good church, and it needs a good pastor. Seems logical to me."

David had not heard that Rev. Shackleford would be retiring, and he had certainly never thought about taking over for the old preacher. But there was something about what Cindy had just said that disturbed him, as if he had come in the middle of a play and had missed the story line.

"How do you know I've got enough time in the military to retire?" he questioned.

"Jimmy told me. He told everyone. It was his dream. He wanted you to come back to Clayton to pastor First Community. Said he would love to have his brother in a church where he was a deacon. I think he probably had most of the congregation convinced." She lowered her face for a moment, and when she looked back into David's eyes he saw the glint of budding tears. "He was going to talk to you about it the next time you came home. It wasn't supposed to be like this," she added as the tears flowed and sobs began to shake her body. She fell into David's arms, her resolve melting away with the tears.

David stood with Cindy Tolbert clinging to him and let the tumbling impressions wash over him. The flowers, the funeral, the church—all too much. His life was the military, despite what he said about a country church and a "normal" congregation. He did not need added complications in the midst of the chaos that seemed to have engulfed him here in Clayton.

He could feel his stomach twist into a painful knot as he thought about Jimmy. Then he was brought back to reality by the slight woman he held in his arms.

He guided the weeping Cindy out of the sanctuary and into the hallway of the church, searching for the library he knew was just around the corner. He found it, and after both were seated, he began to comfort the woman that shook before him—not only as another human being in pain, but as someone he cared for.

Too much, he thought to himself. *Too much!*

2

The black eight ball banked perfectly into the side pocket. "That's five you owe me," Lewis Roswell growled.

"Don't get uptight, man. I'm good for it. Let's play another. Give me a chance to get even," Billy said.

"Pay me the five and then we'll play another," Lewis threatened.

Billy backed around the pool table. Lewis was big, mean, and drunk. Those, in Billy Tippett's mind, were the three things that constituted the most deadly combination imaginable. Billy watched as Lewis advanced like a tank out of control. He dug in his pocket and threw a five-dollar bill on the table. "There, man. Your money. Don't go nuts on me!"

Lewis Roswell scooped the bill from the green felt surface and pocketed it. "Now we play again," he said.

Billy started to tell the big man to forget it but thought better of it. When Lewis was drunk, you played whatever he wanted to play. Tonight it was eight ball, and Billy grabbed the wooden triangle and racked the balls as Lewis chalked his stick. Thick smoke hovered just above the table. Lewis swigged from a long-necked beer bottle and placed it on the edge of the pool table. Water rings surrounding the table marked where Lewis had rested the sweating bottles as he shot. Billy removed the triangular rack and stepped away from the table. He had seen more than one person lose teeth when an inebriated Lewis blasted the balls from the table with one mighty break shot. This time the balls remained on the table, with only the cue ball falling into one of the end pockets. Billy retrieved the ball and placed the white ball on the table, lining up his shot.

He sighted on the two ball and sank it in the side pocket. "Solids," he announced, as the ball settled into the leather pouch.

"Just shoot, man," Lewis slurred.

Billy ran three more solids before missing and relinquishing the table to Lewis.

"All over but the shouting, man," Lewis said, wobbling to the table.

Billy reached for his beer and sipped it. It was warm and tasted terrible, but when you played pool with Lewis, you drank what he drank. It was his third, and Billy was beginning to feel the effects of the alcohol. It was making him tipsy, he knew, but that was all right. He had thought about it and now he had a plan. A plan that even the big monster Lewis would have to admire, if Lewis was capable of admiring something so cerebral. Billy grinned to himself. Soon, he told himself, he would not have to play for a lousy five dollars a game. He would be in the big leagues. The money leagues.

Lewis missed his fourth shot and Billy stepped to the table. "You guys gonna be surprised one of these days," he began, as he bent over the green expanse of felt. He saw nothing wrong with bragging a little. "Billy boy's gonna come into big money one o' these days," he continued.

"Just shoot, dummy," Lewis said. "Ain't nobody gonna give you nothin' for nothin'."

Billy shot and missed, leaning on his cue as he raised up. "Not nothin' for nothin', man. Somethin' for somethin'. That's what it's all 'bout."

Lewis Roswell staggered around the table, not missing as he worked his way through the striped balls and finally sank the eight ball in an end pocket.

"You didn't call that last shot, Lewis," Billy said.

"I called it, man. You just didn't hear it 'sall," the big man slurred.

"No way, man! You gotta call the shot, and you didn't do it!"

"What of it, wimp? You gonna pay up or not?"

Billy Tippett saw it was useless. Even drunk, he knew enough not to argue with Lewis. He jerked a bill from his pocket and tossed it on the table. "One day! You'll see! One day! I got it figured," Billy screamed as he backed toward the door. "One day those idiots out at that *new-clee-are* place gonna pay *me*, Billy Tippett, for what I know! Not for what I can do! You wait and see!" he shrieked, as he made his way down the deserted street. "Wait and see," he mumbled to himself as he turned the corner and stumbled into the darkness. "Wait and see. . . ."

3

The smallish, evil-looking man raised the front brim of the hat that covered his eyes. He smiled as he pushed himself from the chair. He had been in the same position for more than three hours, and he was stiff. He stretched, his long spindly arms reaching into the smoky fog that hovered above him. He pulled a cigarette from the almost empty package and lit it, adding to the suspended pollution. It had been a good night. He had been successful, and success meant money. In this case, lots of money.

He took one last look around the pool room, making certain he had not attracted undue attention to himself. The men at the tables were busy with their games. The drunken Lewis Roswell was shooting at the same table but with a new sucker. It was beyond his comprehension that a man could drink as much as he had seen Lewis down in the course of the night and still manage to shoot pool. But that was not his worry, he reminded himself. He had been assigned to follow Billy Tippett, and that is what he had done. His only orders were to keep his eyes and ears open and report anything out of the ordinary. He had no doubt that Billy Tippett's remarks on exiting the pool hall would be classified as "out of the ordinary." Just how much "out of the ordinary" he did not know, but he did know that the remarks were the stuff that made live men dead.

He pushed through the door and into the street in time to watch Billy stumble around the corner. He would let him go. He had what he needed for the night. If it came to it, maybe he would get the contract to make Billy disappear. That's where the real money was, after all. He smiled, his stained teeth showing under the street light.

Maybe, just maybe.

CHAPTER
FIVE

1

Wayne Young chewed on one of the chalky tablets he had just extracted from the roll of antacids on his desk. Things were going well, and it worried him. The Michaels funeral had gone off without a hitch. The appropriate representatives from CCI had attended the funeral and, while the family had not been overly joyed at their presence, they had all been polite, even the navy commander-chaplain, David Michaels.

Carlton Graham had conducted the hearing into the cause and liability of the Jimmy Michaels death and ruled that CCI was not to blame and bore no responsibility. The widow would receive the normal death benefits from the life insurance, but that was all. CCI was cleared of any culpability in the incident. The appropriate reports had been filed with Worker's Comp, the insurance carrier, and OSHA. Summaries had been sent to Emerson Collins in the twentieth-floor executive suite. That should have been the end of it, but for some inexplicable reason, a problem he had yet to define lurked somewhere in the darkness, a vacuous, uncomfortable feeling.

Now, as the security man removed another tablet from the roll, he turned his attention to the twin problems of Foster Crowe and Billy Tippett. If he could deal with them successfully, he would have his house in order—except for the nagging worry that would not seem to go away and was not connected to either Crowe or Tippett.

Foster Crowe had followed Billy last night and had called Young at home. Young's suspicions had been correct. Billy Tippett *did* know something he had not revealed to the CCI investigator when he had talked to the boy about the death of Jimmy Michaels. Or, Young corrected himself, he was *saying* he knew something about the death, and intimation at this point could be as deadly as truth. Young could take no chances. Too much was at stake.

Young realized he would have to deal with Foster Crowe as well. The slimeball screwed up. Young suspected Billy Tippett had seen Crowe doctor Jimmy Michaels's coffee the morning of Jimmy's death. Maybe Tippett even knew Crowe had doctored the leather climbing harness as well. In any case, it was not worth the risk to think otherwise. He would pay Crowe to take care of Tippett and, with just a little luck, he would then eliminate Crowe. Loose ends were not something Wayne Young accepted.

The security head picked up the profiles he had assembled on the principals in the case. Jean Michaels was the bereaved widow. Young was certain she would take the meager insurance settlement and forget about pursuing the matter further. James Michaels, the father of the boy, was too old to do anything, Young was sure. The one and only brother, David Michaels, was a commander in the navy. Young had been concerned about him until he discovered the commander was a member of the chaplain corps. "A military preacher," Young had ridiculed. "Nothing to worry about there." The navy man's demeanor at the funeral seemed to bear out his assessment. Young was sure that no problems would arise from the family arena.

No, the only loose end seemed to be Billy Tippett. As Young leaned back in his desk chair, he began to form a plan to deal with him. He felt a calm power envelop his being. The plan was forming quickly, and he liked what was materializing. Collins would not like it, he knew, but the redneck Tippett was his problem, and as long as he took care of it, Collins would go along.

Young got up and walked to his window, stopping to pour another cup of coffee and down two more antacid tablets. He gazed out on the Arkansas morning. He loved his job and he loved the South. Things were slower, people nicer, problems not as intense. As the caffeine entered his bloodstream, it added to the overall euphoria he was beginning to feel, knowing that his current problems were well in hand. Even the insistent apprehension he had experienced only minutes earlier was succumbing to the combination of antacid tablets and black coffee.

He returned to his desk and placed a call from his private line.

"'lo," a voice answered.

Young instantly recognized the lazy speech pattern of Foster Crowe. Young despised the man, but he also needed him. "Listen good, Crowe. This is your last job before you head back north." Young relayed his instructions to the small man, feeling better with every syllable. With each word uttered, the problems that plagued the big man took one step closer to resolution.

2

Jean Michaels watched the sun rise on her third day without Jimmy. She reached for her Bible and turned to Matthew 6:34. The verse was one of Jimmy's favorites, and she read the short verse three times before putting the Bible on the table beside her chair. *Don't worry about tomorrow,* she thought, *Just take care of today.* She would do her best to do just that, but it would not be easy. Jimmy had been her life, her companion, her lover. Most of all, he had been her best friend, and nothing could fill the void she now felt. It was as if a part of her had been ripped out and flung to the far reaches of the earth. The sun was well above the horizon when she padded into the kitchen to begin breakfast for the boys.

She had mixed feelings about the papers she had placed in her safe-deposit box at the bank. Maybe she was overreacting, she argued with herself. But had not Jimmy told her there was something strange going on at the construction site, and didn't the papers prove that? No, she told herself, the papers were only reports; copies of reports that Jimmy had written. They were not proof in themselves, only suspicions. She pondered the reports and the papers as she fried eggs, made toast, and set the table. She would talk to David today. Jean had told Dad she had some papers she wanted David to see, and she knew Dad had talked to David because he had mentioned it just after the service yesterday at the graveside. "Today," she muttered, "after the boys are off to school."

3

David awoke with a headache pounding in his temples and a brassy taste in his mouth. Sitting in the second pew of First Community Church had proved to be more of an ordeal than he had anticipated. Rev. Shackleford had conducted the service with a sense of caring and understanding. The music had been perfect, the message appropriate. The church service had lasted less than twenty minutes, and the ride to the cemetery had taken only ten minutes. The grave-side service had lasted little more than the time it had taken to drive to the small country cemetery nestled among rolling hills and towering pines. All in all, David reflected, it had gone quite well, if you could forget that the person in the polished oak casket was your only brother.

David knew why his head was pounding. He was angry! Angry with CCI, angry with his brother for working at such a high risk job, and angry with God for allowing Jimmy's death!

And there was Cindy Tolbert. Her frank admission of past feelings had taken him by surprise, and he had to admit to himself that he had thoughts of her during the funeral service.

Women had never been important in David's life. He had gone on a few dates in high school and college, but other things were always more important to him than women. The military had become his home and his wife. For the first time in his life, he wondered if he had shortchanged himself.

He had watched Cindy at the funeral and at the graveside. She had moved in and among the people, thanking them on behalf of Jean, comforting those who needed it, and taking charge when necessary. David saw in her the things he had missed over the years by allowing the military to dominate every aspect of his life. But then he thought better of it. The military would never have exerted such force on him had he not allowed it. Anything that had happened over the past years had occurred because he had wanted it to. He had orchestrated his life to the point of exclusion, even seclusion. He had run from life, from involvement, from love.

The headache hammered and David knew he would have to take some aspirin. But he also knew there was nothing he could take to rid himself of the thoughts that he seemed to have at odd moments—thoughts of Cindy.

David swung his legs over the edge of the bed and fumbled for the clock on the nightstand. Six o'clock. He had slept a full hour past his normal waking time. FMF marines rose even earlier than David. But they made allowances for a middle-aged navy chaplain and allowed him an extra hour of sack time. The extra sleep made David think he would be better off out of FMF and aboard a nice, quiet aircraft carrier sailing somewhere in the Mediterranean or the Pacific. He made a mental note to look into the possibilities when he returned to Pendleton. The First Community Church was really not an option, he reminded himself. Not for him. He stumbled into the bathroom and found the aspirin.

David heard sounds coming from the kitchen. His father was already making coffee and fumbling with the cast-iron cooking utensils that hung from the old, overhead rack. David entered the kitchen.

"Mornin', Son," his father greeted.

"Morning, Dad."

"You got plans for the day?" his father asked.

"Nothing special," David answered, remembering as he spoke that Jean had said she had the papers she wanted him to see. "Jean said something about meeting her at the bank this morning, but she never said what time. I'll call her a little later."

"Call her now," his father insisted. "She'll be awake. She's still got two boys in school."

David poured a cup of coffee from the old percolator and walked into the living room. He picked up the phone and dialed the number. It was answered on the second ring.

"Jean? David. Dad said you would be awake so I called. How are you? Except for yesterday, we haven't had much of a chance to talk."

"I'm fine. I've been reading my Bible."

David winced, knowing that he had already neglected his daily meditation and that he would not make it up before the day got away from him.

"What about this bank thing?" David asked, not knowing what else to call it. "You say you have some papers?"

"Like I told you yesterday, I'm not sure they mean anything at all. They're some of the reports that Jimmy was working on. Some notes too. Some are drawings or sketches. I'm not sure what to make of them, if anything. I looked at them, but they didn't make much sense to me. The thing that concerns me is that Jimmy thought there might be something funny going on out at the site. He used to talk about it at times. Nothing definitive, just hints. Odd words here and there—that sort of thing. If I didn't know Jimmy so well, I wouldn't have thought to save the papers. It's probably nothing at all. I just thought you could take a look."

"I don't know what good I can do, but I'll do whatever you want. What's a good time for you?" he asked.

There was a pause and then Jean said, "How about ten this morning? That'll give me time to finish up here and maybe look decent."

"Ten o'clock is fine with me. See you at the bank." He hung up and walked back into the kitchen where his dad was busy scrambling eggs. "I'm meeting Jean at the bank at ten. What do think about what she said? About Jimmy thinking there may be something strange going on out at the construction site?"

James Michaels dumped the yellow mass of eggs into a bowl and came to the table where David was sipping coffee. "I don't know, Son. I do know that Jimmy was not his same old self lately. Seemed preoccupied. Worried even."

"That's sort of what Jean was telling me. Whatever was going on, it was enough to raise her suspicions," David told his father. "But he never told you why or what was bothering him?"

"He never told me he was worried or bothered. That was just a dad's observation. I could sense that sort of stuff with him. Jimmy never told me anything about what was going on out at that nuclear place. Come to think of it, that's unusual in itself," he added.

David sat on the edge of his chair, looking up from his coffee. "How do you mean, unusual?"

James placed his coffee cup on the battered kitchen table. "He always used to tell me what was going on. He's done it since he was a kid. He could never keep anything to himself. He even used to tell me when you beat him up and told him not to tell me," James Michaels smiled. "Every job he's ever had, he'd come back and tell me what he did, how he liked it, and such. But this was a new job. Something strange about it too. He got it, I guess, because heights didn't bother him. I didn't like the idea. Jean neither. Tried to talk him out of it, but he said it was something he had to do. I didn't understand."

"*Had* to do? That's what he said? Those particular words?"

"His exact words. It was like he *knew* something and didn't want to burden me. Don't add up," David's father concluded.

David thought for a moment. "It might, if he wanted to keep you in the dark for your own protection."

"That could explain the worried look I kept seeing on his face too," Mr. Michaels added, spooning eggs onto his plate.

"Could. We're probably jumping to conclusions, Dad. I'll probably find that those papers Jean has are just normal situation reports and that'll be that."

"I hope so," David's father added.

David could tell by his father's tone of voice that he wasn't convinced.

"One more thing, Dad. What do you know about Cindy Tolbert?"

James Michaels looked up from where he was working. "The cute gal with the green eyes? Used to come over here and play basketball with Jimmy. She had a crush on you in high school."

David laughed spontaneously. "Did everyone know that but me?"

"Probably. She was just a kid then. But she's special. Always busy at the church or doing something around town. Works out at the retirement home too. I always thought if I ended up there, at least I'd get to see her once a week."

"She sounds special," David agreed, not willing to continue the conversation he'd started. What was he thinking? He had a job he loved and peers who respected him. At forty-seven, there was no room for anyone else. Not even Cindy Tolbert.

4

Attorney Jerry Kennedy threw the papers across the room. They had been delivered by overnight courier and were waiting for him when he arrived at his office that morning. The large manila envelope bore the seal of OSHA and was lying on his desk along with the rest of the mail. The seal had drawn his attention, and he opened it first. It had taken almost an hour to plow through the documents and the government's legal phrasing he had found inside. The bottom line, though, was easy enough to determine: The family of Jimmy Michaels, according to a closed investigation conducted within OSHA guidelines, was entitled to exactly $1,292.20. There was no mention of the calculations involved nor the basis for the award. The one thing that did stand out in the papers—it was repeated on almost every page—was the fact that OSHA had cleared Collins Construction International of any and all blame in the death of its employee, Jimmy Michaels.

Jerry Kennedy fumed around his office, retrieving the scattered papers, arranging them as he went. He fully intended to talk to Jean Michaels and maybe her brother-in-law, David, about the responsibility that CCI would have to bear under the Worker's Comp and OSHA laws. Now, according to the papers in his hand, the company was effectively off the hook. There would not be another investigation—no open forum to determine what had really happened. It was inexcusable!

Kennedy called to his secretary in the outer office. As she came through the office door the lawyer said, "Get me the director of

Worker's Comp in Little Rock on the phone. His name's in this directory," he said, handing her the small book. "And don't take no for an answer. I want to talk to him now!"

The young secretary went back to her desk to make the call. Jerry Kennedy sat in his leather armchair and breathed deeply, trying to stem the frustration that he knew was just beginning. He would have to talk to Jean soon. But first he would talk to Worker's Comp.

CHAPTER SIX

1

The brick facade of the First National Bank of Clayton had been the same as long as David could remember. The building, along with the old courthouse, anchored the downtown area. Both structures served notice to the casual observer that Clayton was a town built on tradition and solid values, values as solid as the brick and stone structures occupying its geographical center.

The bank reminded David of the many First Baptist church buildings throughout the South. White columns supported a covered portico at the main entrance, and white-painted trim framed the rest of the red brick structure. White shutters adorned each window, each shutter open as if exclaiming the building open for all to enter. No secrets here. And, David remembered, the bank really was a brick structure, not just a wood-framed structure with a brick veneer. The bank, along with the stone-and-brick courthouse, formed the center of the town square. The rest of the town wrapped around the two larger edifices on four sides. It was a typical southern county seat town. A good place to grow up. A good place to live.

David parked his father's truck in a space in front of the town's only drugstore. Some of the locals were lingering over final cups of morning coffee in the booths that lined one side. The old-fashioned soda fountain lined the right side of the store, and David remembered that handmade milk shakes were still served there.

David checked the time. Ten minutes before Jean would show. Just enough time to say "hi" to the men in the pharmacy and maybe have a cup of coffee. He pushed through the glass door into the store.

"Mornin', Dave," one of the men greeted.

"Hugh. How's it going?"

"Same as always. Sorry about Jimmy. I don't think he had an enemy in this county."

David took the one empty seat next to Hugh Bowling. Hugh was a poultry farmer a few miles out of town and wore blue denim overalls. If David remembered correctly, the farmer had an agricultural degree from the University of Texas. "So I've heard. It's good to know he was so well liked."

The clerk placed a cup of coffee in front of David. He had not ordered it, but there was nothing strange about that. Everyone who sat in the booth got a cup of coffee. It was tradition, as were the stainless steel sugar bowl and the cream pitcher that held real cream skimmed off the top of a nearby dairy farmer's milk tank. He spooned some sugar into the steaming cup, foregoing the thick cream.

"Here for long?" Benny Chapman asked.

Benny was the local barber and the fifth generation of his family to cut hair in the county. David tried to calculate his age but gave up. "Don't know, Mr. Chapman," he answered. "Probably be heading back in a couple of days."

"Too bad. Been a long time since we seen ya," the old barber said, then added, "There's Jean, if you're waitin' for her."

David turned around and looked out the plateglass window. Jean had just parked next to James Michaels's truck and was looking around. David waved through the glass and rose to leave, reaching for change to pay for the coffee.

Benny Chapman held up his hand. "On me this time, Dave."

"Thanks, Mr. Chapman. I owe you one."

"See that you stay around long enough to pay up, ya hea'?"

"I'll do that," David said, as he left the drugstore, wondering if he would be able to keep that small promise.

Jean met him on the sidewalk. "Already got you drinking coffee again, I see."

"Seemed impolite not to," David said, wondering why he was sounding defensive. "Besides, you can't be in the navy and not drink coffee."

"Just joking, David. Let's get to the bank. The sooner I get this out of the way, the better I'll like it."

David and Jean strode across the one-way street that circled the town square and entered the bank. It seemed extraordinarily busy for a weekday morning. All the tellers were busy with customers, and several people were waiting in line.

"Busy today," David remarked to Jean, as they moved in and around the long lines of people eager to do their banking business.

"They're always busy these days. The nuclear power plant needed more labor than we could provide. CCI had to ship workers in from around the state, set up temporary housing for them and everything. Lots of folks in town I don't know, but the upside is that unemployment here is virtually zero."

"Then why aren't these people working instead of standing in line at the bank?" he asked.

"Collins Construction International—that's the name of the company building the cooling towers, containment buildings, and generating stations—is running three shifts and operating twenty-four hours a day. Big time stuff. I'm not so sure I like all the changes prosperity has brought with it."

"I guess I'm a little out of touch," he marveled.

"Money talks," Jean said.

Jean and David worked through the crowd to the security entrance where the safe-deposit boxes were located. A lady David recognized, but whose name escaped him, sat at the desk just outside the vault.

"Good morning, Mrs. Dixon," Jean greeted the lady.

"Good morning, Jean," the lady replied. "Sure sorry about Jimmy. We'll miss him around here."

"Thanks, Mrs. Dixon. You remember David, Jimmy's brother?"

The gray-haired lady turned to David. "I remember him," she answered, offering her hand to David. "Saw you at the funeral. Sorry it was this type of homecoming," she said.

"Thank you," David said. So far, Jimmy didn't seem to have an enemy in the world.

"We need to get into my safe-deposit box, Mrs. Dixon," Jean continued.

"Certainly, Jean. Do you have your key?"

Jean fished the key from her purse, signed the register that Mrs. Dixon offered, and both she and David followed the lady into the vault. Jean inserted her key, and Mrs. Dixon opened the box for them and placed the metal container on one of the tables in the vault area.

"Take your time. I'll be outside," Mrs Dixon said.

Jean raised the lid and removed twenty or thirty pieces of paper and laid them on the table. "I haven't really gone through these, so there's no particular order," she said. "Mostly reports and stuff like that. Most of it in Jimmy's handwriting. I want you to look at a few things toward the bottom."

"Let's see what we have," David said, as he picked up the first small stack that Jean had laid out.

David paged through the sheets of paper. Some of the sheets were loose pages from a yellow legal pad containing rough notes David recognized as Jimmy's handwriting. Others were preprinted documents, forms, some with the seal from the state of Arkansas and some with the seal of the United States printed at the top. There was a stack of about ten pages with the seal of the Nuclear Regulatory Commission on it. David laid these aside and began with the yellow sheets from the legal pad.

David read the notes slowly, absorbing the information and its significance. Mostly they contained rough sketches and penciled notations he recognized as some type of concrete inner structure. The reinforcement rods, sublayers, and overlays were unambiguous, identifiable because of his engineering background from the Naval Academy. Another drawing appeared to be a master diagram of the complete cooling tower. On that, Jimmy had circled individual portions of the tower, made a notation to see the detail sheet, and drawn the circled portions in greater detail. David placed the overall tower view on one corner of the table and rummaged through the other notes as he arranged the supporting data sheets.

It did not take long for David to understand that what Jimmy had told Jean was indeed true—if the diagrams could be believed. And there was no reason to doubt his brother's sketches. The diagrams documented the systematic reduction of steel reinforcement rods by Collins Construction International or some of its subcontractors. Rod joints were not reinforced as they should have been and, according to an extensive note written in Jimmy's handwriting, the concrete used was weaker than the required job specifications.

"You look like you've found something," Jean said.

"I have, provided my brother knew what he was talking about when it comes to concrete and steel rod reinforcements," David answered. "Look here," he continued, as he slid the diagrams toward Jean. He explained what he thought he was looking at and watched as Jean's face reflected her growing alarm.

"If this is true," she said offhandedly, "then Jimmy might have been murdered."

The word hit David like a lightening bolt. It had never entered his mind because up until now he had no reason to suspect it. No motive. It was hard to believe that men killed for things such as concrete and steel, but David knew it was so. He had seen worse. After all, two thousand years ago, other men did much worse to a man who had come to save them. Somehow David was having trouble rationalizing his dwindling faith with the current events that swirled around him. His younger brother was dead, and now the possibility of murder had reared its ugly head.

"Let's not jump to conclusions," David said. "In the first place, all we have are his notes. We don't even know if he told anyone what he had found. In the second place, if he had filed reports, they would have to go to several different agencies, not just to CCI. They would be hanging themselves if they killed him. It doesn't make a lost of sense."

"I do know he filed reports." Jean picked up a stack of papers and waved them at David. "These are the copies that Jimmy saved when he wrote his reports. Take a look here," she said, indicating one of the limp, yellow copies. "This is the report that caught my eye, the reason I put everything in the safe-deposit box."

David took the copy and began reading. Jean was right. It was a report stating that Jimmy had found the surface concrete finishing to be unsatisfactory, and he suspected that surface abnormalities might be caused not only by improper finishing but also by the lack of adequate support beneath. Jimmy had even included some of the drawings that David had seen on the yellow legal pad sheets.

David examined the rest of the report copies. Each reported the same basic findings. At the bottom of the form was a distribution list. Copies had gone to CCI's concrete foreman, CCI's main office, the Nuclear Regulatory Commission, the Atomic Energy Commission, and the Arkansas Electrical Cooperatives. Thus others had access to the information. That fact alone should have insured Jimmy's protection.

"Is there a copy machine we can use?" he asked Jean.

"There's one in the lobby."

David bundled the papers and walked out to the lobby's copy machine where he copied all the pages. Then David replaced the originals in the safe-deposit box, and Jean locked it.

"What do we do now?" Jean asked.

"I'm not sure," David answered, looking at the papers he held in his hands. "Maybe God will give us the answer," he said skeptically.

"He might just do that, you know. You're supposed to be a preacher, and it sounds like you don't even have faith in the God you preach."

David squirmed at the rebuke, embarrassed by his sister-in-law's accusation, yet knowing it contained more than a modicum of truth. He was finding it harder and harder to believe in God with his brother in the ground. The fact that Jimmy's death seemed to have strengthened Jean's belief only made matters worse.

"I'm a chaplain," he finally said, as if that explained everything.

"Chaplain, preacher, same thing," Jean said as they both left the bank building.

Nope, David thought. *Not by a long shot.*

"What about the papers? Where do we start?"

"You got a family lawyer?"

"Jerry Kennedy. His office is just across the street. I'm supposed to meet with him later this morning, as a matter of fact. Something about insurance and the government."

"Which way?" David asked.

Jean pointed to the corner building across from the courthouse. "The one with the brick front," she said.

"Let's talk to him first. I don't know anything else to do at this point."

"I do," Jean whispered.

An idea that had occurred to him back in the vault haunted him. It was possible, if the sketches about the substandard concrete were true, that other areas of the nuclear plant might have been compromised in the same way. Even worse, what other plants had CCI constructed using the same techniques? David shuddered at the thought, knowing instinctively that if CCI followed the same pattern in the past, there were nuclear power plants scattered throughout the world waiting for disaster to strike. And disaster, on the scale David envisioned, meant human suffering, death, and destruction.

2

As David and Jean Michaels walked out of the bank, a man seated in one of the end offices picked up the phone and dialed. It was answered on the first ring.

"David and Jean Michaels just left the First National Bank building. They examined some papers from a safe-deposit box, made photocopies, and returned the originals to the box." With the message delivered, the man went back to the task before him.

3

Foster Crowe hated Clayton, Arkansas. The town had no bars, no strip joints, no place for a red-blooded American boy to have fun. He hated the rednecks that drove through town in battered pickups, the cops who kept their eyes on him, and the women who paid no attention to him. He hated the fact that after 5:00 P.M. you were lucky to find a grocery store open. He hated the seedy motel where he passed the days without cable TV, and he hated himself for allowing it all to happen. But he liked the money, and, he continually had to remind himself, he had been in worse places before. It was just difficult to remember where and when.

Crowe considered himself a specialist. After all, a specialist was a person who solved specific problems, problems that no one else could deal with. In that sense of the word, Crowe was one of the best. He had worked for Wayne Young years ago, when Collins Construction was still headquartered in New Jersey. Why a sane, rational corporate executive would willingly choose to leave New Jersey for Arkansas was beyond Crowe's comprehension. Had the small man been at all religious, he might well have bowed and prayed twice daily toward the northeast United States. The South was a different place. But that was not Crowe's worry; he would soon return to his own Mecca. He was here to solve problems, and he was good at it.

Now he had another problem on his hands. That redneck of all rednecks, Billy Tippett, must have seen or heard something at the construction site. From what he had heard, it had to do with that religious freak's death the other day. If that was the case, he, Foster Crowe, was involved too. That meant he would doubly enjoy solving the problem of Billy Tippett.

The redneck had sure sounded like he knew something last night in the pool hall. And when Crowe had called Wayne Young to report, he had almost had his head taken off by the security head for calling him at home.

Foster Crowe was nobody's idiot. Not Wayne Young's and certainly not that redneck, Billy Tippett's. He knew he was the only link between the death of Jimmy Michaels and the head of security at Collins Construction International, Wayne Young. It was a tenuous thread at best, but a thread nonetheless.

He had just spoken to Young by phone. *Idiot,* Crowe thought. Every street punk in New Jersey knew better than to issue orders on open lines, but not Young. The order had come. He would enjoy getting rid of Billy Tippett, redneck supreme. And he would also demand and receive much more than a measly ten thousand dollars. After all, a person should get paid for what he knows, not for what he does. Wasn't that what redneck Tippett had said last night?

Foster Crowe pulled himself from the worn chair where he had been reclining. He opened the door to the small refrigerator that came with the dumpy room he was calling home and retrieved the last bottle of beer. He would have to make a trip to the neighboring county to buy some more or seek out one of the bootleggers who plied the illegal booze trade in the dry county of Clayton and charged an arm and a leg for the alcohol.

Crowe dressed, not caring that he was wearing a dirty undershirt, and left the stuffy motel room. He got in his car and headed south. It would take about an hour to get the beer and return. He would be back just in time to see the only ball game on the only TV channel he could get in this redneck town.

Foster Crowe laughed aloud as he drove. He would leave Clayton and Clayton County before long, and when he left, he would have more money than he had ever dreamed of. Redneck Billy Tippett knew enough to get killed; Foster Crowe knew enough to get rich.

4

"That's not right, Buddy," Jerry Kennedy said into the telephone. "This should at least be considered in a court of law. At least you can admit that the possibility of negligence exists on the part of CCI too."

Jerry Kennedy listened to the answer, his face changing from light red to deep crimson. He restrained himself only with a supreme effort and hung the phone up almost delicately. He wanted to throw the instrument across the office. He wanted to scream at someone. He wanted to crawl through the telephone wires and end up in the offices of Worker's Comp in Little Rock and pound some sense into the people down there.

Kennedy sat, staring at the phone, knowing that he had been outmaneuvered, at least for now. It would be difficult to relay the information to Jean, remembering that she was due in his office in a matter of minutes. It wasn't right. And, he thought, it always seemed to happen to the good people. And Jean Michaels was one of the good ones, as Jimmy had been.

He hated being a lawyer at times.

CHAPTER
SEVEN

1

Emerson Collins was having a bad day. Wayne Young had assured him everything was under control. He had seen the original reports Jimmy Michaels had filed with the various departments and agencies, and he had read the report from Young. The written record produced by Jimmy Michaels had been effectively countered. It had taken the exercise of influence in certain quarters, the threat of violence in others, and sufficient money in every realm to counteract the reports, but it had been done. Everything was falling into place just the way it should. That was what worried the head of CCI.

Jameson and Emerson Collins had built the massive Collins Construction International starting with a small construction company in New Jersey specializing in industrial steel construction. They gradually diversified their areas of interest until they had been forced to create CCI to act as a holding company. With the growth had come the venture into nuclear construction and with that, government contracts. Contracts had led to consulting jobs and overseas contracts, all of which were more lucrative than even Emerson had envisioned. The company had prospered at every level. CCI was the foremost contractor for nuclear generating construction in the world. The company presently had reactors under various stages of construction in France, England, Germany, Belgium, and the United States. Emerson Collins allowed himself a rare, self-satisfied smile. CCI was also working on smaller, subterranean versions of its ultra-high-pressure cooled nuclear reactors in Oman and, Collins recalled with satisfaction, Iran. Using a combination of heavy water and the Soviet RBMK-type reactors, CCI was on the verge of developing one of the most efficient reactors in the world. But the good of mankind was not Collins's goal. As far as he was concerned, it was every man for himself, and that's how he directed the massive company.

Emerson Collins and his brother, Jameson, were among the ten highest paid executives in the United States. Along with the retail giant whose home offices were in Arkansas, that meant three of the country's ten highest paid executives lived and worked in Arkansas.

Emerson heard the door that connected his office to Jameson's open. Jameson walked in. It was always amazing to Emerson that he and his brother possessed even a single strand of like DNA, because they were so different from one another. Emerson was exacting almost to a fault. He was slim and gray and immaculately clothed in a dark, custom-made wool suit while his brother, Jameson, favored a less formal black blazer and slacks.

"What is it, Jameson? I've got business," Emerson Collins snapped.

The other difference between the two brothers was that Emerson was direct while Jameson was diplomatic. "It's the Michaels thing," Jameson answered.

Emerson sat waiting for further explanation.

"Something doesn't feel right, Emerson."

"Give me a clue."

"I can't. It's just not right. It's no more than a feeling, but it's a strong one." Jameson took the chair opposite Emerson. He never liked coming into his brother's office. If he believed in such things, he would have thought the office possessed a profound sense of danger, as if the room itself had a life.

"You've seen the reports from Young?" Emerson asked, pretending to busy himself with some of the papers on his desk.

"According to him everything's fine. I'm not sure I trust him, though."

"Of course you don't trust him," Emerson sighed. "I don't trust him either. That's why I keep tabs on him."

Jameson's head jerked up at his brother's statement. "You're spying on Young?"

Emerson, his hands expansive, said, "Of course I am. That's my job, remember? I don't trust anyone, not even you, Jamie."

Jameson nodded. "You've told me that before." He was continually amazed at the preparedness of his brother, though he knew he shouldn't be. Emerson was the pragmatic one; the doer. He was the dreamer. If he could dream it, Emerson could do it. They made a good team. Except lately Jameson was beginning to suspect that Emerson was withholding certain information. There were things going on, things he'd seen in reports, about which he knew nothing. He could sense that now was not the time to bring it up.

"And you believe things are under control?" Jameson asked.

"At this point they're as under control as we can expect. We are in the clear with OSHA, Worker's Comp, the NRC, the AEC, and the insurance carriers. Some of the underwriters have been making some waves, but they're in line for now. That's all we can ask for at the present."

"What about Michaels family?"

"So far no problems. We'll wait and see. I don't expect any repercussions, though. For now, our major goal is to finish Arkansas Three and Four."

Jameson relaxed, bolstered by the apparent calm of his pragmatic brother.

"Settle down, Jameson. Let me take care of this. I'll let you know if we run into trouble, but I'm not going looking for it. Just remember we have friends in high places, and if necessary, they owe us." Jameson rose to leave. He had great respect for his brother's ideas and political connections. Without the driving force Emerson provided, CCI would never have gotten off the ground. Neither he nor his brother would be billionaires, philanthropists, or political powers.

Emerson sat for a moment after his brother was gone, musing behind his desk, knowing that Jameson was not aware of the whole story. He then reached for his private phone and placed a call to France. He just might have to slow down some of his projects for the time being. He needed to concentrate on the Michaels thing for a few days, touch base with Washington, and assure himself that all possible contingencies were covered.

Emerson grinned. His older brother didn't even know how much each of them was worth, and he knew Jameson would be shocked beyond belief to learn they had just surpassed a Middle Eastern prince as two of the world's richest men. He also knew big brother would be even more shocked at the methods his younger brother had employed to accumulate the vast empire.

2

David Michaels sat in stunned silence. Jean was next to him, saying something he missed. He roused himself from his information-induced stupor in time to hear Jean's question.

"How much did you say, Jerry?" she asked Jerry Kennedy. Kennedy had been the Michaels's attorney for as long as Jean could remember. They'd always had more of a friendship than a strict business relationship, but she had always known that Jerry would be there for her when she needed him. It appeared the time had arrived.

"One thousand two hundred ninety-two dollars and twenty cents," Jerry Kennedy read from the papers in his hand. As he read, he tried unsuccessfully to stop the trembling in his hands. It was largely a futile exercise. He had the figure memorized, but the pretense of reading from the papers gave him reason to avoid Jean's cold stare.

"That's not all," the attorney continued. He would have liked to have been anywhere else at the moment. It was hard enough to tell Jean, but it was doubly difficult to do so with David Michaels present. There was something about the navy chaplain that intimidated him.

"It can't be much worse," Jean countered.

"It is," Kennedy said, avoiding David Michaels's cold stare. "The insurance company has put a freeze on the death benefit payment until it completes its investigation."

David Michaels flew from his seat. "Investigation! For what?!"

"Take it easy, David," Kennedy said, trying to soothe the chaplain and wondering if such outbursts were typical of military preachers. "Just before you two came in, I was talking to the insurance company. I'd already talked to Worker's Comp in Little Rock. I tried to call OSHA, but they wouldn't accept my call. Seems the insurance carrier is concerned that there might have been drugs involved in Jimmy's death."

"That's absurd! Where did they get that idea?" David was out of his chair, moving in the direction of the attorney.

Jerry Kennedy instinctively drew back and tried to stay out of the reach of David Michaels. "I know it's crazy, David. But your explosions aren't going to help Jean or the situation. Sit down. Please," Kennedy said, regaining control of his emotions.

"Let's listen to what Jerry has to say, David," Jean suggested.

David returned to his chair; his blood boiled at the mere mention of drugs in connection with his brother. "Tell us, Jerry."

Jerry Kennedy related his talks with Worker's Comp and OSHA. However, he was at a loss concerning the insurance carrier, who had called just as David and Jean entered the office, thus delaying their meeting.

"Basically," Kennedy continued, "the insurance carrier of the life insurance policy is concerned that Jimmy might have been taking drugs, that he might have been negligent in the performance of his job, or a combination of the two, either of which could invalidate the insurance policy the company carries on all its workers."

"How can they say that?" Jean asked in a low voice.

"It sounded as if the company might have been tipped off by an outside source—an informant."

"A liar. Let's call a worm a worm. What's the bottom line?" David asked, his anger barely under control.

The lawyer cleared his throat. "The company has the right to withhold payment until the matter can be resolved. They will conduct an investigation into the accident and render a decision."

"How long?" David queried.

Kennedy was uncomfortable. "I can't say. Depends on how the investigation goes," he hedged.

"How long?" Jean echoed David's question. She knew Jerry Kennedy well enough to know when he was avoiding a direct answer.

"Jean, I don't know." He swallowed hard. "I've known these things to drag on for years."

"Years! And what is Jean supposed to do until then?" David demanded.

"David!" Kennedy almost screamed. "I'm on your side," he finished in a subdued voice. "Don't you think I know how Jean feels? I'm as angry as you are, but that's not going to help rectify the situation. I have a few avenues I can try. I'll file a petition this afternoon, but I don't hold out any hope for that."

David felt defeated, and he knew Jean had to feel the same way. It was difficult enough to lose a loved one, but then to have to fight for every benefit was absurd.

"We'll get along, Jerry. Jimmy and I had some money saved. The Lord will take care of our needs."

David looked at Jean. His faith in God was dwindling as he watched everything going on around him. Life was out of his control. Faith was nothing more than an exercise in frustration. And the weaker his faith got, the stronger Jean's got. He shook his head. "God expects us to take care of some things for ourselves," he said to Jean.

"Maybe, maybe not," Jean answered.

"Well, I'm not going to sit around and wait. I'm going to do something."

"You'll only make things worse, David," Jerry Kennedy advised. "Let me handle it. Give the law a chance to work."

"The problem with that," David said, as he rose to leave, "is that your law and justice are different entities. One has absolutely nothing to do with the other. Your way takes time. Years. You said it yourself. Well, I don't have years, and neither does Jean. I'll do this myself," he said, then left the office.

"You think he will cause trouble?" Jerry Kennedy asked.

Jean watched David's back as he disappeared from view. "If he's like his brother, you can count on it. Jimmy was the best man I ever knew, but don't try to mess with his family or his religion. He'll make trouble," she concluded.

3

Arkansas Nuclear Units Three and Four occupied almost eighty acres not more than twenty minutes from the city limits of Clayton, on the banks of the largest man-made lake in the state. The twin concave surfaces of the cooling towers could be seen for miles and were already being used by light aircraft as navigational aids. The projected time of construction for the twin power plants had been ten years. Now, in their sixth year of construction, Arkansas Three and Four were less than two years from completion, a modern miracle in itself. They would be the first nuclear plants in the South to be wholly owned by an independent electrical cooperative, and the prospect of having them on line two years early was almost too good to be true.

Allen Stuart had started his career twenty-seven years earlier as a journeyman with the North Illinois Electrical Company. He had done it all in those years, from setting power line poles to designing power grid systems. The move to Arkansas to manage North Central Electrical Cooperative had been too good to pass up. As the general manager for NCEC, he had overall operational control of the seventeen-county power infrastructure. Building the nuclear plants just outside Clayton was a good idea that required genius and foresight. The site had a lake large enough to provide the massive quantities of water necessary to cool the light water reactor, thus satisfying the regulatory hurdles of the state and national governments.

Now, as he examined the computer projections on his desk, he saw that the completion of construction was in sight. The reactors would provide all the power needed to service his seventeen-county grid with enough additional capacity to insure major income from Arkansas Power and Light, a subsidiary of Middle South Utilities, and the servicing company for the areas not served by cooperatives. Stuart smiled at the prospect of the role reversal. Before the light water reactor, NCEC had to buy all its power from the larger company at the set price. Now the roles would be reversed.

The projections were ahead of schedule by more than two years, which guaranteed a return on investment that greatly exceeded even his expectations. He had no doubt that when the board of directors saw this information, he would be rewarded appropriately. And he could use the money. True, he'd received almost five hundred thousand dollars from CCI to ignore changes in plans and shortcuts in non-critical systems, but the gambling losses he continued to incur on his frequent excursions to Tunica, Mississippi, were beginning to bear down on him. Those losses had precipitated the verbal agreement he had made with Emerson Collins of CCI, the contractors for the power plant. *There's nothing illegal about the agreement,* he rationalized.

The death of one of CCI's inspectors had been a slight glitch in the mechanism, but that was already resolved. The plant would be completed two years ahead of schedule, Stuart would be rewarded, and the gambling would cease. He had promised his wife he would stop just as soon as he got even. That day was within sight, and he could hardly wait to pay off the casinos that populated the small Mississippi town.

And then there was the other plan his wife knew nothing about.

CHAPTER EIGHT

1

David waited until Jean's car was out of sight before he turned and entered the county courthouse. He could still feel the effects of the anger generated in Jerry Kennedy's office. He would have to control himself. Anger, under certain circumstances, could be as dangerous as a sniper's bullet. As he pushed through the door, he was disoriented for a moment. With the exception of some cosmetic renovations, the building was as he remembered it more than twenty years ago. He headed for the offices of the county sheriff, tucked away in one corner of the building across from the county treasurer's office. As he approached the glass-paneled door to the warren of offices, he noticed the name painted on the glass—Tom Frazier. David was relieved. He and Tom had played football together in high school before Tom had transferred in his senior year. They had never been best friends, but they had partied together after the Friday night games, and David knew he would be able to talk to the man.

Behind the glass door was a waiting room furnished with an old leather sofa and two matching armchairs. The leather was beginning to crack, and the green tile floor was chipped and scarred. The walls had originally been painted in a two-tone motif, but time and dirt had worked to render the color a monotone brown. A wall of radio equipment was mounted on the far wall. A single deputy sat behind a gray metal desk, her brown uniform starched almost board stiff. She smiled as he entered.

"Good morning, sir. May I help you?" the deputy asked.

"I'd like to see Sheriff Frazier if he's in," David said absentmindedly, his mind still on the less-than-triumphant meeting with Jerry Kennedy.

"The sheriff is with someone at the moment. If you would like to take a seat, I'll tell him you're here," the deputy said.

"Thanks. The name is . . ."

". . . Commander David Michaels," she interjected, before David could say it. "Or do they say 'Reverend' in the navy?"

David looked at the young woman, not willing to believe his eyes. "David is fine."

The deputy noticed the confused look on David's face, and smiled. "I won't ever forget our senior prom," she said.

"Janice Morgan!" David exclaimed, finally identifying the attractive deputy. "I'll never forget it either. You were the prettiest girl there, and I was the luckiest guy. How is the ex-prom queen?"

"Fine, David. I'm sorry about Jimmy."

"Thanks. That's the reason I'm here, to talk to Tom about what he knows, if it's not inconvenient."

"It's not. I think he's been expecting you. He was at the funeral, you know. That's the kind of guy Tom is."

"That's good to hear. I can see him in law enforcement, but . . . so, what's it like being a deputy?"

"It's all right. But I'm going to enjoy being sheriff more."

"You're joking!" David said, instantly regretting it. He'd once thought he was in love with Janice Morgan. They'd dated during their senior year. They had even talked about marriage, the way young people do when they don't realize what the commitment entails. That prom had been their last real date. He'd gone to the Naval Academy, and Janice . . . he realized he did not know what Janice had done. The fact that they'd been so close made this realization all the worse. Now, as he thought back, he found it difficult to remember exactly what had come between them. Too many years had passed.

And now there was Cindy. Cindy? What was he thinking? There had never been anything between them, not like there had been between him and Janice. Or so he thought until the confession by the green-eyed girl. Suddenly he was back in First Community Church with Cindy in his arms.

"You one of those?" Janice Morgan asked.

"Those?" David asked, returning to reality.

"One of those men who believe a woman can't handle a job like sheriff?"

"It's not that," David defended. "It's just that you're so, so . . ."

"Beautiful?" she supplied. "I've got as many years on me as you."

"Maybe, but they look better on you. And yes, you are beautiful, but . . ."

". . . but a beautiful woman probably can't do the job?"

David stopped. "It's getting worse, isn't it? I keep putting my foot in my mouth."

Janice laughed amiably. "You keep going and you'll have your whole leg in there."

David laughed. He was enjoying the conversation in spite of his faux pas. "I think you'd make a great sheriff," he said seriously.

"In that case, I'll tell Tom you're here," she grinned. She picked up the phone on her desk and spoke into it briefly. "He'll be just a few more minutes," she said after she hung up.

David and Janice talked, catching up on the last twenty years. Janice talked about Jimmy's death and the effect it had on the community. David was just about to tell her why he wanted to talk to Tom Frazier when the door behind Janice opened, and Tom ushered another man out.

"Mornin', David," the sheriff greeted him. "This is Allen Stuart, the general manager of North Central Electrical Cooperative. I don't think you know each other."

Allen Stuart extended his hand and David took it. "I was sorry to hear about your brother," Stuart said.

"Thanks," David responded. David could remember meeting people who had an aura about them. Allen Stuart was one of them. David could not place it immediately, but the feeling was distinctively uncomfortable, as if evil exuded from every pore. He shivered inwardly. "Nice to meet you."

"And you. Excuse me, I have to get back to work," Stuart said as he left the office.

"How are you, Dave?" Tom Frazier asked.

"Fine, Tom. How 'bout you?"

"Up to my neck in bootleggers and marijuana growers," he said. "Some things never change. What can I do for you today?"

"Got a few minutes?" David asked.

"Come on in. I'll get us some coffee."

"I'll do it," Janice offered, and she poured two cups from the coffeepot sitting near the radio equipment.

"Wonders never cease," Tom Frazier smiled.

David watched the two law enforcement officers. "She doesn't get coffee, I presume."

"You presume correctly," Janice Morgan said, before the sheriff could speak. "Only for special people."

"Am I to presume that I'm a special person today?" Tom Frazier asked, a wide smile on his face.

Janice Morgan looked first at him and then at David. "I wouldn't if I were you," she answered and returned to her desk.

David and Tom Frazier stepped into the office and closed the door. The inner office was furnished almost exactly as the front lobby. The same worn leather furniture and the same green tile combined to make the office functional, but only barely.

Tom Frazier noticed David's assessment. "We don't pay much attention to the furnishings. Clayton County has a limited budget, and what I get I spend on my people and outside equipment. My real office is that car outside, not this hole. You're just lucky to catch me here this morning."

"You were always interested in law, if I remember correctly," David remarked.

"Yeah. I thought I wanted to be an attorney. I even started at the University of Arkansas Law School. It took about half a semester to discover I was meant to do something else. Now I'm looking forward to the day I can get out gracefully. But you're here to talk about Jimmy, right?"

David sat down, following Tom's lead. "Right. What can you tell me about it?"

Tom Frazier ran his hand over his short-cropped brown hair. "Not much. It's out of my jurisdiction. I probably know less about it than you do," Tom said.

"How's that possible? You're the sheriff."

"Because jurisdiction in this case lies first with the federal government. I'm not even sure if it falls under the FBI, OSHA, NRC, or some other agency with even more initials. All I know is that I was served with an official injunction the day of the accident. I was prevented from going on the site before I even knew that Jimmy had fallen."

"That's kind of strange, isn't it?"

"If you mean, does it seem that there's something to hide, I'd agree with you. Unfortunately, there's nothing I can do about it. Oh, I've asked around. Talked to some of the men on Jimmy's shift. Everyone saw the same thing, those that saw anything. Sounds like an accident, I have to admit. Still, I would have liked to have conducted my own investigation."

"But you're not convinced? That it was an accident, I mean?"

Frazier shifted uncomfortably in his chair; he sipped the coffee and grimaced. "No, I'm not sure. I'm not sure of anything concerning this case. But don't read anything definitive into the lack of evidence."

David had said nothing to Jean or his father that morning, but he was curious about a number of points, one of which he was about to ask Tom about. "What about the equipment Jimmy was using? Do you have it or have you seen it?"

"No to both questions. I heard that it was impounded and was being kept until the OSHA investigation, whenever that is. Carlton Graham is in charge of OSHA here in Clayton County."

"It's already over," David said. "The official judgment is with the company, and CCI has been cleared of any negligence or wrongdoing."

"Over! Just like that? Jimmy's barely in the ground!" the sheriff blurted and instantly regretted his outburst. "I'm sorry, David."

David winced at the statement. "It's all right. I understand frustration. Nothing makes any sense. According to Jerry Kennedy, it's standard operating procedure for OSHA. Falls under the same category as eminent domain, more or less. Probably the same reason you can't get in to investigate. Seems OSHA has the right to rule in these cases when the greater good of the government is the primary factor."

"That explains what Stuart was doing here," Frazier said. "He was worried that you might cause some trouble concerning Jimmy's death. I don't like the man. There's something about him."

"I got the same feeling. But why is he worried?"

"Nuclear Three and Four are Stuart's babies. He's got NCEC hocked to the rim of those cooling towers out there. If this doesn't fly, it's his hide the board of directors is going to start hollering for. It's his company as far as he's concerned, and he doesn't want any slowdowns. The job is almost two years ahead of schedule. That means Stuart will have them on line early. And *that* means more money—for NCEC and for him. His contract contains bonus clauses; the sooner the plant is finished, the more bonus money he collects. But he didn't tell me OSHA had already cleared Collins International."

"That's not the whole story," David continued. He was warming to the large man across the desk. Even at 6'2", David had had to look up into Frazier's eyes when they shook hands. He had forgotten how large the man was. But he remembered Tom as being strict and honest. He didn't appear to have changed, and David told him about the insurance investigation and the withholding of payment to Jean and the boys.

"That's nuts!" Tom Frazier barked. "Jimmy never touched drugs. He wouldn't even take an aspirin without good reason. Those boys are way off base on this one."

"That's what I thought, Tom, but I can't prove it." David hesitated. "Tom, is there any way to get our hands on the equipment that Jimmy was using that day?"

"Not that I know of. You might check with Graham, but I've already requested access to the equipment and been refused. The only way to get our hands on that stuff would be to break into the construction site, assuming we knew where the stuff was."

"Are you telling me that I can't even see the stuff?"

"I'm telling you *I* can't even see the stuff! Government regulations and federal laws have got this thing wrapped up so tight, nobody's going to get their hands on that stuff. You got no chance."

"Something smells, Tom."

"I'm beginning to agree with you on that. But my hands are tied.

I'm an official of the county, on the bottom of the totem pole. And I can't go around defying court orders and federal law."

"And I can?" David said, half seriously.

Tom Frazier leaned back in his chair, his hands behind his head, and grinned. "No, you can't. But if circumstances were such that you did come into possession of certain . . . items, shall we say? And as long as you were caught outside the official boundaries of Nuclear Three and Four, whose jurisdiction stops with the fence surrounding the site, it would fall under my jurisdiction, and I have a greater understanding of the grief process than most law enforcement officers."

David was stunned. Had he actually heard what he thought he had? Had he heard Clayton County Sheriff Tom Frazier sanction an illegal search for Jimmy's equipment? He was being told, unofficially, that the Clayton County sheriff would look the other way while he found out what happened to his brother. It was crazy, but there it was. And a rudimentary plan was beginning to form in his mind. He rose to leave. David had heard enough veiled innuendo in his military career to know better than to question it. He also knew that there was a very real possibility that Tom Frazier would deny this conversation should events escalate beyond the boundaries of Clayton County, Arkansas. The risk was all on his own shoulders.

"Thanks, Tom. I'll keep you informed."

Sheriff Tom Frazier rose with him. "Please don't," Frazier responded. "Be careful."

David exited the inner office and headed for the outside door.

"Not going to say goodbye?" Janice Morgan asked as she watched David leave, his thoughts obviously somewhere else.

David turned. He'd been preoccupied with what he'd just heard. "Sorry, Janice. I'm not all here."

"That I can see."

David waved. "Take care," he said and left. As he walked down the corridor of the courthouse, he thought about the bizarre conversation he'd just had with Tom Frazier. He had been given de facto permission to investigate Jimmy's death—permission even to break the law at his own risk. It was also becoming clearer that Sheriff Tom Frazier knew something he was not telling!

David felt a shudder race through his body; something *was* going on at Nuclear Three and Four! That was what the sheriff was trying to tell him. But the sheriff's words had also contained a warning. Help would come only if it did not jeopardize the status quo, which meant that such assistance was questionable at best. David realized he would be putting himself in harm's way.

2

As soon as David Michaels exited his office, Tom Frazier dialed a number and waited. A man's voice answered on the first ring of the private number.

"I think we may have what we wanted," the Clayton County sheriff said into the mouthpiece.

"Excellent," the voice acknowledged.

"You realize he could be killed?"

"That would be a tragedy, a calculated risk. It's a risk we're prepared to take," the voice said.

"I wonder if it's a risk David Michaels is prepared to take?" Tom Frazier asked. "Provided, of course, that we asked him."

"I think if he knew the circumstances, he probably would be willing. Unfortunately, we cannot reveal what we suspect at this point. May God be with him."

Tom Frazier stared at the disconnected receiver, knowing the man on the other end was assessing the problem with the cold, calculating objectivity that came with indirect involvement.

3

Wayne Young reviewed his plan to eliminate the pest Billy Tippett and to dispose of the secondary problem, Foster Crowe. Up to this point, Crowe had done what he had been hired to do, and he had done it well. Maybe too well, the head of CCI security thought. Crowe was beginning to think, to scheme, and for a man in his profession, thinking was a dangerous trait. Young had already decided it would be wishful thinking to expect Crowe to return to New Jersey without at least attempting to line his pockets with a little more CCI cash.

Wayne Young had not devised an elaborate strategy. Quite the contrary, it was a simple plan. The first step was the elimination of Billy Tippett. For that he would use Foster Crowe once again. Both men worked at the construction site, and Young had no doubt that Crowe would be able to keep Tippett in sight long enough to do away with him. After that, Young had someone to take care of Crowe, a man who was the epitome of ruthlessness. The security chief didn't like the man who drove the Mercedes sedan, but he'd used him before, and the man was efficient and cheap. At odd times Young wondered who was using whom? The man in the Mercedes always exuded an air of confidence, as if he alone were in charge. It had occurred to Young more than once that the man in the green Mercedes enjoyed his work more than he should.

4

Billy Tippett waited in the congested traffic at Gate Three of Arkansas Three and Four. It was the same every morning during shift change. He had ignored the small hole in his radiator, and his pickup was beginning to overheat along with his patience. He didn't want to be on the job this morning. He had more important things to take care of, but the more he thought about it, the more uncertainty crept in.

He reached into his shirt pocket and fingered the note, just as the early morning sun disappeared behind a dark cloud. He then looked up and grinned as rain began to fall. Rain was a reasonable excuse for him not to show this morning, and the solution to his dilemma had just struck him.

Billy Tippett pulled his truck out of the line of traffic and headed back in the direction he'd come. It had taken thirty careful minutes last night to compose the note nestled in his shirt pocket, and he was not about to waste his masterpiece.

The rain began in earnest as Billy reached the county road that led to the reactor construction site. He turned left, reaching for the radio knob as he slowed the pickup around the next curve. He turned up the volume and began to sing as the old truck rattled down the road. Ten minutes later he turned the truck south and headed for the state capital. He checked his fuel gauge just to be sure. He had enough fuel, he knew, for the seventy-odd miles to Little Rock. He began to whistle to the country song that blared forth from the damaged speaker. As distorted bass notes filled the cab, Billy Tippett began to feel the euphoria that comes with a firm decision. He was his own master.

As the pickup reached sixty miles an hour and the temperature gauge settled in at just below the danger level, Billy failed to notice the black Mustang that had followed him from the construction area.

5

Foster Crowe had been three cars behind Billy Tippett at the entrance to Gate Three when he saw the redneck pull out of line and head in the opposite direction. It had taken him a couple of minutes to do the same. He'd wanted to stomp the woman in the car ahead of him for not moving when he laid on his horn. She finally got the message and pulled up far enough for Crowe to pull out of the line of traffic, flashing him an angry look as he pulled past. Maybe, he thought, he'd just come back and pay her back for that look.

By the time he turned around, Billy Tippett's truck had disappeared. Crowe panicked for a moment and then turned left, toward town. It had only taken seconds for his Shelby GT Mustang to catch the rattletrap of a truck the redneck drove. He settled into a position fifty yards behind Tippett and turned on his windshield wipers to clear the glass of falling rain.

Crowe had left the motel room this morning fully intending to kill Mr. Redneck Billy Tippett. There was always a way to get rid of unwanted personnel on a construction job, but now the country bumpkin was out on the road heading south. Crowe was skittish at the prospect of having to do the job in a place other than the semi-controlled environment of the construction site.

He glimpsed the truck round a bend in the road and lost sight for a second. When he rounded the curve himself, Crowe saw the truck turn onto the highway leading south to Little Rock. Things were looking brighter, despite the cloudy skies overhead. It was possible that the yokel was about to have an accident on a rain-slicked highway. Accidents happened every day, Crowe reminded himself, and dying in a car accident made a person just as dead as dying from a construction-site mishap.

Crowe ran through the channels on his radio and then twisted the knob off. "Country music," he muttered, and made a retching sound.

6

Billy Tippett, blissful in his ignorance, backed off the accelerator slightly and maintained an even fifty-five. No sense getting a ticket for speeding, he reasoned. Not that it would matter much, because in a few hours he would be rich. *Not rich,* he reminded himself. *Wealthy.* Wealthy was better than rich. He had never had any money, not real money. The job at Nuclear Three and Four was the best job he'd ever had, and while that paid him enough to buy his booze and drugs, pay his rent, and keep his old truck running, it was only survival money. Soon he would be beyond that.

Billy concentrated on the highway. The rain was light, but the road was deadly slick. He could feel the truck slip as he rounded a short curve to the left, and he let up on the accelerator a little more.

Better, he reasoned. The speedometer registered slightly under fifty. As soon as he got out of the mountains and onto Interstate 40 he would be able to make better time. Better to hold it down until then. Besides, a lot of construction was going on further down the road, and that would slow him up even more. Today he could afford to be a little more patient.

The rain began to fall harder. Billy grinned and whistled louder, the distorted strains of the latest number-one country hit filling the confined space of the truck cab. From force of habit his foot eased down on the accelerator. The truck responded, the speed crept toward sixty.

Twenty miles more and Billy Tippett would be on flat land, away from the dangers of mountain curves with their drop-offs and on his way to fullfilling every dream he'd ever had.

7

Foster Crowe pulled to within twenty yards of the rear of Billy Tippett's rusted pickup. No doubt, Crowe calculated, the redneck was headed for Interstate 40. From there it was a toss-up, but that was irrelevant as far as the small man was concerned. He was about to see that Billy Tippett never made it out of the mountains.

Crowe glanced at his speed. Billy had eased his way up to sixty and now headed for even greater speeds.

Perfect, thought Crowe. He closed the narrow gap between the bumper of his Mustang and the rear bumper of the truck. The Mustang's radial tires gripped the pavement as well as they could considering the rain-slick roadway. He could see the rear of the truck fishtail left, then right, and finally straighten out as the redneck let up on the gas pedal.

Crowe inched closer.

The truck was once again accelerating, passing sixty-five this time. Crowe stayed with the speeding vehicle, inching ever closer.

8

Billy Tippett had not been paying attention to his rearview mirror, and now, as he glanced in the cracked glass, he was shocked to see a black Mustang on his tail. He let his gaze rest on the black car a little too long and almost failed to see the approaching curve. He checked his speed. Sixty-three! Too fast! He backed off, feeling the truck slow in response. His eyes quickly returned to the mirror. The car was still there, getting closer yet!

Billy Tippett felt his stomach muscles tighten. His mouth was dry, and he wished fervently for a cold beer. The black Mustang was tracking as if tied to the rear bumper of his truck.

"Back off, man!" he screamed in the mirror.

The Mustang kept its distance. Billy felt the beginning of the curve, his body responding to Newton's law and his shoulder pressing into the door panel. The pressure increased as the turn deepened.

The Mustang remained.

Billy tasted bile in his dry throat. He swallowed hard, his throat burning. The guy must be nuts, he realized. The curve was on him; he steered, trying to keep the old truck in the right lane. He felt the rear end give slightly and he lightly tapped the brake pedal.

He looked in the mirror once again. The specter Mustang moved closer!

9

Foster Crowe saw a single brake light come on as Billy applied the brakes in an attempt to keep the rattletrap on the road. Crowe realized that this was going to be easier than he had hoped. If he let the redneck continue, he would kill himself without any help.

Crowe pressed on the accelerator. The Mustang moved closer to the rusted rear bumper of Billy Tippett's truck. The single brake light flashed once again, and Crowe knew opportunity when he saw it.

Crowe backed off slightly as the Mustang and the truck entered the right-hand curve as if welded to each other. The black car was three feet from the truck bumper when Foster Crowe touched the accelerator pedal gently. The Shelby V-8 growled deeply and propelled the front bumper of the Mustang into the left rear corner of the truck's bumper. It wasn't much, not even enough to scratch the chrome of the Mustang's bumper, really just a touch, but it was enough.

The rear end of the truck, its momentum already directed outward, broke free when bumper met bumper. It happened quickly; Foster Crowe was pleasantly amazed.

The rear tires of the truck, their tenuous hold on the wet pavement now broken, accelerated sideways, bringing the truck broadside in the middle of the curve. The tires, old and tortured, withstood the punishment for a few moments before the left rear tire exploded off the rim. The rear of the truck pitched in the direction of the blown tire; the steel wheel bit into the asphalt and temporarily halted the spin. The truck's rear hesitated for a moment, then continued its awful spin toward the outer limits of the curve and the metal retaining rail that traced the edge of a hundred-foot precipice.

Crowe braked lightly and brought the Mustang under total control. He watched the scene with anticipation. He knew that the old pickup could not remain on the rain-coated roadway. His car slowed, and the truck in front of him slid sideways with the terrified face of Billy Tippett clearly visible in the truck's rearview mirror.

The truck hit the guard rail like the two tons of junk metal it would soon be. It took out a twenty-foot section of steel as the vehicle flew through the air and over the edge of the curve.

Crowe came to a stop fifty yards from where Billy Tippett's pickup had disappeared, got out of the Mustang, and walked back to the edge. The truck was still tumbling down the more than one-hundred-foot embankment. The cab was crushed level with the bed. The vehicle rolled and tumbled like a child's toy.

Mercifully, the truck stopped as it reached the bottom of the ravine and came to a stop on the crushed cab. There was no explosion; the rain began to fall harder than ever. Foster Crowe considered climbing down the ravine to make certain the redneck was dead, but he knew it would be better to avoid any connection with the accident; he'd been lucky thus far. He'd not seen a single car during the exercise. Besides, he figured, there was no way anyone could have survived the crash.

Crowe returned to his car, turned around, and was half a mile from the scene before the first car passed the broken railing. It didn't stop. Billy Tippett's truck was not visible from the elevated roadway, so the driver thought it was only a broken rail that would be repaired by the road crew in time.

10

The last thing Billy Tippett did before he died was grab the note in his shirt pocket. His ticket to the good life had turned into his death warrant.

CHAPTER NINE

1

The rain that had started earlier that morning had swelled into a full-blown downpour. Water was already beginning to puddle in roadway depressions as David Michaels turned onto Main Street and headed for Nuclear Three and Four, twenty minutes from the Clayton County Courthouse. He suddenly remembered Cindy Tolbert's office was in the stone courthouse and parked his father's truck in one of the metered parking spaces near the building.

He'd never felt quite like this before, not even, he remembered, when he had dated Janice Morgan, the would-be sheriff of Clayton

County and former prom queen. The recurring thoughts about Cindy were bewildering, at once contradictory yet exciting. Not unlike, it occurred to David, everything that seemed to be happening to him since his arrival in Clayton.

David and his father had spent most of the night discussing the odd conversation David had had earlier with Sheriff Tom Frazier. It seemed bizarre that a law-enforcement officer should condone—however unofficially—breaking the law. But it had happened, and David wondered about the circumstances that precipitated such a stance.

They had not only discussed the strange conversation; David's father had also broached the idea of the pastorate at First Community Church. David had listened to his father into the early morning hours.

He had told his father that it was still too soon after Jimmy's death to discuss the idea with any real rationality. He had hinted that he might be interested in the pulpit to placate the old man, but he knew at the time that the words were just that—words. His life was waiting for him in Southern California with a group of young marines. But, as he recalled the conversation, he wondered if he had told his father of his interest in the position to get him to drop it, or was he really attracted to the church as he'd told Cindy Tolbert? He'd thought about the pastorate after he'd gone to bed. It had a certain appeal, a tug, but only in a fleeting sort of way. It was another dilemma he would have to confront before returning to Pendleton, but this one, he was certain, already had an answer.

David dug a coin out of his pocket, shoved it into the parking meter, and walked up the steps of the courthouse. Once inside, he turned to his right, away from the sheriff's office and toward the office of the Clayton County clerk.

Stepping into the courthouse was like a trip back in time. The same old notices were attached to the same old bulletin boards. The lighting had been updated and new paneling covered the old plaster walls. The textured copper ceiling was still in place. Dark wooden doors with frosted glass lined the corridor where the door read COUNTY CLERK. David stepped into the office. Three women were working at separate desks behind a long counter. The nearest one looked up when he entered.

"Can I help you, sir?" she asked, with a slight southern accent.

"Could I see Miss Tolbert, please?" David requested. For a second he felt a sense of uncertainty, but then, he had never known Cindy by her married name, and Tolbert came out naturally. He glanced in the direction of the door he'd just come through. The name Cynthia Tolbert was prominent on the upper third of the translucent glass. David smiled to himself, a strange sense of contentment flowing through him.

The young woman, no more than twenty, David guessed, looked at a door in the corner of the open office space. "It will be a few minutes. She has someone in the office at the moment. Would you like to wait?"

David was about to say he would return when the corner door opened and Cindy emerged. "David," she waved. "You here to see me?"

"Not if you're too busy." Had her question contained a note of expectation or was he reading something into the slight nuances that really did not exist? He hoped it was the former.

"Won't be more than a minute," Cindy smiled.

David sat in on one of the mismatched wooden chairs in the small waiting area that contained battered copies of *National Geographic* and assorted hunting magazines, none less than two years old. He noticed a large aerial photograph on the far wall and got up to examine it. He faintly remembered a similar photo adorning the same wall almost forty years ago. But this one was different. The key indicated it as a photo of Clayton County. In the center was an obscene scar glaring white under the sun. David read the key more closely. The photo was current. That was the difference. This photograph was taken after Nuclear Three and Four had been under construction for several years.

The white, glaring scab on the countryside was the construction area surrounding the reactor site.

David heard movement behind him and turned to see Cindy Tolbert and Allen Stuart, the manager of NCEC, exit the corner office. David had the same uneasy feeling he had felt yesterday when he'd first met the man in Sheriff Tom Frazier's office.

Stuart walked through the swinging gate of the counter. "We seem to be running into each other rather frequently, Commander Michaels," Stuart said, not offering his hand.

"Seems so, Mr. Stuart," David replied, grateful that he did not have to force contact with the distasteful manager.

"Allen and I were just going over the titles of the land contiguous to the new generating station," Cindy Tolbert interjected.

David noticed a slight twitch in Stuart's face at the mention of the site. "Buying more land, Mr. Stuart?"

"Just keeping abreast of things. Never can tell when we'll need more. North Central is a growing company."

"I can imagine, with your own nuclear generating plant. Sounds ambitious for a rural electrical cooperative."

"Nothing wrong with ambition, Commander."

"I didn't mean to imply there was. Just curious, is all."

Cindy Tolbert stepped through the gate into the waiting area. "What did you want to see me about, David?"

"Nothing important. I was going to tell you I'll be around for a while. I'm going to help Jean settle the estate and get all the legal stuff finished for her and Dad."

"How long will you be staying?" Stuart asked.

"Shouldn't take more than a few weeks," David answered.

Stuart turned to leave. "Good seeing you again, Commander. If there is anything I can do, please do not hesitate to call me."

David watched the man as he left. He had the feeling that Allen Stuart did not mean what he said and then thought to himself, *I'm going to ask some questions, Mr. Stuart. I'm not satisfied with what OSHA and Collins Construction have decided about Jimmy's death.*

"He seems to be in a hurry," David noted, hoping his distaste for the man was reflected in his speech.

"That's just Allen. He's from up north. They're all like that."

"Do I hear the voice of prejudice?"

"The voice of experience. I've dealt with Allen quite a bit. And to tell you the truth, he's probably more worried about lawsuits stemming from those contiguous lands than he is about acquiring them for future expansion."

"*That* would make more sense," David chuckled, instantly knowing Cindy's intuition was on target. "Corporate paranoia. Anyway, I'll be around. Uh, maybe we can get together while I'm here. Go to a movie. Supper. Whatever."

"I'd like that," she said, genuinely pleased. "And I'm glad you'll be here for a while. I know Jean and the boys will be glad too."

David turned to go. "I'll call you."

"Where're you headed now?"

"Tom Frazier said I might want to talk with Carlton Graham, the OSHA representative out at Nuclear Three and Four. I want to see what he knows about Jimmy's accident."

"I wish you luck. I've dealt with him on occasion. Graham always seemed uninterested in anything other than Collins Construction. Seems more of a company man than a government official."

"He from up north too?" David grinned, detecting the same feelings for Graham she'd displayed for Allen Stuart.

"Let me rephrase that," Cindy said, her hands on her hips in mock rebuke. "He's strange, but he's from the South. We have them down here, too, Commander."

"I'll remember that. And thanks for the warning. Call you later."

As David exited the courthouse, he felt a twinge of nervousness. What was it? The upcoming conversation with the OSHA representative?

The seemingly chance meeting with Allen Sturart? Neither made much sense. He was not the nervous type. Then he realized he'd just asked Cindy Tolbert for a date; that was the source of the quivery feeling. The only other time he could remember such a feeling was the night of the senior prom and his date with Janice. He smiled to himself. A United States Navy commander and chaplain, assigned to one of the toughest units in the history of modern warfare, and he was getting sweaty palms at the thought of phoning a beautiful woman.

2

Cindy Tolbert stood in the middle of her office and watched David Michaels walk away. She had replayed the same scene over and over in her mind countless times in the past—junior high, high school, and then when he'd left for the Naval Acadamy. After Robert had died, she thought she'd died too. Robert had been husband, friend, and adviser. For more than three years, she'd just been going through the motions, arriving at work each day, doing her job, and at night returning to a house devoid of everything she had loved except the memories.

The change had come midway in the fourth year; that had been almost six months ago now. It had been gradual, almost imperceptible, a gentle persuasion that life continued and she was part of it. She realized then that she could love again. Reaching this point had taken prayer, work, and determination, but it had happened. She felt a fullfillment in what she was doing. At the same time, she still felt an emptiness when she thought about Robert, but it was no longer the debilitating vastness it had once been. Robert's memory had been transformed into a burnished patina that exuded warmth when she thought about him.

Cindy had not consciously sought the company of another man in the last year. It would have been a struggle to entertain such a thought in Clayton, Arkansas. Not that there were no eligible bachelors in town, but she'd been the wife of Robert Faulkner, and to everyone in the small community she would always be just that. Off-limits.

Now another change accompanied her new feeling of freedom. It was a longing, a need, which she recognized immediately. She was in love with David.

The self-admission took Cindy Tolbert by surprise. How was it possible? David Michaels had been in town only a few hours, and yet here she was, admitting to loving a man who was little more than a stranger. What had gotten into her? Whatever it was, she knew she did love David, and for the moment, that was enough.

As she watched him disappear down the courthouse corridor, she vowed she would not let him walk out of her life again without telling him how she felt.

3

The anonymous call reported only that there had been an accident on the Hollow Mountain curve. Deputy Sheriff Janice Morgan was working dispatch and took the call. She notified Sheriff Tom Frazier via cellular phone, then called Arkansas State Trooper Joseph Castro.

Frazier reached Hollow Mountain curve within twenty minutes. The blue reflection of rotating emergency lights from the state police unit in front of him bounced off his windshield. He could see Sergeant Joseph Castro getting out of his car.

Joe Castro belied the stereotypical Latin temperament. He was easygoing and, even at 6'4", 270 pounds, difficult to anger.

The ten-year veteran of the Arkansas State Police had toyed with the idea of ignoring the call from the Clayton County dispatcher. He was coming off a twelve-hour shift and was tired. Clayton County, Arkansas, was not a hotbed of criminal activity, but Castro had dealt with more than his share of drunks in the past twelve hours. While he sometimes questioned the political wisdom of maintaining an alcohol-free county, he never disputed the killing and maiming effects of the drug. The answer, in Castro's view, was not to make every Arkansas county "wet." The answer was to ban alcohol; every other such drug had been banned. But that, he knew, had been tried.

Now, as he surveyed the wreckage of Billy Tippett's pickup a hundred feet below, he thought it would be the perfect finale to a totally appalling day if he discovered the driver of the truck had been drinking. He again wished he had ignored the call. It'd take two or three hours just to get the mangled truck up to the roadway. If a body was found in the pile of junk—which surely there would be, judging from the appearance—that'd put him well into the afternoon just completing the paperwork. He turned as he glimpsed a blue light approaching.

Clayton County Sheriff Tom Frazier stopped one foot short of the trooper's bumper and got out of the car.

"What we got, Joe?" Tom Frazier asked.

The big trooper shook his head toward the bottom of the ravine. "Looks like they were in a hurry. Wet road. You know the rest."

"Been down there yet?"

"I was just starting down when you drove up. You call the paramedics and the wrecker. I'll see what gives."

Joe Castro hated automobile accidents. Usually the innocent died. Drunks accounted for the majority of wrecks in Clayton County—a strange statistic since it was illegal to buy or sell alcohol in the dry county. Residents had to drive more than an hour to get the booze, or they had to ferret out a local bootlegger and pay a premium for the alcohol. But, by the looks of this one, the driver had been going too fast into the wet curve.

The dead grass on the slope was slick from the steady rain, and Castro slipped and hopped the entire hundred feet, ruining a perfectly good uniform. As he approached the truck, he could just make out the driver. The old truck, twisted like a pretzel, was resting on its crumpled top. The driver was pinned in the cab, and the sergeant had seen enough accidents to know the paramedics would not be needed.

He worked his way around the twisted wreckage, watching to see if Tom Frazier had started down yet. He tugged on the inverted driver-side door. It refused to open. He moved to the passenger side and pulled on the door handle. It creaked, resisted temporarily, and then gave way under the man's power.

"Looks like Billy Tippett's truck," Tom Frazier said.

Castro looked up. He'd not heard Frazier descend the slope, and the voice surprised him. "It is. Dead as a doornail too."

"He alone?"

"Yeah. Both doors were closed. No way for anyone to fly out."

"How fast you figure he was going?"

Joe Castro crawled into the mangled pickup, tearing his shirt in the process. "Who knows? Fast enough to take out a twenty-foot section of railing up above. Sixty or better would be my guess from the way the railing let go and the impact of the vehicle."

Tom Frazier shook his head. "Had to happen. Billy wasn't wrapped too tight."

"Give me a hand, Tom," Castro said. "We can move him. He's as dead as he will ever get."

"You okaying the move?" Frazier asked. He had been involved in one wrongful-death lawsuit that involved moving an injured person and was not anxious to ever see another.

"I'm okaying it," Castro affirmed.

Frazier moved to assist the trooper. It took them only seconds to remove Billy Tippett from the demolished truck. He'd not been wearing a seat belt. They were laying him on the wet grass when the paramedics and the wrecker broadcast their arrival with lights and sirens.

Two paramedics struggled down the embankment, slipping and sliding the entire way. One carried a fishing tackle box full of first aid paraphernalia. The wrecker driver remained near the fractured railing one hundred feet above and waited to be called.

"Who moved him?" the first paramedic asked.

"I did," Joe Castro answered.

"Dead?" the paramedic asked, noticing the first aid and paramedic training badges on the trooper's uniform sleeve.

"As your grandmother's grandmother."

The paramedics bent over Billy Tippett. "Neck's broken, along with other obvious injuries. Probably died instantly." The paramedic turned to his partner. "Get a stokes. We'll have to haul him out of here with a rope."

"Use the wrecker's winch. Save a lot of work," Tom Frazier suggested.

"Good idea. Do it, Jackson," the senior medic directed. He looked at Billy Tippett and shook his head. "Had to happen. Billy never was too careful."

"Yeah," Castro said. "I'll show it as a one-car. Excessive speed."

"Any marks up above?" Frazier asked.

"I just scanned the area. I'll take the measurements when we're finished down here. There's a rutted mark on the pavement that I figured might be from a wheel. The left rear tire blew," Castro said, pointing to the upturned truck and the blown tire. "The mark's probably from that."

"Let me write it up, Joe," Frazier offered. "You look like you could use some sleep."

The trooper considered the offer momentarily before saying, "Naw, I better do it. Can't tell when you'll end up in court on one of these things. Better to have all the answers than have to guess at them two years later."

"Guess you're right."

The paramedic looked up from where he'd been examining Billy Tippett. "Either of you guys interested in this?" he asked, pointing to Tippett's right hand.

"What is it?" Joe Castro asked.

"Paper. I don't know. You tell me. Note maybe. He's holding it like it was life and death itself." The paramedic pried the paper from Billy's hand.

Castro took the wet piece of paper and read it, then handed it to the sheriff. "What do you make of this?"

Frazier took the paper and handled it carefully. He read the note twice and looked up at Joe Castro. "Looks like Billy was trying to play in the big leagues, doesn't it?"

"Could be," Castro said.

"You got enough to do, Joe. I'll run this down."

"Your county," the big trooper shrugged. "I'll do the accident report."

Frazier nodded and carefully placed the note in a plastic bag he pulled from his pocket. He could still see the words through the clear plastic and knew without a doubt that they were the words that had killed Billy Tippett. He'd have to notify the correct people when he got back to the office.

4

David Michaels approached the sprawling construction complex with apprehension. This time he knew the feeling did not originate with Cindy Tolbert, but with the huge construction site. On the aerial photograph in Cindy's office, it had been a wart on the landscape, a festering scab, but at this distance it appeared more like massive malignant cancer metastasizing in every direction. The trees were gone, sheared as if by an immense hand, sacrificed in the name of progress. For the life of him, David could not figure out why it had been necessary to cut every tree on the eighty-acre site. A twelve-foot, industrial chain-link fence, its razor wire glinting with beads of rain, disappeared to the right and left, snaking out of sight over the rolling hills. He knew the fence enclosed the entire area owned by North Central. Huge industrial lamps were mounted on sixty-foot aluminum poles. Night and day would be indistinguishable within the confines of the fence.

He stopped at the guard house that straddled the four lanes at the complex entrance. A uniformed guard, covered head to foot in rain gear, came out with his hand held high.

David stopped and rolled his window down. "I'm here to see Mr. Graham," he told the guard.

"Do you have an appointment, Mr. . . . ?"

"Michaels," David supplied. "No. I was hoping to see him for just a few minutes if possible. You can tell him I'm the brother of the young man who died here last week."

The guard wrote on his clipboard and returned to the guard shack. He was gone almost five minutes. David watched the activity within the compound until the guard finally returned.

"Mr. Graham can see you. Go to Building Twenty-two," he said, indicating the direction. "You can park in the visitor parking. Mr. Graham's office is just inside the building and to the right. The secretary will show you." The guard handed David a hard hat and a small plastic bag containing what looked like two pieces of wax. "You have to wear the hat and the earplugs while in the area, sir," the guard explained.

David thanked the man, donned the hat and earplugs, and drove deeper into the complex. The construction effort was leviathan, dwarfing even the giant machines that were being used. David could see the gigantic cement plant with its triple mixers standing over ten stories high. The equipment reminded him of the construction projects he'd seen along the highways of Arkansas back in the sixties, when the nation was being linked by concrete interstate systems. But these machines were larger, monstrous in relation to the trucks and graders he'd seen then. Paved roads crisscrossed the area. Even traffic lights were placed at designated intersections to control the enormous volume of vehicles. Twin containment buildings sat just north of the cooling towers, their typical generator-style structures squat and rounded. David could not begin to estimate the number of workers. Thousands, to be sure. Prosperity had indeed come to Clayton County, blown in on the winds of industrial progress.

Building Twenty-two was a large, two-story metal building, obviously intended to be temporary; its usefulness would be terminated with the completion of the construction. David pulled into the parking area designated for visitors.

When he got out of his car, the volume of noise struck him immediately, even with the earplugs in place. Large dump trucks, land graders, mechanical cranes, and diesel equipment generated a cacophony of dissonant grating sound. Even in the rain, men with hard hats scurried like ants among the pieces of equipment. All wore ear protection and David understood why.

The dominant structures on the site were the twin cooling towers rising almost thirty stories into the gray, weeping sky. They loomed like great concrete sentinels over the construction site. David could not imagine that his brother had worked and died on the face of the colossal structures, whose bases alone covered acres. The sides rose majestically, curving inward for the first two hundred feet and then gently flaring the last hundred to form what looked like a giant plant vase. Large hoists were perched on the rim of each tower, making them look like prehistoric birds of prey. Equipment operators appeared as dots within the massive context. David had never seen anything approximating this scale, not even aboard an aircraft carrier.

As he continued toward the office building, he was feeling something that he'd only felt in Vietnam and Iraq. He knew he was in enemy territory, but somehow this enemy territory was different. It was less defined and more dangerous. In 'Nam and Iraq, he knew who the enemy was. Here, but for the feeling, he was not certain an enemy even existed. Then he recognized the feeling for what it was—evil. An all-encompassing feeling of terror gripped him for an instant, and then it was gone as quickly as it had come. David Michaels entered building twenty-two.

5

Wayne Young, head of security for Collins Construction International, ignored the exasperated look from his secretary as he stormed through her office and into his. She had paged him to tell him he had a visitor waiting for him in his office. Young knew it could only be one person, and he was not happy at the prospect of meeting the man at this particular time. That, and the fact that no one was to be in his private office without his presence, combined to magnify his escalating anger.

Young slammed through the office door, barely able to contain himself at the sight of the small, ferretlike man who sat behind his desk, feet resting on the rich walnut top.

"You'd better have a good reason for showing up here," Young whispered menacingly, both ham-sized fists resting on the desktop.

Foster Crowe smiled at the implied threat. "The best reason in the world, Wayne, my man."

Young swept Crowe's feet from his desktop with a massive hand and moved around the large desk. Crowe remained seated, his smile fixed in place.

Young grabbed the small man and lifted him from his chair. Two buttons popped off the front of Crowe's shirt and bounced across the polished hardwood floor.

"Easy, big man," Crowe said. "I've got news you want to hear. Good news, Wayne."

Wayne Young loosened his grip on Crowe and let him drop back into the chair. "Talk to me, vermin," Young hissed, his face inches from Crowe's.

Foster Crowe slunk out of Young's chair and moved away from the bigger man. "The job is done. Just like you wanted. Not only does it look like an accident, it *was* an accident. Mr. Redneck is lying at the bottom of a hundred-foot gorge right this minute, providing the cops ain't found him yet."

"Hold your voice down, idiot!" Young commanded. "You sure he's dead, then?"

"Has to be. Nobody could survive that fall."

Young, now sitting in his vacated chair, rose at Crowe's words. "You mean to tell me you didn't make sure?"

"Hey man, we're talkin' a hundred feet here. That old pickup looked like it had a run-in with a trash compactor. No way the redneck survived."

"But you didn't check! Right!"

"No man! I didn't check! But he's dead. I guarantee it," Crowe retorted.

"*You* guarantee it! *You!* Did it ever occur to you to check the truck for any evidence that might incriminate us? No, of course not," Young accused sarcastically. "You're a fool, Crowe."

Crowe sat back in one of the leather chairs facing Young's desk. "Then I'm a fool who you owe fifty thousand dollars to, Mr. Young, my man." Crowe crossed his arms, his signal that this was an ultimatum.

The security man felt his face redden and the veins pop out on his neck. "Fifty thousand dollars!" he rasped. "You've lost your mind!"

Crowe smiled at the effect he'd had on Young. "I don't think so, Mr. Young, sir. You see, I know more than you know. I'm sure, if it came down to it, I could plea bargain my way out of this thing. You, on the other hand, are in it up to your fat neck."

Young gained control of himself with effort. "You may be right, Crowe," he relented. "Really, you're a bargain at that price," he said concillatorily. "But you've got to give me some time. I'll have to go to a higher authority. I don't have that kind of money in my budget—not that I can spend without creating audit dangers."

"How much time we talkin' 'bout, here?"

"Give me a week. I need to see some people first."

Crowe shook his head. "No way, man. I could catch a bad case of dead in a week. You got forty-eight hours. I'll be in touch. You won't be able to find me. Forty-eight hours. Right here in your office."

Wayne Young nodded his agreement. "Forty-eight hours. That should do it. I'll just have to extol your value as a colleague."

"Yeah. You do that. In the meantime, I'll exercise my skill as a magician and disappear for forty-eight hours. You should know, Wayne, my man, that I've protected myself in case of any accidental mishap, if you get my meaning."

"I understand you perfectly, Foster. Give me forty-eight hours. I don't see any problems," Young assured the man.

Foster Crowe smirked. "If you don't see no problems, man, you're too nearsighted to be in this job."

Young smiled coldly. "Let's say that I've covered contingencies myself. Problems are nothing more than opportunities in disguise. Be back in forty-eight hours."

Crowe moved toward the door. He turned and said, "Forty-eight. No more. After that the price goes up." He closed the door as he left.

Wayne Young punched a number on his desk phone and waited for the call to go through. When the call was answered, he could picture the man on the other end of the line sitting in a dark green Mercedes in front of the Collins building. "The contract has been signed, providing you've not lost sight of him since the accident. He says he's prepared for contingencies."

"He's lying," the man in the Mercedes responded. "I've been with him every minute since you told me, and he's gone nowhere to prepare for such contingencies. He's bluffing."

"I hope so, for my sake and yours," Young said. "Just do it." He hung up and sat back in his chair, satisfied with his performance. Billy Tippett was gone, and Foster Crowe was on his way out. Life was beautiful.

6

Computer printouts and massive spreadsheets littered the top of Emerson Collins's desk, spilling onto the floor. Harmon Douglas, the chief financial officer for Collins Construction International, sat across from him, perusing some cost accounting reports pertaining to Arkansas Three and Four. Each man was deep in his own thoughts when the private line on Collins's desk rang. Each man looked at the instrument because it was something out of the ordinary for a call to come in on the reserved line. Douglas rose and left the room without a word passing between the two men.

Emerson Collins answered the phone.

"Emerson?" Allen Stuart said.

Collins sighed. "Of course, it's me. This is my private line. No one answers it but me. What is it, Allen?"

"You'll have to do something about Michaels's brother. He's staying here to finish up some business and snoop into his brother's death," Allen Stuart said nervously.

"You know that for a fact, Allen?"

"I heard him say it. I was in the county clerk's office this morning when he came in. He was on his way to talk to Carlton Graham then. Heard him tell that Tolbert woman he'd be staying around for a while. What will we do?"

"Don't panic. We don't know why he's staying, if that's all you heard. Let's wait and see. What else did you hear?"

"Just that he'd be handling the estate for his sister-in-law and father."

"There you are, Allen," Collins said soothingly. "That only makes sense. When he's finished with that business, he'll be gone."

"You've got to keep an eye on him, Emerson. I tell you, he's going to be a problem." Stuart's voice was near panic.

"Two Michaels brothers turning up dead within a week of each other would be a problem. Think about that. Besides, there's nothing he can learn. We've taken care of that. Just relax, and if you hear anything more, let me know." Collins replaced the receiver and cursed to himself. Stuart was already more of a problem than Commander David Michaels might ever be. He would have to keep tabs on him.

7

Temporary barriers had been erected in place of the railing demolished by Billy Tippett's pickup truck. Yellow lights perched on black-and-yellow wooden barriers flashed caution to oncoming motorists. FBI Special Agent Morton Powell slowed his car as he neared the lights. Whoever had flown through the railing could not have survived the fall that followed unless he was extremely lucky, and Morton Powell did not believe in luck.

Since Powell talked with Warren Rodale, special agent in charge of the Organized Crime Task Force (OCTF), he was beginning to have second thoughts. It was bad luck that Jimmy Michaels had died, regardless of how it had happened. He wanted to talk to Billy Tippett, the man who had been working with Jimmy when he died. He hoped to extract information that the boy didn't even know he possessed. He would have to be careful though. No one in Clayton knew who he was, and he wanted to keep it that way. With the exception of one person, he wouldn't tell anyone who he was. He would have to figure out how to contact Tippett without revealing his own identify.

Morton Powell shook his head as he passed the flashing yellow lights and the stripped barriers. *Wonder who it was,* he thought, then he accelerated away from the shattered railing.

CHAPTER TEN

1

The metal exterior of Building Twenty-two camouflaged an expensive and expansive interior, belying the building's temporary utility. When David Michaels walked through the glass door of the building, he was struck by the incongruity of the furnishings. The first thing he noticed was the complete absence of outside noise. Whatever had been employed to isolate the giant machinery noise from the interior of the building had worked wonderfully. David could hear the soft strains of Chopin coming from hidden speakers. The walls were covered in richly appliquéd wallpaper. The furniture was modern, highly polished chrome. A single secretary sat behind a starkly designed desk. David immediately compared the woman to Cindy Tolbert. It was a strange feeling to have those—what was it his father called them? cogitations?—cogitations interrupted by the thoughts of this woman. It was a new experience, and one David was not certain he enjoyed.

"Commander Michaels?" she asked.

David nodded, willfully expelling the images of Cindy from his mind.

"Mr. Graham can see you immediately, sir. Follow me," and she got up from the chrome desk.

David followed her down a wide corridor whose walls were covered in the same expensive paper. The doors were unmarked—security in anonymity, David thought—and he wondered briefly how she knew where to stop.

Graham's office was behind the fifth door, just around the first corner in the hallway. David entered through the door and was surprised to find himself standing in yet another waiting area, this one Graham's personal outer barrier. It resembled an expensive physician's waiting room.

"Have a seat, Commander Michaels," a second secretary said, pointing to more of the modern furniture lined against the wall.

David sat down, admiring the artwork on the walls and hoping for the sake of taxpayers that they were copies. In less than a minute he heard a buzzer sound behind the glass partition that separated the waiting area from the secretary.

"Mr. Graham will see you, Commander," she said.

David walked through the open door to the secretary's left and was greeted by Carlton Graham. David noticed the expensive suit and Italian loafers the man wore. "Mr. Graham, I'm David Michaels, Jimmy Michaels's brother."

"Please, Commander, sit down. I'm delighted to meet you," the impeccably dressed Graham greeted David.

David glanced around the office and observed the same luxury he had seen since entering the building. Though the walls blocked the noise from the outside, they did not block the feeling of evil, which seemed amplified in the confines of Graham's office. David prayed silently.

"It's good of you to see me on short notice, Mr. Graham," David began.

"Carlton, please, Commander," Graham insisted. "Allow me to extend my deepest sympathies in the loss of your brother. It's my job to see that those things don't happen, and when they do, that they will not recur."

"I appreciate the concern. I'm really here on behalf of my family. We're curious as to what exactly happened to Jimmy. The official explanation is disconcerting, to say the least."

Graham pushed away from his desk. "I can appreciate your family's position, David. The truth is, I can't divulge any information at this time. I'm bound by OSHA and Worker's Comp restraints until after the accident has been completely investigated."

"I was under the impression that an investigation had already taken place, Mr. Graham," David said, refusing to become familiar with the man.

"It has, David, in a way. We've conducted preliminary investigations, but those are just to lend direction to the overall investigative process."

"Our attorney says OSHA—I assume you—has already cleared Collins from any wrongdoing in the death. Is that correct?"

"Essentially correct, yes," Graham admitted uneasily. "I conducted the investigation myself, as required by law. I found no culpability on the part of Collins," he explained.

"That doesn't leave much to investigate, does it?" David asked caustically.

Graham held up his hand in response to David's question. "Take it easy, Commander. I don't understand what you're getting at."

"I mean, if you've already cleared the company, who, other than my brother, does that leave to shoulder the blame?"

Graham hesitated. "Well, I see your point. It does throw a lot of responsibility in that direction, but it still leaves the company that manufactured the safety equipment, the handler who was working with your brother on that day, and anyone else who may have come into contact with him on the day of his death. You can see that I will have my hands full trying to run down all the possibilities."

David smiled thinly. "I can appreciate your problems, but my sister-in-law has one too. She's not going to receive any compensation for this accident until you've rendered your report and found Jimmy innocent."

"This is not a trial, Commander," Carlton Graham said. "There's no one to find guilty or innocent. It's a matter of determining facts and causes."

David was quickly becoming frustrated talking to the man. "What about the equipment he used that day? Can I see it?"

Graham stuttered for a second. "It's . . . not here, Commander. It's already on its way to Washington to be examined by our lab. I'll let you know when I get the results."

"You do that," David said, rising. "I assume the equipment was Jimmy's personal property, and I would like to have it back."

"You're wrong, Commander. The equipment belongs to Collins Construction, and, as such, you won't be entitled to it," Graham said, instantly regretting his statement. He had been caught and knew it.

David smiled. "Tell me, Mr. Graham. How is it that you cleared Collins Construction of any wrongdoing without having conducted a complete investigation? If that belt belongs to Collins, and you don't yet have the results from your lab, how can you find the company blameless? I find that a rather interesting dilemma. Don't you?" David asked, then turned and left the office.

As he passed the secretary's desk, he remembered a book he'd noticed when he entered. He wanted a closer look at it. As it happened, opportunity knocked. David saw the secretary heading down the opposite corridor.

He waited until she was out of sight and quickly scanned her desktop. The thick book with a parcel shipping company's name on the front lay open at one corner. It was the book he'd noticed earlier. David turned the book around and thumbed through it. The dates of shipments were in the upper right corner; he checked the dates beginning with the day of Jimmy's fall. Several packages had been picked up and shipped, but nothing was sent to OSHA in Washington.

David knew that the gear Jimmy had used was still in the CCI complex. He could feel it as surely at he felt the evil in Carlton Graham. David instinctively knew Graham had lied to him, and he determined to find the gear.

2

Cindy Tolbert looked up from the documents littering her desk. Two of her employees, both women, were in whispered conversation in the records vault. She could hear the voices but could not make out the words. Were they talking about her and David Michaels? As if there were something to discuss in quiet conversation.

Since she had confessed to herself her feelings concerning the navy commander, it seemed as if every person in the world knew what she'd only just discovered. Of course, she knew the whispered conversations and quiet words spoken behind raised hands were not all about her, but she could not help but think they were.

Is this the way love really begins? she wondered. It hadn't been like this with Robert. Their romance had followed what seemed to be a blueprint laid down just after they had met.

It was different with David, more spontaneous. She felt like she was back in junior high, bouncing basketballs off the wall of the Michaels's home, hoping David would react to the "thump thump" against the wall and come barreling out to complain. He rarely did, but that had not stopped her.

Sitting at her desk now, she had the same feeling. Only this time, she knew she had David Michaels's attention. She was no longer the thirteen-year-old tomboy, and he could no longer ignore her.

She forced herself to concentrate on the papers before her, knowing that in a few short minutes her thoughts would once again turn to the tall navy commander.

3

Foster Crowe left the Collins Construction building in downtown Little Rock, walked two blocks to where he'd parked his car, and pulled the black Mustang into the morning traffic. He paid no attention to the green Mercedes sedan that fell in two cars behind his Mustang at the first stoplight.

Crowe crossed the Broadway bridge over the Arkansas River, heading into North Little Rock. He had formulated his plan as he left Wayne Young's office, and even if he had conjured it up on the spur of the moment, it was a good one—simple. *And simplicity is the key to success, is it not?* Crowe thought.

He worked his way through the city, heading for the ramp to Interstate 40 just to the north. He would pick it up and head west toward Oklahoma, take 71 north just before Fort Smith, head into Fayetteville, Arkansas, and lose himself among the students on the University of Arkansas campus. Crowe hummed to himself as he drove. He might even find some young female student willing to help him kill the next forty-eight hours. Life was looking good; in two days he would be rich.

Foster Crowe picked up Interstate 40 and turned west. As he drove, the topography gently changed from the flattened Arkansas River valley to the timber-blanketed rolling foothills of the Ozark Plateau and the Boston Mountains.

Even to Crowe, the beauty of the land—hardwood and pine-forested hills—was impressive, and he began to whistle as he moved westward. He started to relax; the scenery worked as an intoxicant on his spirit.

A little over an hour out of Little Rock, Crowe recognized a familiar shape—cooling towers of a nuclear generating power plant. He was just outside Dardanelle, Arkansas, looking at the first nuclear plant ever constructed in the state. For a moment, the huge concrete towers jolted him from his reverie, and he looked around, almost like a man waking from a dream. Crowe checked his rearview mirror. Traffic was moving normally. He'd held his Mustang exactly at seventy, not wanting to attract the slightest interest of a county sheriff deputy or an Arkansas state trooper. He was surprised at the number of large trucks plying the interstate, and he held to the right lane, only occasionally having to pull into the left to pass a slower-moving vehicle.

The towers of Arkansas Nuclear One and Two slid past on his left, and he forgot them as soon as they disappeared in his mirror. The ribbon of highway stretched to the horizon, nestled between the twin blankets of forest on either side, and Crowe settled once again into the bucket seat of the Mustang. He checked his mirror once again. He still did not pick out the green sedan that held station two hundred yards behind him.

Forty-eight hours. Life was getting sweeter with every passing mile.

4

David Michaels left the barren landscape of North Central Electric's newest generating station behind. He was still overwhelmed by the magnitude of the project. In addition to the land that had already been ravaged by Collins Construction and North Central, Allen Stuart had been in Cindy Tolbert's office investigating the possibility of procuring more land adjacent to the plant. Cindy had raised the possibility that Stuart was interested in contingency lawsuits, but David was not so sure. He could not imagine why the electrical cooperative would want additional land, but he had a bad feeling in his gut about the whole thing.

David drove into Clayton; an idea came to him as he made his way toward the center of town and the courthouse. He had told Cindy he would call her. He would do better than that. He would stop by her office again. There were some questions he wanted to ask her in her official capacity as county clerk. One thing he wanted was a close-up aerial view of the construction site, if one existed. The conversation with Tom Frazier lingered in the back of his mind, along with the beginnings of a plan.

He parked in the same spot he'd used hours earlier and got out. As he entered the courthouse for the second time that morning, he felt uneasy. His plan involved subterfuge, a talent he'd never developed. Even minimum deception caused David discomfort. Sure, he'd tried to lie to his father on occasion while growing up. He could never do it, and, he supposed, the twinge he felt every time he attempted to lie was something that later helped him decide to enter the ministry. There were times, David mused, that being a minister was counterproductive to achieving a desired goal. People had certain, preconceived notions as to how ministers—and chaplains fell into that group—should act. David couldn't blame them. He'd seen enough self-righteous, self-serving preachers to last him a lifetime; he could not fault the public perception of what a man of God should be. Trouble was, ministers were never the way the public viewed them, not because they did not want to be, but because they were as human as anybody else—more so at times. But people never understood that part.

The interior of the old courthouse was cool, like the caves he and Jimmy used to explore down by the river. The memory jolted him like a bolt of lightning. As he approached the county clerk's office, he told himself that what he was about to do, he was doing for Jimmy.

Even though he would not like doing it, he was about to lie to Cindy Tolbert to get the information he needed.

5

Carlton Graham cursed as he reviewed what had happened. First the troublemaker, Jimmy Michaels, was dealt with. Next, Billy Tippett, the main witness, was dead. Just when he thought everything was covered, Commander David Michaels showed up sticking his authoritative, religious nose in business that didn't concern him.

It had always been the same, Graham thought. People couldn't leave well enough alone. It had happened in the army. He'd done his job, but that wasn't enough for his superiors. Reductions in force. Cutbacks. Forced retirements. It had all been aimed at him, Graham was sure. He'd had twelve years in the United States Army when he was fired. That's what it was. He could think of no other word that better described what had happened. They'd called it "discharge for the good of the service." Fired was what it was.

He'd come out of Vietnam and the army a bitter man. Bitter, but smarter for the experience. He'd taken the civil service exams and used the extra points gained by his military service to get on the payroll of the citizens of the United States. That was all he needed. Somewhere along the line, opportunity would present itself, and he would make the best of it.

When Wayne Young, the burly security officer of Collins Construction, had proposed the latest scenario, Carlton Graham recognized the proposal as the ship he'd been waiting for, and he jumped on board.

He'd make a bundle from this one project—a bundle they owed him, money he deserved. But Commander David Michaels could be a problem. He'd have to call Young in Little Rock. This was Young's territory, not his.

6

As David Michaels entered the Clayton County Courthouse, Sheriff Tom Frazier sat at his desk in the other end of the building, placing a phone call that he knew would not be well received. Frazier had dialed the number earlier and listened to the first few seconds of a recording before hanging up. Now, as he waited for the long distance connections to be made, he reviewed what he knew. Billy Tippett, the only witness to Jimmy Michaels's murder—the only one who might have known anything—was dead from an apparent automobile accident. Apparent because nothing was as it seemed in Clayton County, Arkansas. It would have stopped there but for the wet, ragged note the paramedic had pulled from Tippett's right hand. Frazier reread the note once again: *I know who did it and how. It will cost you $100,000.*

Frazier carefully placed the note in his office safe and locked it. It was more than a note; it was confirmation. Jimmy Michaels had been murdered. No doubt about it. There was nothing Billy Tippett could have known that would have been worth anywhere near that much money. Frazier chuckled in spite of the circumstances. A hundred thousand dollars was not even close to what Tippett's information was worth. *A million? Two? Who knows?* he thought. Billy always thought small, and his attempt at blackmail was no different.

The phone began to ring, and he gave the call his attention. When it was answered, he said, "Tippett's dead. We were right. He had a note with him trying to blackmail Collins for a hundred thousand. They made it look like an accident . . . no, I've got the note. Right. I'll get it to you today. What about Michaels's brother, the chaplain? He'll be in danger if he presses too much. Yes, sir, I know all that!" Frazier said, raising his voice for the first time. He was embarrassed by his outburst. "Sorry, sir. But he'll be in danger, and the only thing I can do is sit back and watch. It ain't right. Yeah," he sighed. "I know we're talkin' about bigger fish than just Collins Construction or even some disgruntled OSHA agent. I just don't like it. I'll keep my eyes open, but if Michaels gets in too deep, I may not be able to protect him. . . . Right, I'll keep you updated. Just like when we were huntin' the ridges, right?"

Frazier glared at the instrument in his hand. He loved being Clayton County sheriff, but there were times—like now—that he would rather be doing something else. If it were anyone else, he would tell the person to can it, but friendship carried a certain obligation.

Bigger fish. That's what he kept hearing. But how much bigger did they get than Collins Construction International? Not much, he wagered.

Sometimes the federal government can destroy an iron girder, Frazier thought. The realization that he was part of it was unsettling.

7

Morton Powell would notify only one man of his presence in Clayton, Arkansas, and the agent wanted to keep it that way for the time being. The FBI had transferred Powell to Arkansas as part of the task force headed by Warren Rodale. Powell still did not see the connection between Collins Construction and the Columbian cartels, but he assumed one existed or the OCTF would not be involved. But from where Powell stood, all he saw were questionable trade practices on the part of CCI. He also accepted the fact that what he knew was on a need-to-know basis. The big picture was in some computer in the Hoover Building in Washington, D.C.

As Powell drove into Clayton, he marveled at the view the small Ozark Mountain town presented. It was squeezed between two mountain ranges in a long and narrow valley. The valley ran north and south with a river on each end of the canyon encircling the city limits. The town, at slightly more than twenty thousand inhabitants, was the largest in the county. A nearby lake pulled people from all parts of the state to its recreational waters. *A good place to live,* mused Powell, as he watched the city limit sign flash past.

Powell turned on the same street he'd used every time he came to Clayton. He wondered about the other men who might be on this case. It was possible for things to get out of hand very quickly in an investigation like this. He hoped someone was holding a tight reign, or the mountain valley town would be a good place to die too.

8

Arkansas Highway 71 was the worst road Foster Crowe had seen in all his years of traveling. It had taken him longer to reach Fayetteville and the University of Arkansas campus than he'd anticipated, and he was tired. His original plan was to lose himself among the student population for the forty-eight hours Young needed to produce his money. He was confident he could mingle, maybe even sit in on some of the huge freshman classes, knowing that no one would even realize he was not a student.

Crowe guided his Mustang through the streets of the university's main campus, noting the names of fraternities on Fraternity Row and filing them away in the back of his mind. He watched the students come and go, busy about the work of learning. He marveled at the cars he saw parked on the streets and in the full parking lots. Everything from Mercedes and BMWs to ragged pickups that reminded him of Billy Tippett's old clunker. He smiled at that thought. One down. One to go.

Crowe left the campus and headed north. He would find a small, out-of-the-way motel for the next couple of days, hole up in it, and maybe make a few forays onto the campus and classrooms just to bask in the feeling of youth and vitality of the environment. It would be a good two days, he knew.

The green Mercedes pulled out as Crowe passed.

CHAPTER ELEVEN

1

A worn, green spread covered the sagging double bed. Two ladder-back chairs were pushed under the small, round table that sat in front of the only window in the dingy room. The room smelled musty and damp. A lone, ventless gas heater, its dappled rust revealing years of neglect, was located on the back wall. The paint had at one time been white, Crowe could tell, and spots of black vinyl showed through the threadbare carpet.

Perfect, he thought.

Foster Crowe had chosen the motel because it reminded him of one he'd seen in an old Humphrey Bogart movie, before Bogie had become a big star. The rooms were located in individual cabins, two rooms to a cabin, built, he calculated, in the 1940s, maybe even the '30s. Whenever it was, they were just what he was looking for, away from the big chain motels that dotted the highways.

Crowe threw his jacket on the old bed and twisted the knob on the black-and-white TV, then followed his jacket to the bed. He needed some rest after the drive up Highway 71. Foster Crowe was asleep even before the green Mercedes pulled into the graveled parking area at the motel.

2

The headache already had a good start when the phone on Wayne Young's desk rang. No doubt the call would exacerbate the pain. Young was beginning to hate the device.

"Young here," he said into receiver. It was the call he'd been waiting for. "What's he doin' in Fayetteville? Yeah, that makes sense. He'd want to be out of the way for the next two days. You gonna have any problems with the job? Good. This will work out better than I thought. Crowe's done half the job himself; he removed himself from the immediate area. No one's gonna pay any attention to what happens in that direction. If he'd stayed here and ended up dead, we might have had a hard time explaining why three men from Nuclear Three and Four ended up dead within a week of each other. This way Crowe just disappears. Take care of it and call me only if there's a problem. Otherwise, contact me when you get back to the city." Young smiled in spite of the pain that was shooting through his temples.

Crowe, my man, you made it too easy.

3

With three large, heavily bound books laying on the floor beside him, David Michaels opened the fourth in the series. He had been through the title and title changes that concerned the acreage where North Central Electric and Collins Construction were erecting the nuclear generating plant. All he had learned was that the land had been sold to NCEC, at times for exorbitant prices. But there was nothing illegal about high prices.

David pulled out the large aerial photographs bound in the fourth book. They included several overall shots of the entire area of CCI's construction site. Most had the distorted look that came from shooting the photos with a wide-angle lens. The distortions were greater at the edges of the photographs, something David had not anticipated and, for his purpose, something that worked against him.

The fourth book also contained a folder of smaller photographs, each labeled according to legal descriptions. David extracted the smaller photos and examined them. They were shots taken with an ordinary lens from an aircraft; and they had references appended to them referring to particular environmental impact studies conducted prior to the inception of construction on Nuclear Three and Four. Each photo represented a smaller portion of the eighty-acre construction area. He flipped through the photos, looking for one in particular.

Bingo! It was halfway down in the first stack. The photo showed the lower portion of the area—about two acres, David estimated. He could see the chain-link fence, the southeast corner of the site nearest the lake, and the old drainage ditch that cut across the corner of the site. *The area is far enough away from the main activity of the construction. Maybe as much as a half mile,* David thought. *If the fence is up over the ditch, there may be a way into the compound by way of the ditch.* It was worth a try.

"Find what you're looking for?" Cindy Tolbert asked, approaching the desk where David sat. She rested her hands lightly on David's shoulders, a much more intimate gesture than either would care to admit. The county clerk had been supplying David with the title books he'd been examining, and he had been lost in concentration for the last few hours. She found that she enjoyed his presence, even if he had not said more than a dozen words in all that time. His presence seemed to add a solidifying factor to the office.

"Not really," he lied, feeling a twinge of guilt as he spoke. Cindy's touch was electrifying, and David was keenly aware of the faint scent of her perfume. Doubt about what he was planning was already creeping in. He'd been involved in such operations in the military, but that had been different, and then he'd been only a participant, not the strategic planner.

Now, with Cindy so near, he had a perceptive interruption of his thought processes. With her hand resting lightly on his shoulders, he seemed to have a link extending all the way back to his high school years. He felt almost as if he were betraying her in some obscure fashion.

David turned his attention back to the project at hand, the books, and particularly the photographs.

"These photos are interesting, though," he resumed. "You got a magnifying glass around here?"

Cindy pulled open a drawer at David's right elbow. "Right there," she pointed. "We need them to read the small print on some of the abstracts we get in here."

David took the magnifying glass and examined the photo more closely. He couldn't be certain from this angle whether or not the ditch had been closed off when the fence was erected. It was a question that would have to be answered.

"If I didn't know you were a preacher, I'd say you were about to cause some problems around here," she grinned. She'd loved her husband, but that was in the past. Things had changed. Now the memories of warm nights at the Michaels's home flooded her memory. They had been good times, and in spite of the fact that David had paid her little or no attention, she'd relished the times she'd spent just being in the same house with him. His proximity had been enough in those days. She had felt the same feeling that now astonished her as David poured over the aerial maps. *Puppy love memories?* she wondered. *First love? Anticipation? Apprehension?* David's next response forced her back to reality.

"Never underestimate the ability of a good preacher to cause problems," he bantered. "It comes with the job."

"Not the way you're going about it, if you're going to do what I think you are."

"How would you know what I'm going to do?" he questioned jokingly, enjoying the warmth of her presence and the easy way she smiled, but disburbed by her intuition.

"Give me a break!" she said in a low voice, trying to contain the conversation between the two of them. "I'm not stupid. You're not scrutinizing those pictures because you think they should be framed and hanging in your living room. Does Tom Frazier know what you're planning?"

David flushed despite himself. He'd not realized his actions were so transparent. He would have to remember that for any future encounters with Cindy. "Both you and Tom will be better off not knowing anything about this. Trust me, Cindy. When I leave this office, forget I was ever in here."

Cindy pulled a chair from the next desk and sat down, the new closeness comfortable, accepted by both. "Listen, David. I liked Jimmy too. I don't for one minute think that everything going on out at that nuclear site is legitimate. I don't for one minute think that what he did was not dangerous, in more ways than one. Too much has happened—accidents that shouldn't have happened. Strange behavior seems to go hand-in-hand with that place. Jimmy is only one of many, but his death is too much. Allen Stuart is so puffed up with himself, he thinks I can't read an abstract or a title. He's wrong. As wrong as you are if you think I don't know, or at least suspect, that there's something rotten going on out there."

David relented, turning to face Cindy. "I *think* there is something wrong, terribly wrong," he explained. "But I don't have any idea what it might be. Hints. Insinuations and implications. That's all I have. That and the fact that I know Jimmy was too smart to get killed the way he did. I know that OSHA has already cleared CCI in the incident, and I suspect the OSHA agent out at the site lied to me when he said he'd sent the equipment that Jimmy was using that day to his lab in Washington. If it's still out at the construction site, I want to find it," he said, as he pointed to the photos. "I have a feeling that the equipment will tell us something. OSHA wouldn't even let Tom Frazier see the equipment Jimmy was using that day. I think I can get in there and find it. That's what I'm looking for here, a way in."

David turned back to the photo. Even from the air, he could see the security measures were impressive. He noted the fence with razor wire crowning on his trip to see Graham. Guards dotted the barren landscape like wildflowers. The guard towers appeared strategically located, more from the air than they first appeared from ground level. *A POW camp,* David thought. *That's what it reminds me of.*

"Thinking about Johnson Creek, then?" Cindy said, moving closer to David.

"The drainage ditch in the southeast corner?"

"The same one."

"Then that's the one I'm thinking about using," David confessed, uneasy that he had inadvertently pulled Cindy into his scheme.

"Forget it. It's closed off with razor wire and concrete. I saw it once when I was out there talking to a survey crew. They weren't that stupid. Johnson Creek was too large for them to overlook. If you're going in, you'll have to use the overflow piping across on the other corner."

David looked up, surprised. "What piping?"

Cindy thumbed through the photos in front of David, stopping at one particular photo. "Right here," she indicated a spot with her finger. "There's piping here that leads out into the lake. The idea was to use it for overflow purposes in the original plans, but for some reason, they scrapped those plans. The piping is still there, though. Right now, with the lake low, the upper portion, the part inside the fence, is dry. The other end is in the lake, covered with a grating. You can find the grating with your feet about ten feet from the shore. Shouldn't be any problem for a marine. You *can* swim, can't you?" she chided.

David pushed the photo under the magnifying glass. Cindy's nearness was disconcerting. He was having trouble concentrating. He could barely see the grating inside the compound fence. The other end—the end he would use—was hidden beneath the lake's surface.

"Right about here," Cindy indicated on the photo. "It's the only way in I know. If," she added, "you don't want anyone to know." For a moment her arm brushed his. The touch seemed somehow natural.

"Pretty sharp for a rural county clerk. How do you know it's a way in?"

"Rumors mostly. Kids from the high school use it. It's sort of an initiation ritual for the football team. All freshman players have to do it, or so I heard. Drives the security guards batty. They've talked about closing off the piping but just haven't gotten around to it. They guard it during spring training to keep the kids out. That only adds to the challenge. Other times they're too busy staying ahead of schedule to pay any attention to it. Right now, there shouldn't be a guard within a mile of the place. Anyway, as long as you do it when the lake is at low levels, there's no problem. Or so I hear."

"So you heard, so you hear. Great." *Facedown in water again,* David thought, remembering the Panamanian swamps he'd left behind, how long ago? It already seemed like eons, not just days. Why was that? He was certain Cindy Tolbert was part of the reason time seemed to be expanded.

"When are you going?"

"I didn't say I was. I'm exploring my options right now."

"That's as obtuse an answer as I've ever heard. Give me a break! You're going," she accused, softly. The other workers in the office had not exhibited any curiosity in what David was doing, and she didn't want them to start now. She could not keep the trace of worry out of her voice as she whispered, "Those people out there are not playing around. You could get hurt."

David studied the photos, ignoring the tone in Cindy Tolbert's voice. "Can I get copies of these?"

Cindy retrieved the book and carried it to the copier. She had the copies in minutes and handed them to David.

"These are perfect, Cindy. You won't get in any trouble over this, will you?"

"I'm the boss around here. No trouble." She started to say something else, but stopped. She couldn't trust herself not to reveal how she felt if she spoke now.

"Thanks," David said as he got up from the desk. He thought about setting a time and place to take Cindy out but dismissed the idea for the moment. "I'll call you a little later. Maybe we can go into Little Rock for prime rib. I hear there's a great place down there."

"I'll be here," she said, looking into David Michaels's tired eyes.

David's hand went to her cheek. It was an instictive action. He felt his face redden. "I'll remember," he said as he left the office, the soft feel of her cheek still with him.

4

The house was as he remembered it. But something had changed. A subtle, irrevocable transformation had taken place. Even from the outside, Morton Powell could tell the man living there had experienced a grievous loss. He turned into the concrete drive and shut off the car. James Michaels was the only person he would inform of his dead son's involvement with the FBI investigation. He was clutching at straws, Powell knew, but it was all he had with Jimmy Michaels dead. Without more information, the FBI investigation of CCI and OSHA would quickly grind to a halt. Witnesses had disappeared before, but never one Powell had been close to. The FBI agent had liked young Jimmy Michaels. He'd been a gregarious, fun-loving person, devoted to family and friends. He'd also been one of the best informants Morton had ever met. The man had been fearless. What seemed to Morton Powell to be extreme risks had been no more than games to Jimmy Michaels. Games to be played and won. Or lost. That was what he had never been able to make Jimmy Michaels understand. In this business, Powell knew, the last game was always the one you lost, unless you were smart enough to quit first.

Powell knocked on the door of the Michaels's house. James Michaels answered almost immediately. Powell could see the resignation on the old man's face.

For a brief moment Morton Powell thought that this might be the time to quit—the smart move, the sane move—but sanity rarely ruled. "Mr. Michaels, my name is Morton Powell. I'm with the FBI. I think I have some information you need to hear."

The old man stepped back, and Morton Powell stepped into the house.

5

As David Michaels turned the corner next to the First Community Church, his mind flashed back to the conversations he'd had since arriving in Clayton. The church would be needing a new pastor very soon. He could have the position if he wanted it, but did he want it? He'd been a marine and was now a commander in the navy. His life revolved around the military. He was a chaplain, not a preacher. Most people could not make the fine distinction, but David knew the difference, and he was not too sure that his experience in the military would translate to the civilian community. Nor would he want it to. It would be nice, though, to give his full attention to a specific ministry and not have to worry about the swamps of Panama, the deserts of the Middle East, or the mountains of Peru and Ecuador.

Middle age had a way of opening one's eyes to the realities of the world, and David realized that he had passed true middle age several years ago. Most men his age had long ago retired from the military, taken up positions in the civilian world, and allowed their middles to begin the inevitable march toward expansion. He would think about it when he had the chance. Right now, he had more pressing problems.

It was a government car. The no-frills, four-door sedan was conspicuous in its simplicity. David had seen enough of them to know that much. But what was it doing here? The hairs on the back of David's neck began to prickle, as if he were back in the Panamanian swamps still pinned down by an OPFOR.

David parked the pickup directly behind the FBI car, noticing that the license plate did not overtly indicate it as a government vehicle. He scanned the interior of the auto as he passed. Government. No doubt about that, despite the license plate. David pushed the kitchen door open and stepped into the room. His father and a stranger sat at the kitchen table drinking coffee.

"David," his father began, "I want you to meet someone."

David felt an involuntary chill run down his spine as he slowly lowered himself in the chair across from Morton Powell.

"Mr. Powell, this is my son, David. He's the man you're looking for."

6

Emerson Bradford Collins stomped into his office. He'd spent the last hour updating his brother, the president and figurehead of CCI, on the happenings at Nuclear Three and Four in Clayton. The meeting had not gone well, and Emerson was angry. He cursed his brother under his breath as he entered his office on the twentieth floor of the Collins Building in downtown Little Rock.

Wayne Young sat in one of the two chairs fronting Emerson's massive walnut desk. He could feel the anger flowing from the operating head of CCI. He waited until Collins sat behind the desk and acknowledged his presence before beginning.

"What is it, Young?" Collins began.

"An update on the events in Clayton."

"Go on."

Wayne Young consulted the notes in his lap before speaking. "First, the project is still on schedule."

"I know that!" Collins barked in exasperation. "Get to the other," he ordered.

Young cleared his throat. "I've spoken with Graham. He's worried about this David Michaels fellow. Michaels went to the construction site to talk with him. Graham sounded excited when he called me about it. He says Michaels is pushing to see the equipment his brother was wearing when he fell."

"So what's the problem? I was under the impression that Graham had taken care of that part."

"Yes, sir. The equipment is locked up in his offices. Seems he told Michaels that OSHA had given CCI a clean bill of health and the equipment his brother had used that day was at the OSHA lab in Washington being examined."

Emerson Collins sat forward. "Are you telling me that Graham admitted he made a decision exonerating CCI in this case and then told

Michaels that the decision was made without first having the lab report from Washington, which, by the way, is not forthcoming?"

"That's not the way he stated it," Young answered. "But according to Graham, that's the way Michaels took it."

"Of course that's the way he took it!" Emerson Collins screamed. "Michaels is not an idiot. Obviously not as stupid as Graham. What else?"

"Allen Stuart is worried about Michaels too."

Collins sighed. "I'm beginning to think we have chosen the wrong people for this project. What has Stuart said?"

"Not much, sir. Just that Michaels has been spending time at the county clerk's office and at the project site. Apparently, Stuart heard about the meeting with Graham, and he's worried about that too. He said he tried to find out what Michaels was doing in the clerk's office. One of the employees in the office told him that Michaels and Cynthia Tolbert, the county clerk in Clayton County, were friends from high school. Stuart didn't sound convinced. He wants us to do something about Michaels."

"I take it he means he wants us to eliminate Michaels?"

"That's the impression I got, Mr. Collins."

"That would cause some problems, would it not?"

Young knew what the man was referring to. "Yes, sir, it could. We've taken care of the Billy Tippett problem. That's going in the books as a one-vehicle accident, according to our sources at head-quarters," Young said, referring to Arkansas State Police Headquarters on Roosevelt Road in Little Rock.

"And can we assume that our sources from the state police are reliable?"

"One hundred percent reliable, sir. The other problem—Foster Crowe—has taken himself out of the immediate area, and I don't believe he will be associated with us in any way."

"Has he been taken care of?"

"As we speak, Mr. Collins," Young stressed.

"Then the problem I see is with Michaels. What do you propose, Mr. Young?"

Young cringed at the use of "mister." It meant that Emerson Collins wanted the "official" solution to the problems David Michaels's presence was causing. Young held no illusions. It was his place to solve this problem and get Graham and Stuart back on track. That was the reason he earned six figures. Solving problems was his specialty.

"I think I know what Michaels is up to. I'm planning to neutralize him. He's a meddlesome military preacher. He shouldn't be too much trouble. I'll let you know as soon as he's out of the picture."

"You do that, Mr. Young."

Wayne Young rose and moved toward the door, glad to withdraw from Collins.

"And Mr. Young. Do it quickly, please."

Young nodded, dabbing at the sweat with his handkerchief as he walked to his office.

7

Morton Powell had made a decision, one he was not happy with, but one he knew he had to make. He and David Michaels had talked for more than an hour. James Michaels had excused himself when he'd realized the bent of the conversation. Powell had been relieved.

Powell had listened to David Michaels, interpreting the conversation for exactly what it was: a covert assault on the construction site of Nuclear Three and Four.

David Michaels had been candid, despite the fact that Powell was an FBI agent. He told the man about his suspicions, the strange conversation with Carlton Graham, and the aerial photos he'd procured from Cindy Tolbert's office. He showed Powell the copies he and Jean had made of the drawings from Jimmy's safe-deposit box. The sketches had been self-explanatory, and Powell had been aghast at the inferences.

David had expected the FBI agent to put a stop to the plans as he outlined them. To his surprise, Powell said nothing at first; then he approved the plan and even offered to accompany him. Powell had argued, quite correctly, that it was a two-man job and he was the perfect second man. David wondered about the offer until the agent had explained that Jimmy had been the only connection he'd had between CCI, OSHA, and the conspiracy he saw arising within the government and Collins Construction International.

"You're sure about this?" David asked Morton Powell.

"I'm sure. I'm operating independently on this one. I do need to make one phone call, though."

David pointed to the phone on the wall. "I'll go sit with Dad while you call."

Powell waited until David was gone and dialed the Washington, D.C., number.

Warren Rodale, special agent in charge of the OCTF answered his private line.

"It's Mort," Powell said into the receiver.

"Go ahead," Rodale urged.

"The investigation is taking a new twist since the death of Jimmy Michaels. I may need you to cover for me in the next forty-eight hours."

"You'll have whatever you need, provided you're alive to use it."

Powell understood what the agent was saying. Rodale was savvy enough to know when not to ask about an operation and intelligent enough to know when that operation might go sour.

"Mort. Remember one thing. This investigation goes a lot higher than you know. CCI is not the only one involved in this thing. There are individuals connected to this that can make you and I both disappear without a trace with no questions asked. Do you understand what I'm saying?"

"I understand, Warren. Thanks for the information. I'll be in contact." Morton Powell hung up the phone and sat back at the kitchen table. Warren Rodale was not prone to exaggeration. *There are individuals connected to this who can make you and I both disappear without a trace.* That's what he'd said. Someone high enough to make Warren Rodale disappear without questions meant only one person that Powell could think of. Powell felt his head spin at the thought.

David Michaels returned to the kitchen. "You make your call?"

"It's done," Morton Powell affirmed.

"You look a little pale."

The FBI agent smiled weakly. "Happens in this business," he said.

"Are we set for tonight, then?" David asked quietly.

Powell nodded in the affirmative. "Tonight. I've arranged for what protection I could should something go wrong. But don't count on too much support. This case is bigger than either you or I know."

"I'm only interested in what killed Jimmy," David said.

"Then let's get ready," Powell answered.

There are individuals connected to this who can make you and I both disappear without a trace.

Powell felt himself tremble. He was sure he knew who the individuals were. He also knew they could make David Michaels disappear just as easily.

CHAPTER
TWELVE

1

Lightning played across the darkening sky in wide, bright flashes as Cindy Tolbert made her way home. It was not hard to deduce what David had in mind. She knew it was illegal and possibly dangerous, and she wondered whether she should pray for the success of an illegal act. She also wondered about the feelings she'd experienced as she sat with David in her courthouse office, the feeling she'd had when she touched him. She'd only been teasing with him when she saw him for the first time after so many years just outside First Community Church. Since then, she had become aware of her roller-coaster emotions. It was as if time had reversed itself, sending her back to the years when she thought she loved the older of the Michaels brothers—back to when things had been simpler. Now, if the sensations overflowing in her mind were any indication, life was about to become very complicated.

Cindy switched on the lamp by the front door. Her Bible was on the end table, and she picked it up. She turned to the front, which contained an index of Scripture for particular situations. She settled on Psalms 37:23: "The steps of a good man are ordered by the LORD . . . ," she read aloud. She was aware that she was taking the verse out of context, but it was the only relief she could find at the moment, and she would hold onto that until something better came along, until the swell of emotions had time to settle down.

She sat in the large, worn, wingback chair that faced the blackened fireplace. Logs were laid for a fire, and she rose, retrieved a fireplace match, and touched it to the crumpled newspaper and pine kindling that lay beneath the oak logs. Within minutes the warmth and light of the fire chased the darkness and cold from the room.

She returned to the worn, leather chair. It had been her grandfather's chair. She'd been a teenager, searching and experimenting in the social circles of school, church, and work for answers to the hollowness she felt. Her grandfather had sensed the desperation in the attractive teenager and sat her down one night and explained exactly what life was about and how God fit into the picture. He'd spoken not only of the wrath of God but also of His love; of lostness and salvation; of truth and error. He'd laid it out for her in a simple manner—a manner she understood instantly as the truth. She had decided to follow Jesus as Lord and Savior that night, right at the feet of her grandfather and the old, battered leather chair.

He'd died years later, and when her father had contemplated selling the chair, she'd stepped in and salvaged it. There was nothing magical about the chair, she knew. But it was a place of comfort in a world that knew too little of it. It was her special place, and she needed it now.

She curled up in the depths of the old chair and let the warmth from the fire play over her. As her eyes slowly closed, she felt a warmth that went beyond that of the crackling oak logs and the dancing flames of the fireplace. And as sleep overtook her, she thought she could just make out David Michaels's face forming in the gentle flames.

2

The man reviewed the setup in the room next to Foster Crowe. His plan was an adaptation of a basic infantry trick requiring a wooden clothespin, a roll of all-purpose wire, and a six-volt lantern battery. The man cut two lengths of wire about five feet long, stripped the ends of each piece, exposing the copper, and attached one piece of bare wire to each jaw of the clothespin so the bare wires could make contact when the pin's jaws were closed. He then attached each wire to opposite poles of the battery, one to the positive terminal and one to the negative, and checked his circuit by opening and closing the clothespin's jaws. He was rewarded with a spark each time he let the jaws snap shut.

He then ran a length of wire from the doorknob of Foster Crowe's room to a plain, white index card he'd placed between the jaws of the clothespin to prevent contact of the bare wires. The crude apparatus was attached to the old gas stove with common wire from a hardware store. The wire attached to Foster Crowe's motel room door ran beneath the door of the adjacent room and was attached to the index card by several staples.

The man opened the gas valves of the four surface burners and the oven of the kitchen stove and then left the room. The sole purpose of the apparatus was to create a spark in a gas-rich atmosphere.

One way or the other, whether from the smell of gas or from natural urges, Foster Crowe would open his door. When he did, the string would pull the index card from between the point set and create a spark.

It would be the last spark Foster Crowe ever created.

3

The only light in the room came from the TV screen. The bed was rumpled, and the green bedspread lay in a heap on the floor. Foster Crowe ambled to the window. It was dark now. Safe enough, he reasoned, for his inaugural foray onto the campus of the University of Arkansas. He had plans to keep himself busy for the remaining thirty-six hours until he contacted that large, pompous head of security for Collins Construction, Wayne Young.

Crowe went to the bathroom, examined himself in the cracked mirror, and combed a wisp of unruly dark hair back into place. He approved of what he saw and switched off the bathroom light. He moved to the TV set, started to turn it off, and then thought better of it. Leaving it on would give the illusion of occupancy. Protection. He ignored the fact that he was the single most deadly force residing in the cabins. Crowe was about to exit the dilapidated room when he smelled gas!

Idiots, he fumed. Someone had left the gas on, probably in the adjoining cabin. He would report it to the management on his way out.

Crowe pulled his door open. The index card in the next room was pulled from its resting place between the metallic points, creating a single, bright yellow spark that lasted only a split second. That was enough.

Witnesses to the explosion would later say it was the largest fireball they had ever seen in the northwest Arkansas city.

Foster Crowe felt as if he were being crushed by a huge hand squeezing the very life from him. He was pushed back into his room by the explosion and felt nothing after the initial pressure. The two-room cabin went up in a detonation so massive that homeowners for twelve surrounding blocks reported broken or cracked windows. The initial fireball rose to a height of over one hundred feet. Every cabin in the small motel complex sustained some form of damage, from fire damage to shattered glass and cracked plaster. The two nearest cabins, thankfully empty, ignited instantly and burned to the ground.

No other fatalities were connected with the explosion and subsequent fire. The single male occupant in room twelve was eventually identified through automobile registration forms from the New Jersey State Police as Foster Lincoln Crowe, a part-time, petty crook with no family. The matter was never pursued further.

No one noticed the green Mercedes sedan slipping through the fire trucks and police cars at the scene.

4

"Hope you don't mind getting wet," David Michaels grunted.

"I always mind getting wet," Morton Powell replied.

"Can you swim?"

"If I have to. Learned at Quantico."

David allowed a smile to crease his face. "You have to," he said.

"I was afraid of that. Those extra clothes you brought along were a dead giveaway."

David Michaels and Morton Powell were threading James Michaels's old pickup down the side of a slippery mountain road that would bring them to a remote part of the nuclear reactor complex. The earlier rain had turned the road into slithery clay. The tires were having difficulty gripping the surface. The rear of the truck had more than once tried to overtake the front. David battled the wheel as he peered into the creeping darkness. With no streetlights, it seemed gloomier in the forest than on the open road. The weather conditions, he knew, might force them to postpone their attempt to enter the Nuclear Three and Four construction site.

"Tell me one thing, Powell," David queried.

"What's that?" Powell asked.

"What we're about to do is illegal. I know why I'm doing it, but what about you?"

"Against the law, sure. That means technically, I'll have to arrest you and me both," Powell laughed.

"Something like this could cost you your job."

"Under normal circumstances, you would be right. But these are not normal circumstances. Nuclear Three and Four are not normal generating facilities, and Collins Construction International is not your normal, run-of-the-mill construction outfit. This investigation goes far beyond this project here in Clayton County and the state of Arkansas. As a matter of fact, it goes beyond the borders of the United States."

"Are you telling me something I shouldn't know?"

"Absolutely. Nothing highly classified, if that's what you mean. Even so, this information could be dangerous to you. But I want you to know at least what I know, and that's not much."

"I'm listening," David said, as he fought with the steering wheel once again, forcing the truck back onto the rutted road.

Morton Powell laid it all out for him. "I can't tell you how far this thing goes. My responsibility is to the special agent in charge of the OCTF in Washington. My assignment involves Collins Construction International exclusively. Even that is limited to CCI's domestic operations within my region. That means I'm essentially investigating just the Arkansas Nuclear Three and Four project. Your brother was helping me with that. The drawings you copied at the bank are just the tip of the iceberg. Jimmy had already supplied me with documents and drawings that showed CCI to be using inferior products, scaled-down dimensions, and even alternate blueprints."

"Are you telling me that Jimmy was working with the FBI?"

"Not *with* the FBI . . . *for* the FBI. Jean and the kids will be receiving all the benefits of a G-14 government worker if you're interested. And if this turns out to be murder, then CCI will go down for the murder of an FBI agent. The courts do not look upon that very favorably."

"I never had any idea." As incredible as it seemed, his brother had been an agent for the Federal Bureau of Investigation. David felt a swell of pride.

"Jimmy was the best I've ever worked with. He knew his job. That's why I don't buy this junk OSHA is putting out about his being negligent. The only way Jimmy Michaels would have been negligent in his work would be if he'd been drunk or drugged. I know the first isn't possible, not for Jimmy. But I'm not ruling out the second. They could have slipped him something. Anything to make him overlook the obvious."

"Who is *they*?"

"Who knows for sure? CCI hired guns. Someone at NCEC who has a stake in this. Suppliers who knew he was getting too close. The list is endless in an operation like this."

"Is that all of it?"

"Not quite. The next part is pure speculation on my part. It will be up to you to provide your own perspective, but I think CCI is doing this same thing around the world. The company grosses billions of dollars. It's an international, multinational conglomerate. What's to keep CCI from doing the same thing in England, France, the Middle East, East Asia, or Australia?"

"And people could be getting killed all over the globe. Is that what you're saying?" David challenged.

Powell let out a slow breath. "Precisely, just for the sake of profit."

"And how far do you suspect this goes?"

"What do you think? Perspective, remember?"

David paused, contemplating the ramifications. "It would have to be high. CCI would have to have State Department interference at least,

I would think, because of trade agreements and commercial treaties. A trail has to exist. No company of the size you're describing can operate in anonymity. Here in the states it seems that OSHA is in the company's back pocket just from what we've seen here. It could go all the way into the White House, I suppose."

Powell glanced at Michaels, and David caught the inference.

"No!" David exhaled the word in agony. "The president of the United States?! That's not possible, is it?"

Powell shook his head. "You tell me. The president is from Arkansas. CCI's domestic headquarters are in Little Rock, Arkansas. The president was governor when he offered CCI the moon to move down here, and CCI accepted. It all seems pretty convenient to me. CCI moves to Arkansas, and the company's stock skyrockets. The governor becomes president, and CCI goes international with contracts throughout the free world, the Middle East, and most of free Asia. There are connections, threads, coincidences. And I have a problem with so many coincidences."

The steering wheel jerked in David's hand, and he wrestled with the truck. It was raining harder now; lightning streaked the sky. David had chosen a route that would put them behind the farthest point of the nuclear site and about half a mile from the possible entry point and the abandoned piping Cindy had told him about. With the rain pounding and the entry method they were about to use, it would be a cold, wet night. David wished he could concentrate on the objective at hand but the information Powell had just revealed made it difficult.

"It's still all circumstantial. We need proof."

"Proof? What constitutes proof?" Powell grunted as the truck bumped once, almost throwing him into the overhead.

"I have no idea. I started out to prove that my brother's death was not just an accident. All of a sudden I'm in the middle of an FBI investigation. My brother turns out to be working undercover for the FBI, and the construction company is no longer just the company building a power plant in my hometown; it's a multinational company extorting billions from every country on the face of the earth. And you ask me what I think proof is?" David was letting his voice rise, and he caught himself as the headlights illuminated a boulder in the road. He dodged it and calmed down. "You tell me. You're the expert. At least, I hope you're the expert. What is proof?"

"I'm looking for documents. Links. Connections. Something that will tie CCI to other projects around the country. Relationships to suppliers. Contracts. Papers that will show how they operate. With whom. Anything I can come up with," Powell said.

"Unless I'm mistaken, that stuff couldn't be used as evidence in a court of law."

"You're right about that. But I'm not looking for evidence; I'm looking for connections, pure and simple. We need some place to go from here. Quite frankly, without Jimmy, my investigation is stymied. While you're scouting for the equipment your brother was using, I'm going after papers—anything that looks interesting."

David downshifted at the approaching curve. They could be no more than a mile from their destination. David fell silent. He felt as if his whole existence was beginning to tumble out of control. Life in the military was simple, ordered, orchestrated. Here, lurching through the stormy night, nothing was as it should be. Chaos ruled. He needed to concentrate, to focus, but it was becoming more difficult, and he knew lack of concentration could prove fatal.

Morton Powell felt the atmosphere within the closed cab of the truck change as he finished talking. Some of what he'd told David Michaels was true. Most of it was speculation on his part—deduction and speculation. But he had to have Michaels's help. There was no place else to turn at this juncture, and he wanted whatever information he could get on CCI and its operations. This was the only way. CCI was connected, very well connected. Protection came in the form of congressional and executive branch pressure. Normal legal channels were no longer available. Protection had been offered and accepted.

What he had not told David Michaels was that should they be caught inside the construction compound of Nuclear Three and Four, they could easily end up dead and no one—not the FBI, OSHA, the president of the U.S., or even God in heaven—could help them.

Powell reflected on his last thought. Jimmy Michaels had believed in a God in heaven. Since David was a military chaplain, it was obvious that his older brother believed in the same God. As for himself, Powell could find no logic that dictated an omnipotent being who was in control of the entire universe. It made no sense to him. If he needed any additional verification . . . well . . . Jimmy Michaels believed and Jimmy Michaels was dead, wasn't he?

The two men passed the remainder of the ride in silence as the pickup careened and rattled down the road.

Morton Powell wrestled with the opposing forces that fought within him and David Michaels pondered his calling from God and the urge to avenge his brother's death. And he thought about Cindy. When David stopped the pickup at what appeared to be a graveled turn-around at the end of the road, neither man had settled the questions in his own mind.

"This is as close as we go," David informed the FBI agent.

"How far are we from the reactor site?"

"Not more than a mile."

Morton Powell consulted his watch. "How long do you think it will take us to make it to the site?"

The rain continued to hammer at the surrounding countryside. "Considering this rain and the dense forest, probably an hour or so."

Powell peered through the rain-spattered windshield. He could see nothing but tall trees, limbs barren of leaves, and wet. The ride had taken the better part of an hour, and he figured David Michaels had done his best to skirt the most traveled roads to come up behind

Nuclear Three and Four. They'd not seen another automobile since they had turned off the pavement miles back. The approach resembled a military action, and then Powell remembered David was military.

"What branch of service did you say you're in?" Powell asked with obvious bewilderment.

"Navy."

"Chaplain corps. Right?"

"Right."

"Assigned where?"

"At the present, FMF, Camp Pendleton," David answered, as he continued to pull on his rain suit and adjust the waist band.

"FMF?"

The rain pounded loudly against the old truck, forcing David to raise his voice to answer Powell. "Fleet Marine Force. I'm the chaplain to some recon marines."

"Great," Powell sighed to himself. "I'm teamed up with a super soldier."

"Make that a middle-aged, not-so-super soldier," David shot back. Then he almost added, . . . *one who is thinking seriously about quitting.* David was astonished at the thought. "Got your rain gear on?" he asked, as he did a final check on his own suit.

"It's on," Powell grumbled.

"Let's go. While we're out there," he ordered, indicating the forest, "you listen to me. Got it?"

Powell nodded his affirmation, noticing the character transformation the situation had induced in the chaplain.

"No talking, you follow me, and don't let me get more than ten yards ahead. In this rain and light, you could lose me in seconds. I don't need to go searching for some FBI agent lost in the forest." David pulled at his rain suit one last time before stepping into the now blinding rainfall.

Powell followed David, noticing immediately that the navy chaplain moved through the thick woods as if he'd done it before. Each step was deliberate, calculated to cause the least amount of noise, despite the sound-deadening effects of the downpour.

Morton Powell could hear nothing save the beating of the large raindrops against the landscape. He followed David, having more problems than the navy chaplain. Ten yards was too much in the available light, and Powell closed the distance to just under five as they slogged their way through the swampy forest floor. This was a place where Morton Powell was uncomfortable, and it had as much to do with the surroundings as it did with the steady seepage of the rain suit he wore. He'd been brought up on the streets of Memphis, Tennessee, and contrary to the popular belief that anyone from Memphis was a "country boy," he knew that without David Michaels, he would have no hope of survival in these woods.

David moved slowly but purposively, avoiding overhanging branches that might whip back into Powell's face and cause the agent to cry out. He'd checked on the FBI agent moments ago and noted that the man had closed the distance between them to less than ten feet. David smiled to himself. The agent had never worked in low-light conditions and obviously did not know how to use his night vision. David, on the other hand, moved confidently, gracefully even, his eyes darting back and forth, not letting them remain static lest he overlook something in the dark. Night vision, he'd been taught, was better at the periphery of a person's viewing area, and he kept up the eye movement to allow him to better scan the terrain. He also reminded himself that the most apparent thing in the dark was movement. Colors and contrast were virtually nonexistent in such conditions. Movement was the single most important detection factor in the dark. That meant the best progress, in and near any opposing force, was slow and deliberate. David recognized that he now thought of anyone associated with CCI as an opposing force: the enemy. The realization was as chilling as the rain that continued to drop from the sky in sheets.

The going was miserable. Both men's feet were wet, despite the waterproof boots each had borrowed from James Michaels. They perspired heavily, and the perspiration was accumulating beneath their waterproof suits. David knew that they would be chilled to the bone by the time they reached the outer perimeter of the reactor site.

The forest was becoming lighter as they moved through it. David signaled for Powell to stop. He stood for a moment, letting his eyes adjust to the increased light. They were no more than four hundred yards from the perimeter fence, he calculated.

His eyes focused, David moved slowly, checking the trees and the forest floor for some type of infrared motion detector or surveillance camera. He didn't think CCI would be so paranoid as to have installed such devices, but he was cautious. If there was indeed something happening with CCI and NCEC, detectors would not be out of the question. He scanned the trees, the junctures of trunks and limbs, and the bases, places where a sensor could be concealed. He detected no devices, and the two men climbed the gently rising topography leading to the site.

The lights were brighter, the horizon illuminated by a halogen glow, and David moved slowly to allow his eyes to adjust to the increased light level. The top of the rise was heavily wooded, and as the rain poured from the heavens, David considered that he was being overly prudent under the circumstances. This was a civilian establishment, not a military objective, and the perimeter security, although substantial by civilian standards, was not that to be found around a military compound of the same size.

David struggled to the top of the rise, maintaining a prone position. He glanced back at the FBI agent. Powell was understandably reluctant to prostrate himself in the pouring rain, and he stood at the base of the rise, looking bewildered. When he glanced up the rise toward David, David motioned him forward with a flat hand. They had come too far to risk discovery.

It had been a long time since Powell could remember feeling this wretched. He was soaked inside and out. The mild chill in the air now felt like a winter blizzard. He could feel the beginnings of muscle twitches, the forerunner to hypothermia. The temperature, he guessed, was in the low sixties, maybe the high fifties. Certainly not excessive, but dangerous under present conditions. His teeth chattered and his head ached. He found it difficult to concentrate. He was beginning to think he'd made a mistake in accompanying Michaels. The navy chaplain seemed to be able to completely ignore the conditions.

Powell was on his belly now, every muscle protesting. He'd have to start some form of exercise other than that mandated from the Hoover Building. He crawled to the top of the ridge, moving next to David Michaels, and peered into the fenced compound that was their objective.

From the top of the small mount, David could see the massive shadows cast by the three-hundred-foot cooling towers. He and Powell had come out of the forest exactly where he'd wanted—the remotest portion of the fenced compound. Multiple halogen lamps perched atop sixty-foot aluminum poles, their severe white light playing over the huge area, illuminating virtually every square foot. Few portions of the compound escaped the cold, probing light. Workmen and heavy equipment moved about the construction areas as if it were daylight.

David could distinguish three separate areas of major construction: the cooling towers to the north, the smaller rectangular reactor containment building situated a hundred yards south of the towers, and the elongated control building to the west of both the towers and reactor building. Large, yellow earthmovers lay idle near the fence below where he and the FBI agent were positioned. Ponderous cranes dominated the construction areas, lifting and placing heavy equipment in and around the reactor buildings and the cooling towers.

The enclosed perimeter was totally barren. The only cover, as far as David could see, consisted of the equipment and the structures themselves. The men moving about the area were clad in an assortment of rain-repellent clothing. There was no uniformity. *That is our first break,* David thought. *We can blend in with the rest of the workers.*

Powell fidgeted next to Michaels. David understood the meaning of the motion and turned as Powell pointed in one direction. David followed Powell's point. To the east of the construction area, along one of the many blacktop roads within the fence, stood one of the guard towers. Powell pointed again, and David picked out three more towers along the fence's perimeter. The tower closest to them would be the one to worry about; the others were just shadowy shapes, their edges softened in the fog.

David tapped Powell on the shoulder and moved off to his left, toward the lake. They moved in the shadow of the ridge for ten minutes.

The surface of the lake was as dark as the sky above it, each blending into the other, its invisible horizon lost in the night. Raindrops sent ripples out in every direction.

"The pipe entrance is just below the marker there," David said as he pointed to what appeared to be a small buoy marker.

Powell didn't like it. He could swim, but only because it was required by the FBI. For him, swimming was nothing more than survival in water. Barely.

It was time.

David moved into the lake, a man totally comfortable in the water, and stopped short of the buoy. The water was waist high. Powell watched as Michaels ducked beneath the surface. At first the agent thought Michaels had been sucked into the pipe by some unseen hydraulic force. Then he reappeared, looking more like a sea serpent rising from the depths than a man. Powell shuddered as Michaels motioned him forward. Powell swallowed his fear and stepped into the water.

The agent was pleasantly surprised to find the water warm. At least it was warmer than he was. He waded to where the navy chaplain stood, dreading what he knew the former marine was about to say.

"This is the way in," David whispered.

"I was afraid it might be," Powell concluded miserably.

"I've already removed the cover, so be careful not to fall in. The pipe is at least three feet in diameter. Shouldn't be too much of a problem."

"You ever do a stint with the SEALS?" Powell asked, not knowing why he'd brought up the amphibious branch of the navy.

"Two years. I hated it."

"Yeah," Powell muttered to himself. "I can understand that."

"I'll go first," David said. He quickly hyperventilated, ducked beneath the surface, and forced his 6'2" frame into the bowels of the pipe.

Powell turned his attention inside the fenced area and began counting, "One thousand one, one thousand two. . . ." He counted almost seventy seconds before he saw David Michaels reappear within the compound. He looked like some creature appearing from the depths of the earth as he exited the other end of the pipe. Michaels waved and touched thumb and forefinger together in a circle to indicate it had been easy.

Powell cursed to himself, hyperventilated, and plunged beneath the dark water. The agent swam down and into the pipe, his eyes closed. His head thwacked against the pipe where it made a ninety-degree turn inland. He momentarily panicked, losing orientation. The agent shook off the blow and swam through the unobstructed pipe. Thoughts of death in the claustrophobic pipe raced through his mind; he could feel panic rising, sucking at him like a whirlpool. He'd started counting when he dove beneath the water and had lost count when his head struck the pipe. What was it now? Thirty seconds? Seventy? His lungs were almost at their limit, the burning spreading throughout his chest, when he felt a strong hand grasp him and pluck him from the abyss.

"Not so bad, was it?" David Michaels whispered.

Morton Powell gasped for air, thinking briefly, as his conscious thought processes returned, that he would like to punch Michaels in the nose. The idea quickly evaporated. He had no doubts that the middle-aged chaplain could destroy him in short order. The hand that had pulled him from the darkness and water had a viselike quality about it. David Michaels was deceptively strong.

"This is where it gets dangerous. Stay with me," David commanded.

The two men had just started for the building complexes, their movements matching those of the workmen that moved within the complex, when they heard a sound behind them.

"Stop right there!" the voice hissed menacingly.

Powell and Michaels froze and then slowly turned to stare into the silenced muzzle of an Ingram submachine gun.

5

Tom Frazier had guessed right, but then he was used to that. He'd made a career out of being in the right place at the right time. He'd become the youngest deputy sheriff in Arkansas and the youngest agent in a government agency few people knew about. When the grizzled sheriff of thirty-four years had retired, Frazier had become the youngest sheriff to take office in the state. He'd been lucky in sports, in finance, and in love—his wife of twenty years was just as lovely now as when he'd married her, and they were just as much in love. In the financial area, Frazier had followed the advice of friends who knew what the stock market was all about—nothing illegal, no inside trading tips, just rock-solid advice and in-depth valuations of new-start companies. He'd made a killing buying start-up stock in small electronics firms that were later purchased by huge conglomerates at exorbitant prices.

Tom Frazier was a millionaire. The fact that he did not live like a millionaire would have endeared him to his constituents had they known his net worth. Only the monetary funds manager who had direct control over Frazier's assets and one other man knew that the law-enforcement officer was independently wealthy.

But Tom Frazier was much more—more than even the people of Clayton County, Arkansas, knew.

Frazier had been looking out his office window when David Michaels left the Clayton County Courthouse earlier. He'd ambled down to Cindy Tolbert's office and talked to Cindy about a land dispute that was pending in municipal court. Cindy had not had the time to replace the folios the navy chaplain had been using, and Frazier took note of them. He'd dealt with the large, hardback books enough to know the one that Michaels had shown interest in was the one that contained the deeds, photos, and lease agreements of the construction site at Nuclear Three and Four.

Leaving the courthouse, he'd driven by James Michaels's residence and noticed the strange car pulled into the drive. Government, no doubt, he'd deduced correctly. He also knew that Michaels had been to see Carlton Graham, the OSHA representative at CCI. It didn't take much to figure out that Michaels, and possibly some government agent as well, were going to try to enter the CCI nuclear construction area. But even with that information, he still did not know when, how, or where.

Frazier had driven by the Michaels home once again to find the government car still parked in the driveway. James Michaels's pickup was gone. He called and talked to Mr. Michaels. It did not take long to discern that neither the unknown government man nor David were at home. Frazier had already evaluated the possible points of ingress and settled on one area. He'd guessed right.

Sheriff Tom Frazier lay prone just to the right of where David Michaels and the unknown agent had been moments earlier. The bone-chilling rain was making life wretched at the moment. Frazier had arrived a full ten minutes before Michaels and the agent. He'd hidden his car in a short turnoff just off the county road and had walked to the top of the ridge. The sheriff had been startled by the approach of the two men. The rain had dampened not only his spirit, but the sound coming from the forest, and Michaels had been on top of him before he could react. Luckily the rain had also served as natural camouflage, and he had not been spotted. He did not need the added aggravation of trying to explain his presence.

Now, as he lay on the crest, he watched David Michaels and the FBI man work their way into the lake, and one by one, disappear. It had been a strange experience until he saw David Michaels reappear inside the fenced construction area as if by magic.

The pipe! he remembered. Rumor had it that the Clayton High School football team used it as sort of an initiation, a rite of passage. Frazier had dismissed the stunt as foolish, but seeing Michaels disappear and reappear, and then the second man disappear, he made a mental note to be out here next football season, if he was still around. The way things were going, he doubted he'd be in Clayton County next year.

Frazier scanned the area with the Zeiss binoculars he'd carried from his patrol car. What Michaels expected to accomplish was beyond him, but under the circumstances, doing anything was better than sitting on your hands and waiting to react to events that may prove to be beyond control.

Frazier twisted in the soft earth, trying to stop the itching that was beginning to annoy him. The rain continued, but much of its ferocity had been spent and it had settled into a gentle downpour. He moved the field glasses slowly over the lighted, fenced-in area, watching the workmen and machines go about the task of constructing a nuclear plant.

Frazier picked up movement to his left. He repositioned the glasses in that direction. Michaels and the second man came into focus in the twin lenses, hands behind their heads; they were being held at gunpoint by an armed guard. *Man,* he thought, as he recognized the silenced Ingram. *This is getting out of hand more quickly than I thought it would.* Frazier continued to watch, struggling to devise a plan that would extricate Michaels and his partner from the situation. After all, he had virtually forced David Michaels into this situation. This was the logical outgrowth of the conversation he and David Michaels had had in his office. It had been a calculated risk, a gamble. He'd tacitly approved this very thing.

As Frazier watched, the guard ordered Michaels and the government agent—Frazier wondered why he instantly thought of the second man in such terms—to turn around and lie on the ground. Frazier scanned the forest floor, searching for any object that might be of use. His eyes locked onto a rock just off to his right. He rolled in that direction, carefully maintaining visual contact with the guard. The rock was slightly smaller than a football but weighed more. He hefted the rock and stood slowly. Then he hurled the miniboulder into the perimeter fence. The rock struck the wire mesh fence with the force of a small asteroid. The sound, even in the sound-dampening rain, reverberated across the compound.

Frazier was rewarded as the guard involuntary reacted to the sudden noise, swinging the Ingram in the direction of the source, and then, much to Frazier's disappointment, recovering just as quickly. Neither Michaels nor the agent had time to move. The sheriff dropped to the ground and rolled behind the crest of the ridge, out of sight. He got to his feet and headed for his cruiser. He'd done what he could. Now he would have to report his actions for the night. He hoped he would not have to later report the death of David Michaels and an unknown second man.

6

The lights in the Oval Office burned into the night. President Donald Farmington Adams paced around the outer edges of the deceptively small room. He circled the twin wingback chairs at one end and then the desk at the other. Pacing was one of his habits when he had a problem, and he had one tonight. Having a problem was nothing new for the president, but this problem did not concern foreign policy, domestic tranquillity, or world peace. This problem was much closer to home.

Right now he was waiting for the phone to ring.

The door connecting the office to the outer secretarial spaces opened, and T. J. Kirby entered. He was the only person allowed complete access to the president, and as chief of staff, he was also the only person privy to most of the thoughts of Donald Adams. Most, but not all.

Kirby and the president had grown up within hailing distance of each other back in Arkansas. Kirby was a balding, overweight—he preferred stocky—man in his early fifties. Adams was in his late forties, and the two men had become friends on the athletic fields of the University of Arkansas. The friendship had continued off the fields, mostly because the two were perfectly meshed. Kirby was amiable. Adams was an enigma; a totally honest politician, or so it seemed, and honesty was a difficult commodity to deal with in the rarefied environs of Washington.

"Mr. President," T. J. Kirby stopped when he saw the expression on the president's face. "Don," he smiled, "I thought you had gone to bed." The use of the president's first name was a perk allocated only to Kirby, and only when the two were alone.

The president shook his head. "Not yet, T. J. I've got something on my mind."

Kirby scowled. He was privy to most problems that plagued his boss, but this was something new. He'd not heard of anything that would cause such consternation in the president. "Anything I can do?"

"Not tonight, T. J. I'll let you know, but thanks." Don Adams resumed the pacing he'd halted at Kirby's entrance.

T. J. Kirby backed out of the Oval Office. Whatever was worrying his boss, it was serious, that much was certain. He'd seen Adams under pressure many times, but this was different. Now he was worried too.

The chief of staff went to his office and dialed the Arkansas area code and a number.

7

Water dripped and formed a puddle at the feet of Sheriff Tom Frazier as he listened. He had come directly from Nuclear Three and Four and placed the phone call. He didn't put the conversation on the speaker phone; it was too private.

"I understand," he answered. "There were two of them. Michaels was one and the other was some sort of federal agent. FBI, perhaps. I don't know his name. There was a government vehicle parked in the Michaels's driveway. Could be GAO, NSC, anything. I have no way of knowing. You could look into that for me, if you would. Good, I'll call later if I learn anything. In the meantime, you better tighten up on your end. This is really big, isn't it? I'll keep my eyes open. Good night."

Frazier hung up the phone and sank heavily into the worn chair. He was cold and tired and wet. He'd not bargained for this when he'd begun. Now he was in deep; too deep to back out. Even worse, now others were involved as deeply as he was. He could take care of himself, but he was not so certain about the others.

8

Carlton Graham crumpled the report in anger. Then he let the anger subside and straightened the paper so he could feed it into his shredder. The machine hummed as Graham pushed the paper into it.

Random, crosscut, eighth-of-an-inch shreds fell from the machine and into the security burn bag attached to the shredder.

Mr. Murphy knew exactly what he was talking about, Graham thought at the moment. *If things can go wrong, they will.*

David Michaels was Murphy's law incarnate, Graham fumed. The navy chaplain had all the markings of a man who stuck his nose in where it did not belong. Graham finished with the papers, satisfied that the shredded material was now safely destroyed.

The OSHA inspector let his breathing return to normal and his pulse regulate. He'd always been able to solve any kind of problem, and this was another opportunity to prove it. Given time, he was confident he could resolve the situation. The first thing to do was to get rid of the climbing equipment Jimmy Michaels had used the day of the accident. He had made a mistake by talking to David Michaels. The man had picked up on the point of a closed investigation without definitive results from tests on the equipment. Graham had tried to mitigate the damage, but he had seen the light in the eyes of the chaplain. That light meant trouble.

He left his office and walked down the corridor of the building until he came to an unmarked office door. He retrieved a key from his pocket and opened the door. When the light illuminated the room, it revealed a labyrinth of articles Graham had impounded over the course of his investigations for CCI. None of the paraphernalia piled in the room had ever made it to the OSHA lab in Washington.

Graham fumbled through the pile, searching for the belt and rope. He'd just found it when he heard the door behind him open.

The last person he wanted to see at this moment was Commander David Michaels, but here the man stood, with water streaming from his clothing as if he'd been swimming. Behind him stood another man whom Graham did not recognize. The two men advanced into the room.

"Nice collection, Mr. Graham," said David Michaels.

"Shut up, you," a voice from behind ordered.

Graham recognized one of the perimeter guards, but couldn't recall the man's name. The black bulk of the silenced Ingram demanded obedience.

Graham began to feel better.

Then David Michaels moved with almost blinding speed.

CHAPTER THIRTEEN

1

The guard holding the silenced Ingram was shocked by David Michaels' speed. He'd not expected so middle-aged a man to move with such catlike precision and quickness. The error was costly.

David Michaels's right leg shot out straight and locked, the power of his hips behind the kick. His right boot caught the guard's hand and forced the Ingram upward, but not before the rattle of the bolt operating signaled the weapon's discharge. David half-stepped into the man and brought his foot up a second time, this time higher, catching the man in the throat with all the force of a battering ram. The man's scream was silenced in mideruption; he crumpled against the wall and lay still. David turned quickly; Morton Powell was bending over Carlton Graham. The OSHA inspector had gone suddenly pale.

Powell looked from David to the unconscious guard and back to David. "You did that rather well," Powell said. "As if you may have done it before. But one of the bullets got our friend here."

David moved beside Powell and the stricken Graham. In just a few short seconds, Graham's clothing below his waist was soaked with blood. "How bad is it?" he asked, knowing the answer.

"Bad enough. The bullet got the femoral artery, I think," Powell answered as he pressed his right hand against the wounded man's right inner thigh to stem the bleeding. The maneuver worked.

David directed his attention toward Graham as Powell kept pressure against the wounded man's inner thigh. "Where's the equipment my brother was using the day he died?" he asked coldly, ignoring the wound.

"You have no right to be here!" Graham insisted, wincing as the initial shock wore off and the pain began to set in. The man was nothing if not obstinate.

David Michaels met the FBI agent's gaze as the man looked up from the stricken Graham. Both knew what had to be done, but David did not like it. The chaplain within wanted to console the stricken man, to provide comfort, assuage pain, but the brother of Jimmy Michaels wanted to make the man talk.

"Mr. Graham," Powell began, "you have a choice. You can help us now, or I can let you bleed to death."

Graham's eyes widened in panic as he looked into the agent's eyes. "You wouldn't do that," said Graham.

Powell smiled menacingly. He released the pressure he was holding against Graham's femoral artery, and bright red blood spurted from the bullet's entry hole. Powell smiled coldly as he reapplied pressure to the pressure point. "Your femoral artery was nicked. Interesting artery if I remember my anatomy correctly. It's the second largest artery in the body, next to the aorta. You could bleed to death in just under a minute, I believe. Maybe two minutes, but the timing is not the important thing. You would be dead."

"I can hold the pressure myself," Graham argued weakly.

Powell grinned. "You could. But take a look at yourself. You've been shot. It won't take too long before you go into shock. You might be able to hold the pressure until then. Say two or three minutes. After that, you would pass out and bleed to death. No, Mr. Graham, your life is in my hands, literally."

"You wouldn't da . . ."

"Of course," the FBI agent interrupted, "I could be wrong. If you care to try, I'll be more than willing to oblige."

Carlton Graham searched the agent's face for compassion. There was none. He turned to David Michaels, "You wouldn't let him," Graham pleaded.

Powell spoke before David had the chance. "No, he wouldn't. He's an honorable man despite what he's doing here. I, on the other hand, am not quite so compassionate. I have no reservations at all about letting you bleed to death."

"I . . . it'd b . . . be murder," Graham stuttered.

Powell laughed. "Think about it Graham. You've been shot by your own guard. He'll wake up and find you dead. We will be gone. If my suspicions are correct, he'll be long gone before anyone even knows you're in here. That silenced Ingram he's carrying is a mercenary's weapon, and I'll bet my pension that our sleeping man over there is nothing more than a hired gun. Oh, and before I forget it, that particular weapon is illegal, but then I suspect you already know that. Your choice, Graham."

David Michaels turned and walked from the room, his head reeling. The warm, pungent scent of Graham's blood permeated the room, but that was not the problem. He had seen and smelled worse. It was the idea that he could allow such inhuman behavior that disturbed him. Man's inhumanity to man, and he was part of it. He'd seen enough for the time being. *Powell is right,* David thought, *I couldn't do what he is doing now.* It wasn't part of his makeup, no matter how much he wanted to avenge Jimmy's death.

Graham was close to panic, his mouth forming words he could not utter.

"Let me help you decide, Mr. Graham," Morton Powell said, releasing the pressure point yet again. Blood spurted in pulsating streams from the wound. Graham screamed and fumbled for the pressure point unsuccessfully. "Thirty seconds," Powell said, looking at his watch.

"All right!" Graham screamed hysterically.

Powell moved in and stemmed the flow immediately. David returned. "Get me something to use as a tourniquet," Powell ordered.

David found some leather strapping and a metal rod, and Powell fashioned a crude tourniquet. Minutes later, with the tourniquet in place, Powell began.

"We need some information and we need it now," Powell demanded. "First, where's the equipment Jimmy Michaels used the day he died?"

"I need a doctor," Graham moaned.

"The equipment," Powell repeated.

Graham pointed to a double-doored metal cabinet. "On the right side. It's in a large plastic bag labeled with Michaels's name."

Powell motioned toward the cabinet, and David moved to open it. It was a shelved storage cabinet, the kind found in every office and used for supplies. On the right side of the bottom shelf, a lone garbage bag rested with a masking tape label that read, "Michaels." David removed the bag and opened it. He found the rope and the leather harness inside. Even with a cursory examination, he could see where the leather had separated. It looked as if acid or some foreign compound had eaten through the fibers. David felt the tears begin to form and he forced them back as he turned to Graham.

"You did this?" he asked venomously, jamming the equipment close to Graham's face.

Graham cowered at the tone of voice. "No. I don't know who did it. I was only responsible for ignoring it," Graham offered in a whisper.

"Ignoring murder?" David said, thrusting the leather close to Graham's face.

"I didn't know it was murder," he replied.

David threw the leather harness to the floor. Both Powell and Graham recoiled involuntarily at the ferocity with which Michaels hurled the object.

Powell said, turning back to Graham, "I may have underestimated the preacher. Maybe I should let him continue this interrogation." Powell grabbed Graham by the front of the shirt. "Those," he said, pointing to the rope and leather harness, "are enough to get you the gas chamber. And I believe they still have capital punishment here in Arkansas."

"I didn't do anything," Graham whined. The man from OSHA was growing weaker by the minute. His complexion was a pasty white; small beads of cold perspiration dotted his forehead just at the hairline. He was having difficulty focusing.

"That remains to be seen," Powell said flatly. "You can help yourself by answering the rest of my questions."

"I need a doctor," Graham pleaded weakly.

"The pain will help to keep you alert. Now," Powell continued "tell me about the connection of Collins Construction International and OSHA."

The OSHA man shook his head in the negative. "There's no connection. Not directly, anyway. When OSHA inspections are scheduled, an inspector is assigned to the project. The assignments are usually given to a half dozen or so inspectors who have expertise in the particular field. Nuclear power plants are my specialty," Graham said.

Powell saw the signs of impending shock. He would have to hurry. "And since CCI deals in nuclear power generation, you can be assured of being assigned to them. Is that it?"

Graham nodded. "Basically, yes. Not all of the CCI inspectors are getting paid by CCI. Only one other that I know of. But between the two of us, we can waive millions of dollars in expenses related to employee safety."

"Not to mention the fact that you can hold hearings and make judgments exonerating the companies involved," David Michaels declared angrily.

Graham shook his head. "I know. But that's the easy part. Ignoring the regulations and laws governing operations accounts for millions more than any injury claim ever could."

"And that money goes directly to whom?" Powell pressed.

"I don't know that. I can't even say how the money is accounted for. That's out of my hands." Graham moaned and rubbed his injured leg.

"The sooner I have this information, the sooner you'll get a doctor for that leg," Powell pressed.

"From what I understand, CCI supplies much of its own material from subsidiary companies. That, too, is beyond the realm of my responsibility. Those companies are owned wholly or in part by Emerson and Jameson Collins," Graham volunteered.

"Then it's a relatively simple matter to order material at inflated prices and pocket the difference."

"And falsifying delivery documents for materials supposedly ordered and received—materials that never arrive. And when they do, they don't meet the codes. I've seen trucks deliver concrete reinforcement steel that was the wrong size or sometimes defective. I've even seen signed invoices verifying complete deliveries of construction products that never even made it to the site."

David Michaels stepped closer. "And you're saying that all that money is going into the Collins brothers' pockets?"

Graham looked up at David. "I didn't say that. That's what I suspect, but this operation is so large, there must be hundreds, maybe thousands, of hands in the pie. You're trying to bring down a leviathan with a popgun."

"A Goliath with a single, smooth stone," David Michaels whispered.

"With that many people involved," Powell said, "it would be virtually impossible to keep it quiet. Too many bodies means greed. Someone would have talked by now or wanted in for more of the take. What you describe is impossible."

Graham snickered. "It's happened. I'm telling you. Collins has a way of keeping people in line. The head of security, a man named Young, is responsible for compliance. He's nothing more than a hired gun. The few that stepped out of line just disappeared and that pretty much took care of defections. The guards here are his men." The OSHA representative tried to point to the unconscious guard crumpled against the wall. He could not raise his arm. Graham could not last much longer.

Powell was beginning to worry about the man, but this was a close as he'd ever been to getting information on CCI, so he pressed on. He pulled a Beretta 92 from his shoulder holster and handed it to David Michaels. "You know how to use this?" he asked.

David took the weapon. "Same model MPs and SPs use. I can handle it."

"A preacher with a gun," Powell muttered, shaking his head in dismay.

"Chaplain," David corrected, wondering if the difference was as great as he'd imagined. "Big difference."

Powell checked the battered guard still against the wall where David Michaels's kick had put him. "I'm beginning to appreciate that difference." He turned back to Graham. Powell knew he'd have to get the OSHA inspector to an emergency room soon. He could lose the leg and quite possibly die, and Powell needed the man on the witness stand, should it ever come to that. "One more thing, Graham. I want documents, files, false delivery sheets, faked vouchers, unverifiable inventories, anything I can get to substantiate your story."

Graham shook his head weakly. "No way. Not a chance. None of that's kept here on site."

"Where then?"

"The main offices in Little Rock. I've only been there a couple of times, but the place is guarded like a fort. The only way to get at those documents is with a warrant," Graham said weakly.

"There are always alternatives," Powell responded, as he turned to check on the guard. David Michaels was just out of reach of the man, sitting on a folding chair, the Beretta resting easily in his right hand. Powell could see the pistol's safety was off, and Michaels's index finger was resting gently along side the trigger guard. Michaels did indeed know what he was doing.

"You got a key to the CCI building in Little Rock?" Powell quizzed Graham.

"No. I'm not that big."

"I want a way in," the FBI man insisted.

"There's no way, not even for you two cowboys. It can't be done."

"Yes, it can, Mr. Graham," Powell continued in a solicitous voice. "You've been there. Tell me about it."

Carlton Graham was close to deep shock. His skin was pasty and clammy. His breathing was shallow and rapid as he lay back on the floor. His words were coming in disconnected spurts that made his speech sound like a foreign language.

"You don't have much time, Graham. Talk to me."

Graham gasped, "I . . . was the . . . inspector on the ren . . . renovations of the CCI building. From the roof, the roof . . . there's a central ventilation system. It goes down through the center of the building. If you can get . . . get on the roof without detection, you might be able to . . . penet . . . penetrate the building that way. That's all I know," Graham gasped.

Powell turned to David. "Tie that one up and we'll take him with us."

"What about Graham?" David asked.

"I ought to leave him here, but we'll leave both of them with the sheriff. I think he'll take care of them for a few hours, and he'll make sure a doctor sees Graham."

"And how do we get out of here?" David asked.

"Not the way we came in, I can assure you," Powell emphasized. He'd forgotten how cold he was during the interrogation of Carlton Graham, but now his shivering body reminded him. "We'll just drive out," he said. "I'm sure Mr. Graham's car is well known by the gate guards. We won't have a problem, will we, Graham?"

The OSHA inspector shook his head weakly. "No . . . none."

"Let's go," Powell said to David. "You and I have an appointment in Little Rock."

"There are some things I need to do first," David indicated to Powell. "It'll only take a few minutes."

2

Allen Stuart was close to panic. He'd been sitting at his desk in North Central Electric Cooperative's managerial suites for the past two hours as lightning scorched the night sky. Stuart was paranoid, and the appearance of David Michaels in Clayton had done nothing to assuage his escalating fear. Now, with the office lights fighting the creeping darkness, Stuart was ready to crack. He groped through the desk drawers and the paper stacks littering the desktop. He had his own plan in mind, and it did not include his querulous wife, the barmaid in Tunica, the Collins brothers, or any other person. Three different mutual fund share statements showed he had amassed at least a half million dollars during the process of construction of Nuclear Three and Four. Fully half the money had come from his own inventiveness concerning the accounting system used by NCEC. The other half came from the kickbacks and under-the-table funds he'd funneled from CCI.

Half a million was not what he'd hoped for, but it was better than nothing. Besides, if he acted quickly, Stuart knew he could augment his funds with little trouble. It would require a confrontation with the utterly disgusting head of security of CCI, Wayne Young, but doubling his money made it worth the effort. He'd called Young earlier, and the man was expecting him. The head of North Central Electric Cooperative shivered at the thought of dealing with the CCI security head.

Stuart examined the documents he'd collected. They represented his total involvement in the Nuclear Three and Four fiasco. He stuffed the papers into his briefcase, gathered the mutual fund statements, and went to the cooperative's safe. He extracted ten thousand dollars in cash, inserted previously prepared vouchers to account for the money, tossed the cash on top of the other papers in his valise, and walked out of the office. The vouchers in the safe would not stand up under the careful scrutiny of a company auditor, but they would give him a few hours more that he would otherwise not have. Those few hours were all he needed to entice a payment out of Wayne Young at the CCI offices in Little Rock and lose himself in his carefully prepared escape plan.

When Stuart locked the doors of North Central Electric Cooperative, he felt a slight twinge of disappointment that could not be alleviated by the money he carried at his side. *I deserved more,* he thought. *I worked for it.* Maybe the impending doom he foresaw in the meeting with Wayne Young would never materialize.

In any case, it would be good to escape the religious bigots that populated the small southern town. He'd certainly had enough of people trying to save his soul. Maybe half a million was not so bad compared to the persecution he had endured from the local Christian community.

Stuart climbed into his company car. He'd be in Little Rock in two hours. He'd use the time to formulate exactly how to make his demands to the head of CCI security.

3

The remaining half inch of coffee in the old coffeemaker was beginning to smell like burned rubber. Sheriff Tom Frazier rose from his desk to switch off the appliance. Frazier was cold and tired—no, exhausted and angry. He wanted to be out at the construction site, waiting for David Michaels and the stranger to reappear once again. He wanted to follow them, to determine exactly what it was they had in mind. Whatever it was, the sheriff realized, it was not necessarily legal, and by what he had seen earlier, very dangerous. He had given Michaels carte blanche in the county. The orders had come from higher up, but the tacit approval had come from his office. If this whole thing blew sky-high, he would be the first one to fall to earth in the rubble. But Frazier could understand the state of mind David Michaels found himself in. It was bad enough to come home for your brother's funeral. It was another thing entirely to find your brother was not just dead but probably murdered.

Frazier was not happy with his role in the investigation. He essentially had abdicated his jurisdiction to others. The fact that he had no idea who the others were compounded the difficulty.

The phone rang, and Frazier lifted the receiver. The ring released a jolt of adrenaline that stimulated his system. He'd been on the verge of sleep, brought on by the overheated office and late hour, but now he was wide awake.

When Tom Frazier returned the phone to its resting place, he knew the identity of the strange man with David Michaels. He'd scribbled notes on his desk blotter, and now he tore the paper from the desktop, folded it, and placed it in his shirt pocket.

He'd also received further instructions as to his involvement in the case of David Michaels and the man he now knew as Morton Powell, the FBI special agent working under the umbrella of the OCTF. For Frazier the news was good, and it buoyed his spirit.

The Clayton County sheriff opened the bottom drawer of his desk and pulled out a Glock 17, 9 mm automatic pistol. The Austrian firm that produced the Glock had perfected the process of producing high-polymer handguns that withstood the roughest treatment.

He removed his Sam Browne with its Smith & Wesson 357 magnum revolver and placed it in the drawer. The Smith & Wesson was an excellent weapon: dependable, rugged, simple, and powerful. Its only drawback was its limited ammunition capacity. The Smith & Wesson held six bullets; the Glock held seventeen 180 grain slugs. Frazier loaded his ammunition. The traditional firearm purist argued that six was enough if you could shoot well. Frazier could shoot well enough, but the "six-is-enough" argument didn't hold water if you knew you were headed into a no-holds-barred situation against superior firepower. What had happened in Waco, Texas, to the Alcohol, Tobacco, and Firearms agents would not happen in Arkansas, Frazier promised himself, as he checked the five additional magazine clips attached to the Glock's holster belt. The total came to 102 rounds loaded in magazines that could be slammed into the handle in a split second.

Frazier rose, strapped the belt on, and headed for the door. As he left, he checked his watch. It had been a little over an hour since he left the rain-soaked ridge. Enough time, surely, for Michaels and Powell to exit the compound and be gone. Provided, of course, the men had been able to subdue the Ingram-carrying guard who'd had them in his sights when Frazier had tossed the rock against the perimeter fence. For some inexplicable reason, the Clayton County sheriff had every confidence that they had somehow escaped.

Another hunch. Another guess. Tom Frazier had the feeling he would guess right again tonight.

4

Cindy Tolbert had been true to her word about praying for David Michaels. Not only that, but she called Jean and told her what she knew of the situation and enlisted her prayers too.

Jean had been more than willing to pray for her brother-in-law, regardless of the circumstances. She'd been doing it for several years anyway. She'd prayed for David because Jimmy had once shared with her the difficulty of being a military chaplain. "A hybrid," Jimmy had called him. A preacher-soldier. An oxymoron to Jean's way of thinking, but she'd prayed.

"Meet me at the church," Cindy had told Jean.

Jean arrived at the appointed time. Cindy had been waiting in the cozy chapel just off the main sanctuary.

"What's going on?" Jean asked as she entered.

"I honestly don't know, Jean," Cindy responded. "David was in the office today looking at the area in and around the nuclear site. I know he's been to talk with the OSHA inspector out there, Carlton Graham. I'm afraid he's taking Jimmy's death personally. He wants to know what happened."

"We all want that," Jean interjected.

Cindy shook her head. "Not the way David wants it. It's an obsession with him. As if he were an avenging angel from God."

Jean looked into her friend's face, recognizing what it was that Cindy really feared. "You're in love with him, aren't you?" The words were candid, their meaning natural.

"No! Oh, I don't know. I think so," she admitted. "I'm confused. I still remember him when we were in school together. I had a crush on him then, you know. I thought I'd forgotten him after all these years, but seeing him now brings back a lot of memories. I was just not expecting it to be like this."

"I know how you feel. Jimmy always told me to pray to the Lord when I was confused. Jimmy used to joke that prayer might not settle the confusion, but it sure made it a lot easier to live with."

Cindy Tolbert could see the tears in Jean's eyes well up and spill down her cheeks. "Let's both pray," she suggested. "For David and for those of us who have to live day to day."

Jean Michaels took Cindy's hand, and they bowed in the quiet of the wood-lined chapel. Somehow, just being in a church made things better.

For Cindy Tolbert, the peace that normally came from being in such close proximity to the white church building did not come. Confusion was only part of what she now felt. Jean's question had forced her to voice her innermost feelings. *Love?* God is love, she knew, but what of the emotions she was dealing with in the here and now? What about David Michaels? Did she love him, or was she just recalling more carefree times when love was easier to define?

5

"It's happening too fast," Wayne Young complained. "It's out of control."

"Settle down, Young, and tell me what you're talking about," Emerson Collins commanded. "You're acting like some rookie cop on his first drug bust. What's this about Allen Stuart?"

Wayne Young caught his breath and began, "Stuart called a few minutes ago. He's coming in here to talk to me. He left the impression that he wants out."

"Out?"

"He's leaving the country. I suspect what he would like from us is money."

"The idiot!" the de facto head of CCI roared. "I want to see him when he gets here. The fool shouldn't be coming here in the first place. I hold you responsible for this, Young."

Young exploded from his seat at the accusation. "Me? The man is scared. This David Michaels has put the fear of the devil in the man. That kind of fear can be dangerous. How am I supposed to stop him? Kill him?"

"That's an idea," said Collins slowly.

"Not right now it's not. We have two dead, Michaels's brother and that redneck spotter, right in our backyard, not to mention another body, or what's left of it, up in Fayetteville, which, may I remind you, may or may not be traced back to this office. We can't afford another death right now. Especially not the death of the general manager of NCEC. There's too direct a connection with CCI. The feds would be on us like white on rice."

Collins snorted, "Save your quaint colloquialisms, Young," he said, waving the big man back to his chair. "You're right, of course. We can't afford another death. What do you suggest?"

"Right now I'm at a loss. Stuart will be here in a couple of hours. Let me go over my options until then. I'll have an answer before Stuart shows up."

"Good. That's what I pay you for, answers. Now, down to a real problem. I just got a call from Washington. You're right about this David Michaels. Seems he might pose some sort of problem after all— more than just through Stuart. My sources tell me he is more than just a little interested in his brother's death. He's already created concern with Carlton Graham as well."

"Stuart relayed the same message to me," Young added. "He also said Michaels was in the clerk's office in Clayton County going over area photos of the nuclear site. It's one of the things that spooked Stuart."

"The nuclear site? What's up there that could be incriminating?"

"Not much, Mr. Collins. All the accounting, blueprint changes, and documentation are down here. For Michaels to come up with anything, he'd have to find a way in here, get to the engineering department, the accounting department, and the government licensing office. Even then, he'd have to know what he was looking for. I don't see that Michaels can harm us, if we can contain Stuart, that is."

"Keep it that way. And I want to know as soon as Stuart arrives. You handle him and see what he wants, then relay the information to me, got it?"

"Yes, sir," Young replied and left the office.

"Well, what do you think, Harmon?" Emerson Collins asked his comptroller as the small man entered the office from an adjoining door.

"Young's a fool. All Michaels has to do is tap the computer system to retrieve all the information he needs. Of course, he'd have to be an accountant or a lawyer to decipher the raw data, and I doubt that's the case. Nevertheless, Mr. Michaels could cause a great deal of harm."

"And Stuart?"

"You were right the first time. Kill him. He's turned into a liability. If my guess is right, Stuart is coming down here to pry some money out of Young, and then he's gone—on his way to some Caribbean island or South American country without an extradition treaty would be my guess."

"So?"

"So, if that's the case, he probably left North Central in a mess. He's planning on disappearing on his own, we just help him along the way, is all."

"There's logic in what you say," Collins agreed. "I'll wait to see what Young has to say after Stuart arrives. I have a feeling that we might be able to help Mr. Stuart with his travel plans."

6

Heavy rain was predicted for the Maryland and Northern Virginia countryside. As T. J. Kirby fumed from the Oval Office, the sky was beginning to show every indication that it would be a violent storm. Large black clouds rumbled and boiled in the sky. The storm on the horizon was a summer shower compared to the salvo the chief of staff had just experienced from President Donald Adams.

Adams had been on his private phone for the last couple of hours, and Kirby was worried. Something was going on back in his home state of Arkansas; that much was apparent. It wasn't apparent what the problem was and that worried Kirby.

He trudged into his office that adjoined the Oval Office. His office was sparse, furnished only with his desk and chair, two straight-back chairs that discouraged long visits, and a worn couch that Kirby now fell into. The thickset chief of staff rubbed his temples and recalled the conversation he'd walked in on. The president had been angry—no, *insistent* better described his tone of voice—and determined. That was all Kirby could be sure of with any degree of certainty. What had shocked him was the president's glare; it had stopped him in his tracks. The president had placed his hand over the receiver and waited until Kirby had backed out of the room. Kirby knew it was not business as usual.

T. J. Kirby rose and moved behind his desk. He extracted a key from his pocket, opened the left-hand drawer, and removed a normal-looking black table phone. Looks were deceiving when it came to this phone, however. The instrument was directly connected to every long distance service in the nation. Kirby could reach anywhere in a matter of seconds by dialing any combination of one to three digits. The ultramodern, fiber-optic, computer-controlled electronics bundles located in the basement of the White House automatically connected Kirby to anyone from the president of the Soviet Union to the prime minister of England. Kirby always smiled at the thought that he'd reserved the single digit combination for his mother back in the hills of Arkansas.

The computer made the prescribed connection, and Kirby waited. He needed a handle on what was going on, and the one man who could give it to him should be answering his private line within seconds. After all, as chief of staff, it was his job to know everything, not just the things the president wanted to tell him.

CHAPTER FOURTEEN

1

It had been easy getting the unconscious guard into Carlton Graham's car. Graham, on the other hand, had been less than cooperative. His leg had resumed bleeding, and the pain was beginning to make the man difficult. David Michaels was amazed, even with the problem Graham had presented, that they'd been able to sequester both men in the car without incident. With machinery and workers everywhere, no one had paid any attention to the movement of the four men near the administration building. The workers on the nuclear site went about their business. Most of the major construction was taking place far enough away that no one came close as Michaels and Powell transferred Graham and the guard.

Morton Powell reset the child safety switches on the rear doors of the car so that neither of the men in the rear could open the doors from within. The safety switches made the car a secure vehicle for transport.

David tossed the rope and safety harness used by Jimmy into the trunk of the automobile. Powell was behind the wheel, and David slid into the passenger-side seat. He was still holding Powell's Beretta. He didn't like depending on the black pistol for his feeling of well-being, but he recognized the necessity. Still, he'd always depended on a higher authority, and the thought that he needed the weapon seemed like rebellion on his part. He dismissed the reflection. There were some things a man had to do for himself.

"I'm ready," David informed Morton Powell.

"Tell our passengers to be good," said Powell.

"You heard the man," David relayed to Graham. The guard was just beginning to stir in the rear seat. "Wake him up," David ordered Graham, motioning toward the man with the pistol.

Graham reached over and gently slapped the ex-mercenary-turned-guard. The man opened his eyes and focused on the 9 mm Beretta; he instantly calculated his chances of reaching the pistol before the man holding it could fire.

David recognized the look. He allowed a thin smile to crease his face. "Don't even think about it, pal. And just so you'll know, I'm an ex-SEAL and current recon marine. I'll blow your kneecap away before you get halfway over this seat. Believe it."

The brawny guard settled into the backseat. His gaze never left the black automatic.

The FBI agent started the car and pulled out of the office parking lot, heading for the main gate. All around them the construction of a nuclear plant was in full swing. David could not see any reduction in activity in comparison to the daylight hour shifts. The massive equipment rumbled around the fenced area. Men in hard hats moved in and out of buildings. In the midst of all this, the massive twin cooling towers that would provide cooling for the nuclear reactor stood poised like behemoth temples of a long-dead civilization.

David thought about how much the United States had become like the children of Israel—except that now the icons of power as represented by the twin towers were worshiped instead of pagan gods. Powell's voice yanked David from his reverie.

"Get ready. Hold the gun down so the gate guards won't see it," he warned.

David dropped the pistol to the seat and looked at the guard. "This 9 mm will go straight through this beautiful upholstery," he said. "Don't make me ruin Mr. Graham's seats."

The guard sneered. Graham moaned.

Powell slowed the car for the approaching gate. Four guards were visible, two at the entrance and two at the exit. The agent could see pistols holstered at their sides. There was no evidence of the ugly silenced Ingrams the guard in the backseat had been armed with.

A line of cars stood in front of him, each stopping in turn as it pulled even with the gate guards. The guards were inspecting each car. The FBI agent began to think his idea was less than prudent when his turn to pull up came. He'd already made up his mind that he would not stop. His foot was positioned to jam the accelerator to the floor and shoot by the guards. Once outside the security area, he could be out of sight before the guards could run to the security truck parked at the guard house, and more importantly, outside the jurisdiction of the armed guards.

The guard waved at Powell to pull up, and the FBI man slammed on the accelerator. Then, as if someone were watching over them from above, the guard recognized the car and waved it through, casually saluting the car as if it were a military operation.

Morton Powell glanced sideways at David Michaels. Both let out a sigh of relief.

"Did you notice the salute?" David asked.

"Yeah. What about it?"

"Unless I miss my guess, each of these guards is ex-military, probably active mercenaries. Would that be the case, friend?" David addressed the guard in the rear.

The man smiled wickedly. "You'll never know," the man spat.

David smiled. "You just told me, friend. I have to say, though, that this group must be the most incompetent bunch of mercenaries I've ever seen."

The man's grin turned to a scowl. "Try us again sometime," the man challenged.

"Nope. One chance is all you get and you failed that one. I could have killed you back there, but I didn't. Don't give me an excuse to do it now. Just put both hands beneath your legs and make sure they stay there. This Beretta is faster than you'll ever be."

The man didn't move.

"Do it!" David hissed menacingly.

The man recognized the tone of voice of an officer and placed his hands beneath his legs, sitting on his hands.

"How's the leg, Graham?" David asked, no concern in his voice.

"It hurts like hell," the OSHA inspector groaned.

"Wrong. You'll never know what hell feels like until you get there. And, believe me, a bullet in the leg is nothing like hell will be."

"You sound like a preacher boy," the mercenary said.

"Chaplain," David said.

"Chaplain!" the man shouted. "You got lucky back there, preacher." The man started to remove his hands from beneath his legs.

"You got stupid back there, soldier. Don't compound the error. I know eighteen-year-old privates who know more about soldiering than you do, friend. But if you feel like pressing your luck, go right ahead. Just don't count on my chaplain's benevolence," David warned.

The man had visibly relaxed after he heard that David was a

chaplain. But there was something about the man, the mercenary knew, that was different from the other religious people with whom he'd come in contact. He had no doubt that the pistol was leveled at him, unwavering, just out of sight behind the car's seat. The chaplain's eyes were relaxed but alert. They were not the eyes of a murderer, but they were the eyes of a man who would do what must be done. He knew he wouldn't have a ghost of a chance at the black pistol. He closed his eyes. If nothing else, he could sleep.

2

It had already been a long night, and Wayne Young knew it was not over. His internal alarm system was sending signals throughout his body. The signs that something was going down were everywhere within the high-rise corporate offices of Collins Construction International. Harmon Douglas, the company comptroller, had been in and out of Emerson Collins's office all day long and was still in the building hours after normal closing time.

Jameson Collins, the nominal head of CCI, was off on a Caribbean vacation. No warning. No notice. Things like did not happen under normal circumstances.

Most of the staff in the accounting and legal departments had worked later than usual. They were gone now, except for a chosen few. The security head of CCI was waiting for his intercom to inform him that Emerson Collins would see him. As security head, he was entitled to know if any of the company's actions had a bearing on security. He was also waiting on that idiot from North Central Electric Cooperative, Allen Stuart, to show up. The more he thought about it, the more he was certain that Stuart was bailing out on the project.

Wayne Young cursed softly to himself. He was in charge of security for CCI, and as such, he had hired each of the guards at the nuclear site.

The hiring of guards and the deaths of Billy Tippett and Foster Crowe had been the extent of his real involvement. He had followed orders, but that argument had not worked at Nuremberg and, he knew, it would not work here either. He'd killed and sacrificed for his corporate god, but that would not offer any protection should it be discovered.

Young had done the same kind of work in different parts of the world. He always enjoyed solving problems, though he preferred doing it somewhere other than in the United States. The feeling that CCI's downfall would come in the democratic environment of the U.S. had haunted him for a long time.

Now, as his intercom buzzed, the feeling overwhelmed him.

3

Allen Stuart parked his car in the basement parking lot of the CCI building in downtown Little Rock. He could not understand the attraction the relatively small southern city held for a corporate giant like CCI. For that matter, as he reflected on it, he could not understand the attraction the general manager's position at NCEC had held for him. When he placed his hand on the briefcase in the seat beside him, which contained ten thousand dollars and the mutual fund accounts, he remembered why he'd taken the position.

Stuart picked up the case and stepped from the car. If all went well, he would have an additional half million dollars to augment the cache now resting in the funds accounts. He'd already begun to plan the transfer of moneys from the domestic accounts to higher-paying but more speculative international accounts. He would use the foreign accounts as a short-term holding device until he got out of the country, so the risk was negligible. Once he reached his destination, he would make a few timely withdrawals and some funds transfers, and he would live happily ever after. He'd even instituted a strategy of sorts concerning the overseas holdings of CCI. He had dumped most of the money into a mutual income fund that paid almost 30 percent. The fund manager operated out of Geneva, Switzerland, with reciprocal agreements managed through local investment houses. Stuart intended to take advantage of the 30 percent current yield on the half million he already had and transfer the money from the mutual fund and into a numbered account in Switzerland. One could still find a Swiss account executive who disdained the openness fostered by the international banking community, specifically the United States, prompted by the necessity of tracking laundered drug money. The money would be safe. The best part was that the fund was composed of nothing but CCI stock. *It will be the final justice,* Stuart thought, as he pushed the elevator button that would carry him to the office of security and its overbearing head, Wayne Young.

4

The president of the United States felt as if the telephone was growing out his ear. He had been on it constantly since the early part of the evening, and he was exhausted. Besides the calls he had received from Arkansas, he had to deal with a flare-up in Bosnia that was threatening to spill over into the southern parts of Hungary and Romania. The Muslim religious factions in the area had declared a jihad, a holy war, and attacked a northern village on the Hungarian-Romanian border. The more he learned of the world, the more he was convinced that the only hope for the world at war was Jesus Christ. It was not a popular stance in a modern society whose focus had turned inward, but it was his view. And, he was convinced beyond a shadow of doubt, that what he believed was the truth.

The president shook his head. It was tragic that most of the fighting going on in the world was between so-called religious factions. It was no wonder that people looked on religion in such a circumspect manner. Don Adams bowed his head and prayed. It was his practice— one that few people knew about and one that he did not demonstrate in public. Prayer, for him, was a release and a balm as much as a personal conference with his Lord. Prayer was the one time he knew someone was listening and the place he went for answers.

The gentle knock on the door ended the prayer. "Come in," the president sighed.

T. J. Kirby strode into the Oval Office.

"Why aren't you home in bed?" the president asked his chief of staff.

Kirby hesitated a moment then said, "I need to go to Arkansas, sir."

The president tensed. "What for, T. J.?"

"Personal business, sir."

"Too personal to tell me?"

Kirby shifted his weight from foot to foot. "With all due respect, sir. Yes, sir."

"You know you can leave whenever you need to, T. J. I want you to think about it, though," he added. "I'm on the verge of an important project here and I need you. I can't tell you exactly what is happening at this point, but it's important. I can use your administrative skills on it."

Something important, thought Kirby. "I appreciate the position this puts you in, sir, but it will only be for a day or two," he told the president.

"The world could be at war in a day or two, Kirby. You know that. We no longer have the luxury of self-imposed isolationism. The Balkans could flare at any moment. But if it's that important, by all means, do it," the president responded.

"Thank you, sir," Kirby said. "I'll be back as soon as possible," he added as he turned to leave, thankful that he'd escaped a sermon from Don Adams. The man was a good man and a good president, but he still believed that religion should play a role in modern politics. Kirby had a hard time dealing with that aspect of the president. Even when he reminded Adams of the trouble Jimmy Carter embroiled himself in just because he was a Christian, Don Adams refused to listen.

"You're going tonight?" the president asked incredulously.

"The sooner I leave, the sooner I get back, sir," Kirby assured the president.

"All right, T. J. Have a safe trip. I'll pray for you."

"Thank you, sir," Kirby answered and was out the door of the Oval Office. *Pray for me,* he thought. *The man is going bonkers.* Prayer was not what he needed right now. What he needed right now was a crystal ball. He had contingencies to plan for.

T. J. Kirby went to his desk and pulled a thick file from his locked drawer. He would study the contents on the way to Arkansas. It was deadly information—information that could topple the most influential and powerful man in the world, the president of the United States.

T. J. Kirby hoped it would not come to that. The president was his mentor, his boss, and, above all else, his friend. But even friendship had its boundaries. If sacrifices were called for, he would not make them, Kirby promised himself.

Kirby was booked on the three o'clock flight out of National Airport. He had one stop in Memphis, then one hour to Little Rock. He checked his watch. With one hour difference between time zones, he would land at Adams Field in Little Rock before sunrise. A rental car would be waiting for him at the Hertz counter. Better to travel inconspicuously, he reasoned, especially considering the errand he was on.

Outside, Kirby's chauffeured Cadillac waited. He climbed in the black automobile and gave the driver the go sign and then picked up the telephone attached to the rear of the front seat. He needed to talk.

5

Sheriff Tom Frazier parked his patrol car behind the car he'd followed from the main gate of the nuclear generating station. He'd recognized David Michaels riding on the passenger side of the vehicle. He had guessed correctly. Michaels had indeed overcome the obstacle of the armed guard and escaped from the construction compound. He had missed identifying the driver's face, but assumed it to be the FBI agent named Morton Powell. Michaels had been positioned with only his profile visible, as if looking at something or someone in the rear seat.

Frazier had turned around and followed the car, surprised that it led him directly to the Clayton County Courthouse and his own office. He parked the police cruiser behind Powell, his eyes never leaving the vehicle in front of him. When the passenger-side door opened and David Michaels stepped out, Tom Frazier felt a release, a relief. The relief lasted only until he identified the Beretta model 92 Michaels was holding on two men now getting out of the rear of the automobile. Frazier recognized Carlton Graham. He and the OSHA inspector had had jurisdictional run-ins over Nuclear Three and Four. Frazier didn't care for the man. He found him to be too book-and-regulation oriented.

Frazier drew his Glock 17 and held it at his side, his finger over the trigger guard. The pistol's safety was incorporated into the trigger mechanism, and Frazier held the ready position as he joined David Michaels. "What have we got, David?" Frazier asked curiously.

"I'll have to let Powell give you the legal terms, Tom. Tom," David began, "meet . . ."

"Morton Powell, special agent working under the OCTF headed by Warren Rodale," the Clayton County sheriff finished.

Powell moved around the car and took the sheriff's hand. They shook. "I'm impressed, Sheriff. Glad to meet you. Particularly under the circumstances," he added.

Frazier indicated Graham and the guard with a wave of his free hand. He continued to hold the Glock at his side. "Graham I know. Who's the other one?"

"One of the guards out at the generating station," Powell supplied. "We'd like for you to hold these two for a bit."

"What's a bit?"

"Forty-eight hours should do it. By then I'll have what I need, and we can put them away for good."

"What charge?"

"Let's start with conspiracy to commit murder for Graham and possession of an illegal firearm for Smiley," Powell suggested. "Is that enough to keep them incommunicado for a couple of days?"

"More than enough. And I have just the deputy to take care of the problem too," he smiled.

David looked at the sheriff. "You mean Janice?"

"I do indeed mean Janice. She's the best certified deputy I've got. Best shot, and karate expert to boot. She wants to be the next sheriff, you know."

"I heard," David acknowledged.

"She'll make it too. Shoot, I'm even going to vote for her."

"You're retiring?" David asked Tom Frazier.

"Just as soon as I can. I've got one thing to follow up on and I'm gone. Janice will be a better sheriff anyway."

"Don't do anything for the next forty eight hours," said David.

"If we can leave these two with you, we have something to follow up too," Morton Powell interjected.

"Looks like Mr. Graham needs a little first aid."

"I need a doctor," Graham wheezed.

"Smiley over there," Powell said pointing to the guard, "shot him. Bullet nicked the femoral artery almost certainly. He'll need a hospital."

"I'll call an ambulance," Frazier said. "With that leg, he won't be going anywhere for a week, and Janice will see to it that our boy over there won't be leaving us. Anything else I can do for you gentlemen?"

"Not at the moment, thanks," Powell answered.

"Don't suppose you want to tell me what you're up to?"

David moved around the car. "We'd rather not, Tom, if that's all right with you. The less you know, the better it will be if this thing explodes in our faces. I hope you understand," David apologized.

"Hey. No problem. One thing, David. I was by your dad's house earlier. His lights were on. You might consider at least telling him where you're going."

David was touched at Frazier's concern for his father. "Thanks, Tom. I'll do that," he said, getting into the car.

Powell started the engine, and the car was moving before David Michaels could shut the door.

Frazier herded Graham and the guard into the courthouse. He turned the guard over to Janice Morgan and placed a call for an ambulance. "Janice," Frazier told the deputy, "I'll be in Little Rock. Call me on the cellular if there's a problem."

CHAPTER
FIFTEEN

1

The lights in James Michaels's house glowed softly through curtained windows as Tom Frazier had told David. David pulled Graham's car into the driveway as the impressions of the last few hours whirled and tumbled in his mind. It was hard for David to believe his actions. The thoughts that kept coming to him at odd times, like flashes of old movies, were even stranger. These thoughts came to him as he'd held Powell's Beretta while watching Carlton Graham spill out his life's blood back at the nuclear construction site. The random, almost bizzare thoughts included Cindy Tolbert and the First Community Church, along with a kaleidoscope of intermingled visions. Had the thoughts been a form of escape or a form of denial generated by the conflict of his beliefs and actions? Had he needed something to distract his thoughts and allow him to act in a way contrary to what he believed or professed to believe?

David shrugged off the intruding thoughts and returned to the problem at hand.

Cindy Tolbert and the church were issues he was not going to reconcile in the next twenty-four hours. He had more pressing, immediate problems to deal with. David was becoming aware of his almost maniacal need to find his brother's murderer. For a split second, while Powell had been questioning Graham, David had to stem his urge to tell Powell to release the pressure on the man's artery and to let him die. It would not have been the justice he was seeking, but it would have been sweet revenge. The feeling had come and gone quickly, overridden, David knew, by his own core values and his respect for human life. But the feeling had emerged, nonetheless, and that was frightening.

The FBI agent's car was still parked next to the house. When David saw it, he remembered his father's truck, which was still parked in the forest outside the nuclear site. It would have to stay there for the time being.

"We don't have much time," Morton Powell interjected into David's musing.

David glanced at the clock in Graham's car, grateful for the interruption. It would be dark for the better part of five more hours. Time, he calculated, to drive the two hours to Little Rock and scout the CCI building, particularly the ventilation system that exited onto the roof of the building. Graham, on the way into Clayton, had volunteered additional information about the building. Both David and Powell had been alarmed when Graham told them that the building had a sophisticated alarm system consisting of motion, infrared, and noise detectors, which were controlled by a central panel in the basement. They were relieved to learn that the ventilation system did not contain the sensors. However, Powell pointed out that since the system was vulnerable at that point, it would be heavily guarded should any suspicion of incursion arise. They hoped the security force at the Collins Building was not forewarned.

"Let's change clothes," David suggested, getting out of the car. Their dry clothes were still in the pickup back in the forest.

Before he and Morton Powell made it to the steps of the house, the door opened and James Michaels stepped out. His eyes were red, and his hair was disheveled. He looked tired and worn. He held a cup of coffee in his hand, and David could see the cup shaking as his father waited on them.

"You been up all night, Dad?" David asked.

"Yep. Waiting for you boys to come home."

"You should've been asleep," David remarked, putting his arm around his father and walking into the house, wondering at the same time how many other nights this man had waited up just to be sure his sons were safe.

"I've already lost one son. I don't want to lose another. The least I can do is stay up and pray. I don't know what you're doing, David, but don't expect me to just sit on the sidelines."

"We need more than prayer, Mr. Michaels," Morton Powell remarked as he followed son and father into the welcome warmth of the house.

James Michaels turned to Powell. "I'm sure you think you need more than prayer. But, I'll tell you, son, the rest is minor compared to the prayer."

Morton Powell smiled condescendingly. "You're just like your son. Jimmy was always telling me the same thing. But this is the real world, Mr. Michaels. Not some fantasy that prayer can do anything about."

James Michaels shook his head. "I'm sorry to hear you say that. You're wrong, you know. I just hope you don't get my son killed finding out how wrong you really are."

"I'll take care of David," Powell told the old man. "Besides, in case you don't know it, your son is quite capable of taking care of himself."

"I'll keep praying," James Michaels responded.

"Enough," David interjected. "Dad, we need to change clothes and get on the road. You still have some of that coffee left?" David asked.

"Brand new pot. I'll get it for you," David's father offered, as he moved toward the kitchen. "You two change and come into the kitchen."

David and Morton Powell withdrew to different bedrooms. In David's old room, a complete change of clothes was laid out on the bed: a pair of dark slacks, a navy blue sweater, dark socks, and, to top it off, one of David's old navy watch caps. David shook his head in amazement. His father might not know the details of their plans, but he understood the reality of what they were trying to do.

David smiled at the watch cap. When he'd first joined the navy, he'd called the watch cap a toboggan and had been quickly reprimanded by the officer in charge of clothing issue.

David also realized that his father knew the seriousness of their undertaking. Dark clothing and prayer. James Michaels had always prayed. And always backed up that prayer with action. Tonight was just another example of his father's pragmatic faith.

David slipped into the dark clothes and headed for the kitchen. Morton Powell sat at the table drinking a cup of coffee. The smell of eggs and bacon frying permeated the bright room. David went to the coffeepot and poured himself a cup of the steaming dark liquid. He joined Powell at the table.

"I told your dad we didn't have time to eat," Powell began. "But he insisted."

"We'll take time," David agreed. "I don't know what we'll run up against tonight, but I can promise you that we'll be happy we took the time. Dad's a fantastic cook."

Powell smiled, unconvinced. "Fifteen minutes. No more," he insisted.

"Fifteen minutes," David agreed.

James Michaels brought the food to the table along with three plates. He scooped large portions of scrambled eggs laced with onion and green peppers onto each plate and placed them in front of the two men.

"I'll bless this," Mr. Michaels said, sitting down. "Lord, thank you for this food and protect my son and Mr. Powell. Amen."

"That was a short prayer," Powell observed.

"Don't need to be long," James Michaels said. "Just truthful."

The men ate in silence, finishing the eggs, bacon, and buttered toast in under ten minutes.

Morton Powell rose. "That was good, Mr. Michaels. Thanks. And I hope you don't take offense at my views on prayer."

"Not at all. This is a free country. Everyone has the right to be wrong," he grinned.

Powell smiled. He liked the old man, despite his misplaced faith. Upon walking into the living room he retrieved the Beretta he'd laid on the couch. He ejected the magazine from the handle and checked to see that it was fully loaded, then ejected the round from the chamber and forced it into the magazine. He strapped the shoulder holster on and covered it with his coat, all the while thinking about telling James Michaels that if he wanted to pray for something, to pray for more fire-power. But he stopped himself. Knowing the old man, he would say they already had all the firepower they needed. Powell thought that maybe the old man really had something. He'd like to talk to him after the night was over. Provided, of course, that he lived through the night.

2

Allen Stuart was having second thoughts. The express elevator ride to the twentieth floor of the Collins Building had been surprisingly uncomfortable. Had he had the option, he would have reversed the elevator, gotten in his car, and driven away. But the cursed thing stopped only at the twentieth floor, and he was stuck, at least until the doors opened and he could push the down button that would return him to the basement parking lot.

As the elevator doors slid open, Stuart had already decided to leave the building with his half million-plus. A meeting with Wayne Young would only be counterproductive. He could live well on what he had, knowing that the living was cheap and easy in Costa Rica and South America, the two places he was considering. He would decide where to go after he had retrieved the money from the Swiss account.

As the door came fully open, Allen Stuart was shocked to see the bulk of Wayne Young framed in the opening.

"Good to see you, Allen," Young began. "Mr. Collins wants me to take care of you myself. Let's go to my office."

Stuart had no choice but to follow Young. He exited the elevator and felt the big man's arm go around his shoulders. Stuart did not like the way Young had said, ". . . take care of you," but he decided his imagination was overactive.

The two men strolled down the carpeted corridor, the security man's arm draped over Allen Stuart's shoulders, a reminder that escape was impossible.

Stuart had been in Young's office only twice before, but he remembered it as it was. The massive polished oak desk was positioned almost in the center of the room. The security chief's chair sat slightly askew behind the desk, overstuffed like the man himself, Stuart realized. Two wingback leather chairs faced the desk. A matching couch sat against the far wall beneath watercolor landscapes that Allen Stuart recognized as originals by a local artist. The floor was polished oak, matching the desk, and accented by Oriental rugs. The overwhelming features of the room were the floor-to-ceiling windows behind the desk. The heavy draperies were open, revealing the city of Little Rock. It was a nice office. Not top executive quality, but nice. Much nicer, Stuart thought, than what he'd had in Clayton.

"Sit down, Allen," Wayne Young said, offering Stuart the chair in front of the large desk. "What can I do for you? You sounded a little disjointed on the phone earlier."

Allen Stuart took a deep breath. It had been a mistake to come, and the solicitous attitude the security head now adopted confirmed the error. Young would not be asking what he wanted if he hadn't already figured it out.

Stuart cleared his throat. "It's about the project," he stammered.

"The project?" Young responded, feigning ignorance.

"The power plant," Stuart said, exasperated.

"And what about the power plant, Allen?"

Stuart swallowed. Young seemed detached, aloof. "It's coming apart, is what, Young," Allen Stuart managed to say.

"You mean the buildings and towers are falling down?"

"I mean," Stuart began, his voice rising, "that the cover-up is coming apart. People know what is going on up there, and it's coming down around our ears."

Wayne Young leaned forward in his chair. "What people?"

"David Michaels, for one," Stuart answered.

"What does he know?"

"He knows his brother's death was no accident."

Young's eyes narrowed into slits. "How does he know that?"

"The man's not stupid. He went to see Carlton Graham. Why else would he go there if he didn't already know something?"

"Maybe because Graham is the OSHA inspector on the site and he just wanted to clarify some points. Could that be it?"

Stuart thought for a moment. *That could be it, but I doubt it. No, things are coming apart, and apparently I am the only one who recognizes the symptoms.*

"I tell you, he knows something. He's been in the county clerk's office several times. One of the clerks told me he was examining the records, deeds, and abstracts for the land where the generating plant sits. He's even looked at the aerial photos of the complex. He suspects something, I'm telling you."

"Suspects? You just said he knows something. There's a lot of difference between knowing and suspecting. Of course, depending on what you've done in coming here, Michaels could see it as further evidence that something does exist. It was a mistake for you to make this trip, Mr. Stuart. Mr. Collins has put me in charge of rectifying the situation."

"What situation?" The NCEC manager asked nervously.

"Why, *this* situation, Mr. Stuart. The one you seem to be intent on drawing all of Collins Construction in on. The situation that involves your embezzling some a half million dollars from the construction funds of North Central Electric Cooperative. That situation, Mr. Stuart."

Allen Stuart felt his blood run cold. His worst fears were confirmed. How had Young found out about the money? What else did he know? If things were truly coming apart at the seams, a scapegoat would be needed. It would be a simple matter to place the blame for all that had happened on the NCEC manager, especially if he was nowhere to be found. Wayne Young had orders to kill him, he had no doubt. And he was trapped on the twentieth floor with no means of escape, no options, and limited time.

"Let's discuss our options," Young said, as if reading Stuart's mind.

"You have a half million dollars squirreled away in mutual funds here in the States. Your plan, as I see it, was to come here to add to that stash. Am I right?"

Stuart remained silent.

Young smiled at the silence. "Let's assume I'm right, shall we? You come here and tell us it's time to get out—time to leave a multimillion dollar construction project, shag it to some South American country, and live like a king for the rest of your life. How am I doing so far?"

Stuart fidgeted in the chair.

"You seem to think we would consider abandoning not only the generating plant in Clayton, but the rest of the projects around the world. This is not a fly-by-night outfit, Mr. Stuart. We have multibillion dollar undertakings in every part of the world. No, Mr. Stuart, we'll not abandon the plant in Clayton, anymore than we'll abandon the ones in India, or Russia, or any other part of Eastern and Western Europe. It will be much easier for CCI to eliminate a half-million-dollar problem than a multibillion-dollar one."

There it was, confirmation. He was to die.

Stuart sprang from the chair and swung the briefcase he carried. Wayne Young was taken by surprise. He'd never considered that Stuart would be desperate enough to attack him in his own office!

Young was moving as the briefcase arched through the air, but he moved too slowly, his bulk a hindrance in his attempt to avoid the blow. The corner of the briefcase caught Young a glancing blow on the left temple, and the security man went down hard, sprawled behind his desk. Allen Stuart was out the office door and running before Young could recover.

Young struggled to his feet, his temple throbbing. His hand went to his head and came away with blood! *I'll see Allen Stuart rot in hell for this!* he promised himself.

He pulled himself up, using the desk for support, and picked up the telephone. There was only one place Stuart could go and that was back to the parking basement. Young doubted that Allen Stuart had enough wits about him to contrive an elaborate escape plan in the time he had. The man was running scared. Reacting. Young dialed and waited. There was one guard on duty in the basement, but, like every other guard in the employ of CCI, he was armed with a 9 mm automatic.

The guard answered on the third ring.

3

Wayne Young had been right. The NCEC general manager hadn't thought out his escape scenario. He'd run directly to the express elevator that had brought him to the executive floor and pushed the button for the basement. Almost immediately he realized he was committed to riding the elevator to the basement and chastised himself for his predictability. One phone call, he realized, and guards would be waiting for him as he exited the elevator.

Allen Stuart had a plan that just might get him by the guards who were bound to be waiting.

4

The parking lot guard picked up the phone. He figured one of the few men left in the building was calling to have his car ready at the exit gate. When he heard the harried voice of his boss, Wayne Young, he snapped to attention, not realizing the man could not see him over the phone lines.

"There's a man on his way down the express elevator," Young explained rapidly. "I want him stopped! Understand?"

"Yes, sir," the guard responded. Whoever it was, he knew he'd raised the wrath of Wayne Young, and that was never good. "How important is this?" the guard continued.

Wayne Young knew exactly what the guard was asking when he answered with, "Use maximum force, if necessary. I don't want him to leave this building."

The guard hesitated a minute before acknowledging the order. "Maximum force. Yes, sir, I understand," as he replaced the receiver. He had orders to kill the man in the elevator if it came to that. So he pulled his automatic from his holster and worked the slide, inserting a 9 mm bullet into the firing chamber, and then moved to the doors of the express elevator. He wondered if he could execute the orders he had just been given.

5

Wayne Young stood before the bank of elevator doors on his floor. These doors provided access to the conventional elevators serving every floor of the CCI building. With no one in the building, save the few in accounting and Emerson Collins, the elevator would provide a direct route to the basement in much the same manner as the express elevator. The only difference was that the express elevator operated at a much higher speed than the others. Allen Stuart would be in the basement before Young's elevator covered the first ten floors. The delay caused by Young's phone call to the basement guard added to the head start Stuart had, but barring any unforeseen act, the guard would have the NCEC general manager in custody before Young set foot out of the elevator.

Young punched the parking level button and waited impatiently as the doors slowly slid shut.

6

President Don Adams had tried to sleep after his conversation with his chief of staff, T. J. Kirby. It had proved impossible. He'd returned to the Oval Office and collapsed on one of the two striped couches facing each other in front of his desk.

As he lay on the couch he pondered the events of the last few hours. Phone calls had been routed to and from Arkansas. The president held the evidence in his hand: a computer printout of all the calls made over the last twenty-four hours. Some were his, and he had already highlighted those in yellow. Others, however, he had not made—calls to and from very specific numbers.

He'd suspected, of course, but the proof he now clutched in his hands still brought an ache in his heart. There was little doubt that T. J. Kirby was implicated in the foul situation.

T. J. was a friend and companion. An adviser. All that was by the board now. T. J. Kirby would have to be neutralized.

The president of the United States, Donald Farmington Adams, lifted the receiver of his private line and dialed. His people in Arkansas needed to know that Kirby was on his way.

7

The Boeing 737 aircraft lifted off the runway, leaving the lights of Washington, D.C. in its wake. As the pilot retracted the landing gear, adjusted the takeoff flaps, and trimmed the large twin-engine aircraft for its departure climb out of Washington's terminal control area, T. J. Kirby opened the manila folder he'd taken from his office. He quickly flipped through the loose-leaf pages, stopping to examine the bold-print headings. The report was a result of an ongoing and painstaking investigation. The chief of staff did not like the connotations nor the conclusions drawn by the information.

The 737 began a gradual turn that would set its course for Memphis International Airport.

T. J. Kirby closed the folder. He had to weigh the options. One thing was certain. He'd protect himself regardless of the affection he felt for the man in the Oval Office.

8

"Stop by the church on your way out," James Michaels told his son and Morton Powell. "Some folks you'll want to see are there." The elder Michaels had a strange expression on his face as he spoke.

"Okay," David assured his father, wondering who his father was talking about. His first thoughts were of Pastor Shackleford, but his mind quickly leapt to the green-eyed Cindy Tolbert. A gentle stirring in the pit of his stomach reminded him of his feelings for the Clayton County clerk. He'd never had such an experience. The times he had gone into battle as a military chaplain had always been times of tremendous focus, concentrated toward a final objective. Lately his thought processes were divided between his brother's murder and Cindy. It was a strange situation, one David was not entirely comfortable with.

"No time," Morton Powell said.

"There's always time for the church," David's father said.

"Come on, Michaels," Powell said to David as he slid behind the wheel of his government car. "We're pushing the time frame as it is."

"The church is just down on the right, on the way out," David said, ignoring Powell's protest and praying silently that the reason for the sidetrack was Cindy Tolbert.

Powell pulled the car into the semicircular drive in front of the white church. "Five minutes, no more," Powell fumed.

"Five minutes," David acknowledged. "Thanks, Mort."

Powell fumed all the more for David Michaels's decency and then smiled. He found it impossible to stay angry with the navy commander. Besides, Michaels was still a recon marine, and that spoke volumes. Morton Powell harbored no illusions about completing the night's work without the marine/chaplain. It was a two-man job, and David Michaels was the second man. The agent lay back against the car's headrest and closed his eyes. Five minutes' sleep was better than none.

David tried the front door of the church and found it unlocked. As he moved into the sanctuary and then the chapel, he could see three figures kneeling at the altar. He approached to within ten feet before he identified Cindy Tolbert, Jean Michaels, and Reverend Glen Shackleford, the pastor of the church.

David had entered so quietly that the three had not heard, and when he cleared his throat, they all jumped in unison.

"You could kill an old man like that," Reverend Shackleford accused David before breaking into a wide grin. The pastor came to David and offered him his hand.

"Not you," David retorted, shaking the old man's hand. "I know how far you run each morning and the kind of exercise equipment you have stashed in your spare bedroom.'

The preacher smiled at David's recollections. "I still run three miles in the morning. It's just slower than it used to be."

"That's the case for most of us."

"What are you doing here?" Jean Michaels piped up.

"Dad told me to stop by here on my way out of town," David answered his sister-in-law. "He didn't tell me a prayer meeting was going on."

"Then it's not over," Cindy Tolbert interjected, meeting David's gaze with her clear green eyes. There was no accusatory tone in her voice, only concern.

"What's not over?" asked Reverend Shackleford.

"You don't want to know," David said, speaking to the preacher but holding Cindy's stare with his own; it was a comfortable feeling, one he hoped would be repeated at a later date. "None of you want to know. But to answer you, no, it's not over. It's just beginning."

"Then we'll stay right here and pray until it's finished," Cindy remarked, a feeling of calm coming over her as she spoke. She'd not looked away from David, holding his steady gaze with her own. There was a warmth, a deepness in his eyes, and she reveled in it. She was aware of her pulse beginning to accelerate slightly and once again felt like the young schoolgirl back in the Michaels home so many years ago. She was also discovering that she liked the feeling. Jean Michaels had been correct, she now knew. Without a doubt, she was in love with David Michaels, and she wondered if it showed.

"It could be a long time," David advised, pulling his gaze from Cindy, addressing the old pastor.

"No matter," Shackleford said. "One of us will be here every hour of the day. If I have to get others involved, I will. The community has lots of older Christians who are just waiting for this kind of opportunity."

David felt his stomach knot. "Thank you. All of you," he said.

"We'll keep praying. You be careful," Reverend Shackleford assured David. "Let's have prayer before you leave."

The four approached the altar and Reverend Shackleford led the prayer. It was short and direct. David had always admired the preacher's directness, as if the request, upon being made, was sealed in success. It was the same way his father prayed.

They rose from the altar, and David hugged Cindy and Jean, enjoying the tingling sensation when Cindy's arms tightened around his neck. It was more than a friendly exchange. He shook hands with Reverend Shackleford one last time and left the comfort of the small chapel.

"He's going to need lots of prayer," Reverend Shackleford said. "I'd better make a few calls."

Jean watched the old man leave. Cindy Tolbert watched David until he disappeared through the door, knowing without a doubt how she felt about the navy commander; certain now that he felt something for her as well. Both women turned back to the altar and continued to pray.

9

The elevator door slid open. Allen Stuart felt his heart pounding in his chest. His pulse was racing; sweat gleamed on his forehead. As the door stopped, Stuart saw the muzzle of the automatic the guard was holding; the hole in the barrel looked like the dead eye of a shark. The guard stood ten feet from the elevator door in a crouched position, the pistol gripped in a two-handed shooting stance. Wayne Young's orders had preceded him.

Stuart slowly brought his right hand up. In it he clutched the ten thousand dollars he'd taken from the North Central safe. He tossed the money at the guard. It scattered like leaves in a March wind.

The guard hesitated for a moment, not sure what to do. His pistol wavered.

"That's ten thousand dollars," Stuart informed the armed guard. "It's all yours."

The guard hesitated for only a moment before holstering his pistol and scrambling for the free-floating cash.

Allen Stuart broke into a sprint as the guard fumbled for the money. His car key was already out, and he had the car started toward the exit in short order. He bounded onto the street from the parking basement, just as Wayne Young burst from a side door of the CCI building. Stuart heard screaming curses and shrieking as he accelerated away from the demonic countenance of Wayne Young.

It was minutes before he realized the shrieking was coming from his own mouth.

10

Tom Frazier had traded his marked patrol car for the only unmarked car in the Clayton County Sheriff Department's inventory. He had parked a half block from James Michaels's house and had stayed put as Morton Powell and David Michaels had driven a few hundred yards and stopped at the white clapboard First Community Church. He'd waited until David returned and Powell had pulled back onto the street and guided the car through the residential section of Clayton.

Frazier had followed at a distance, his lights off. He could have driven the streets of Clayton with his eyes closed, he was so familiar with them. He followed Michaels and Powell as they made their way out of Clayton and onto the highway leading south toward Little Rock.

The storm that had struck the county earlier now renewed its strength, sending wide blazes of lightning across the sky followed by booming claps of thunder. Frazier could see Powell's car heading south, lighted intermittently by the lightning flashes.

His orders had been explicit: he was to follow Michaels and Powell until he discovered their purpose. After that, depending on the what he learned, he was free to intervene or withdraw totally. The decision was his. His hand instinctively rested on the Glock automatic in his holster. He reached for the bulge in the seat carrier attached to the front of the seat. The mass that represented his Sig-Sauer 9 mm automatic rifle reassured him for the moment.

He hoped he would not have to use the deadly rifle tonight.

CHAPTER SIXTEEN

1

The lights of Little Rock glowed softly against a starless, rainy sky as David Michaels and Morton Powell crossed the Interstate-430 bridge spanning the Arkansas River. An overturned poultry truck just north of Damascus, Arkansas, on Highway 65 North had cost them thirty minutes. The irony of the Damascus-road experience was not lost on David. It had not amused Morton Powell.

As they entered the city limits of Little Rock, both men were aware that valuable time had been lost. Their one consolation had been reported on the radio: The weather would hold for the next twenty-four hours; continuous rain would be their ally. It also meant darkness for at least an additional hour.

Morton Powell took the Cantrell Road exit and headed east. The Collins Building was just two blocks south of the Arkansas River in the downtown area. Cantrell Road more or less paralleled the Arkansas River, converging with the riverfront as it neared downtown.

David and Powell had discussed various options as they drove. The plan, as it stood, was to check into the Excelsior Hotel that overlooked the river to the north and the Collins Building to the south. The height of the new hotel would provide the perfect vantage point from which to examine the roof and the ventilation system of the shorter Collins Building.

David Michaels glanced over at Morton Powell as the FBI agent drove. "You look worried."

"I am," Powell admitted grimly.

"About breaking and entering the Collins Building?"

"Not that," the agent chuckled. "We've already gone way past any legal rules of evidence that exist. I'm worried about the possibility of getting in the way Graham explained it. I can't see it, not yet anyway."

"The ventilation system? How do you mean?" David asked.

"Look, neither of us is an acrobat. We're talking about a twenty-story building here. Has it occurred to you that we can't even get to that rooftop ventilation system, much less down it?"

"I assumed there would be a fire escape system on the side. It's an old building. It should have metal ladders all the way up the side of it. I doubt Collins would have removed them."

"You think wrong. Remember, I work out of this city. I've been working on this Collins thing for a while too. That building is just like Graham said it was—secure, including the removal of the fire escape stairs on the outside," Powell assured David. "We're looking at a modern fortress here."

David didn't respond.

"I could get a helicopter, but that would be like announcing our arrival over a loudspeaker."

"Maybe something will come to us after we see the roof from the hotel."

"I hope so," the FBI agent remarked, as both men fell silent.

The Excelsior Hotel was the epitome of the modern luxury hotel. The multistoried building of glass and concrete jutted above the south shore of the Arkansas River, overlooking the recently constructed Riverview Park. The park nestled on the south shore of the river between the Broadway Street Bridge and the I-30 South Bridge. Across Cantrell Road, just west of the grand hotel, stood the five-story Capital Hotel. The painstakingly renovated Capital, converted from the Denckl Building in 1876, was the favorite of the nostalgia group, particularly baby boomers. Directly west of the Excelsior on the same side of Cantrell, connected by means of an elaborate tunnel system, stood the State House Convention Center. One block west of the Excelsior, the white-columned facade of the Old State House, Arkansas' first legislative building, stood as a reminder of the grand past of the southern state.

As Morton Powell drove east on Cantrell, memories flooded David as they passed each of the landmark buildings. Powell pulled up to the front entrance of the Excelsior. The liveried doorman rushed to open the door for Powell as David exited from the passenger side.

"I could get used to this," Powell remarked as he and David entered the hotel.

"I hope the government's paying for this foray," David said lightly, aware of the disquiet beginning in the pit of his stomach.

"So do I," Morton Powell joked, then turned to the clerk behind the counter. "One room, top floor on the south side," Powell requested.

"I'm sorry, sir, but the only available room on that floor looking south is one of the presidential suites."

"That's fine," the FBI agent assured the clerk.

"Uh . . . the price is . . . uh . . . $700 a night," the clerk stammered.

"We'll take it," Powell said.

The clerk looked from Powell to David Michaels and back to Powell again, more than a little skeptical that the two men who looked like poor replicas of second-story men could pay for the room.

"How will you pay for this, sir?"

"Credit card," Powell said, tossing the card on the counter.

The clerk took the card, passed it through the instrument that read the magnetic strip on the back, and handed the card back to Powell.

Powell was pleased at the clerk's change of expression when the verification came back almost immediately, indicating, in addition to the requested amount, that the card had an unlimited credit limit.

The clerk handed the registration card to Powell for his signature along with the key to the room.

"Luggage, sir?" the clerk asked.

"None," Powell answered as he and David headed for the bank of elevators to their left.

The room was indeed presidential.

"I've never seen anything like this," David Michaels remarked. "This is not normal navy lodging."

"You're employed by the wrong branch of government," Powell quipped.

"Obviously," David agreed as he took in the rich appointments of the five-room suite. There were two bedrooms, each with its own bath (the larger of the two sported a two-person spa), a central room, a dining area, and a kitchen. Subdued brocade wallpaper added a pleasant ambiance along with dark wood tables and overstuffed furniture. Expensive oil originals adorned the walls. A crystal chandelier dominated the central room along with a bank of floor-to-ceiling windows that faced south. The windows were covered by remote-controlled curtains.

"Look at this," Morton Powell motioned to David.

David Michaels went to the window where Powell had been standing since they had entered the suite.

"See it?" Powell asked.

"The taller of the three buildings across the way?" asked David.

"That's it. What else do you see?"

David scanned the building, looking for anything out of the ordinary. He saw nothing. "Such as?"

"Watch closely."

"Nothing," David said after a minute. The darkness did nothing to aid in his examination of the building.

"Turn out the light," Powell suggested.

David went to the switch, then moved back to the window. The rain had created reflective puddles on the roof of the distant building. As his eyes adjusted to the dim light given off by the street lamps, David picked up a bright flash near the equipment housing on the roof of the Collins Building.

"How did you pick that up and I didn't?" David asked.

"You're used to night vision in the jungle. This is my jungle. I know what to look for," Powell replied.

"A guard?"

Powell hesitated, then responded, "Probably. The light must be glinting off his belt buckle or maybe even a Sam Browne rig. Whatever it is, it confirms that they're waiting for us."

"Maybe he's just smoking a cigarette," David Michaels offered.

"In this rain? Not likely."

"Guess not. What do we do now?" David asked.

Powell walked away from the window, turning on the lights as he went. "We aren't going to get in that building by way of the ventilation system. At least not by way of the roof ventilation system," the FBI agent mused.

"Sounds like you've got another idea."

"Maybe I do," Powell observed. "Try this. We know the ventilation system is the one part of the building vulnerable to outside entry. Graham confirmed that. If that's the case, isn't it vulnerable to inside entry also?"

David looked puzzled. "I don't follow you."

"Simply this. If the ventilation system offers the only area that's not guarded by electronic systems, it makes no difference whether we enter it from the top, the bottom, or somewhere in the middle. All we have to do is get into the building during regular business hours while the security system is inactivated, find a way into the ventilation system while in the building, and wait until everyone is gone."

"How do we get into the building in the first place. Just walk in?"

"Exactly," Powell asserted. "We wait until the building opens for business, choose a time when the guards are overworked, and enter the building. We can call the switchboard later and find out when the building closes for the day. The guards are busy letting people out during that time. They're not too concerned about night workers entering—cleanup crews, repairmen, and such. If we go in tonight, that gives us all day to collect the equipment we will need once we're in. What do you think?"

"Sounds too easy."

"Easy is more fun than hard," Powell joked. "Easy is also usually overlooked *because* it's so obvious."

"Then if we're going in tomorrow night, or rather, tonight, we'd better get some rest. You're paying for this," David said. "You get to choose your bedroom."

"I'll take the one with the big-screen TV," Powell said.

"You gonna watch TV?" David asked incredulously.

"Nope, but it makes me feel good to know I could," Powell smiled, disappearing into the larger of the two bedrooms in the suite. "Six hours. No more," the agent called over his shoulder.

"Six hours," David agreed.

As David lay down on the bed, he wondered for the first time if he would see another day. As his mind and body wound down from the adrenaline high it had been on, he involuntarily thought of the small community church in Clayton and the green-eyed woman he had left praying there a few hours ago. Maybe the church and the woman were what he wanted, what he needed. As he drifted off into a troubled sleep, he saw the soft green eyes of Cindy Tolbert. He could still feel her arms around him as sleep overtook him.

2

Tom Frazier parked his unmarked car in front of the Capital Hotel when he saw Powell and Michaels pull into the Excelsior. The valet for the Capital met him almost immediately, offering to park the car. When Frazier told him he wouldn't be staying, the young man informed the Clayton County sheriff that he would have to move the car. Tom Frazier pulled out his wallet, letting it fall open to an identification card protected by plastic, and showed the card to the valet. The hotel employee glanced at the card, then upon recognition, backed away from Tom Frazier as if he'd seen a ghost. Frazier smiled. The identification card got the same reaction every time he used it.

Frazier waited, weighing his options. After thirty minutes, he left the car and walked across Cantrell Road and into the lobby of the Excelsior Hotel. Tom Frazier wasted no time admiring the opulence of the luxury hotel. The feeling of openness and the glass elevator that ran the entire height of the hotel added to the effect. He went to the clerk on duty.

"Can I help you, sir?" the clerk asked.

"I hope so. I just missed a couple of friends by minutes. We were supposed to meet here, and I was wondering if they'd made it yet?"

The clerk smiled. He'd heard the same story countless times before. His instructions were explicit in this situation. "I'm sorry, sir, but I can't give out that information."

"I don't want a room number," Frazier explained. "Just to know if they made it." The Clayton County sheriff slid a twenty-dollar bill toward the clerk with a blank registration form.

The clerk saw the bill, palming the card and the money in one movement.

"Names are Michaels and Powell," Tom Frazier informed the clerk.

"Just checked in about thirty minutes ago," the clerk informed Frazier.

"Did they say for how long?"

"No, sir. But they took the presidential suite and paid with a credit card that had no limit."

"That's them," Frazier smiled. "Thanks," he said, sliding another twenty toward the clerk. He could have used the same ID he had used across the street at the Capital, but that piece of plastic had a way of starting rumors and, at this point, Frazier preferred anonymity.

Tom Frazier walked out of the Excelsior and back to his car. The rain was lighter but steady and added to his feeling of helplessness. He would liked to have rested, but there was no way to tell what Powell and Michaels would do next, and his instructions were clear. He was to stay with the two men through to a resolution, regardless of what form that resolution took.

3

Though T. J. Kirby held the post that for all practical purposes was the second most influential post in the nation, few people recognized the chief of staff away from the White House and Capitol Hill. His plane from Memphis to Little Rock was late boarding, and his frustration was exacerbated when he realized that it was a commuter flight and not a regular heavy jet. Now some smiling idiot behind the boarding gate check-in counter insisted on rechecking every ticket and boarding pass.

Kirby passed the papers across the counter to the man and waited for the reaction to his name.

"T. J. Kirby," the man mumbled. "Looks okay, sir."

"Thanks," Kirby said.

"You know, there's someone in government with the same name. Odd isn't it?"

"Yeah. Odd," Kirby remarked, and then under his breath said, "Idiot." Kirby hoped the rental car agency in Little Rock was more efficient. He was losing an hour flying the twin-engine commuter plane, and he was beginning to have the feeling that every hour counted. As the plane taxied for takeoff, the pilot announced a delay due to a warning issued by the Little Rock Flight Service Station concerning heavy thunderstorms in the vicinity of Adams Field. This did nothing to diminish Kirby's aggravation.

4

The euphoria that accompanied Allen Stuart's escape from Wayne Young and the Collins Building was quickly supplanted by reality. He needed to be out of the city—no, the country—to really feel safe. As he maneuvered through the rain-slicked streets of downtown Little Rock toward the industrialized airport and riverport areas, his mind raced. He couldn't claim the airline ticket waiting for him at the capital city's airport. Young would surely have men waiting there. Possibly at Memphis International Airport, too, Stuart concluded.

He had to think, to evaluate the situation. Safety would be found in distance. Distance. He needed to put miles between himself, CCI, and Wayne Young.

Stuart took the on ramp leading to I-30 west. Even at this time of morning, the interstate that circumnavigated Little Rock was busy with large trucks moving the nation's goods. He settled in the far right lane, contemplating his situation. The green interstate sign announcing the exit for Texarkana swept overhead, and Stuart made his decision. He could make it to the city straddling the Arkansas-Texas border in under three hours. If need be, he could continue on into Dallas, only another four hours past Texarkana. Not even the head of CCI security would expect him to fly out of Dallas-Fort Worth. And even if Wayne Young was smart enough to think about it, he didn't have enough warm bodies to cover every departure gate at the sprawling mega-airport in north Texas.

Distance and size. Dallas offered both, he thought.

Stuart took the Texarkana exit and settled into the seat as he drove. He flipped the radio on and tuned it to the only easy-listening station he could find. Even after years in Clayton, he'd not developed a taste for the country music that dominated southern airwaves.

5

The head of security for Collins Construction International felt like a fool. He'd let some northern moron whack him in the head with a briefcase and escape. Wayne Young was tired of northerners right now. Tired of Allen Stuart; tired of the dead Foster Crowe; tired of Emerson Collins, head of CCI; and tired of the man in the green Mercedes. His life would be far less complicated with the elimination of all Yankees from his circle of acquaintances. But that was not possible. Not yet. He needed the man in the green Mercedes for at least one more job, and he had issued that order only minutes before setting foot in the office of the Yankee, Emerson Collins. Find Allen Stuart, he had told the unpleasant man in the Mercedes.

"You were to take care of the problem, Young," Emerson Collins raved, "not aggravate it!"

Wayne Young shifted his bulk uneasily as he stood in front of Collins's desk. "It was . . . unavoidable, sir," Young defended himself.

He despised being put on the defensive. "If that guard had not gone nuts over a measly ten thousand dollars, I'd have Stuart in custody this minute."

"Excuses," Collins said, "are not acceptable at this stage. Do you have any idea what we are facing at this moment, Mr. Young?"

"I think so, sir . . ." Young began.

"You have no idea, Mr. Young. With Stuart gone, there will at least be an investigation. To what extent I don't know, but any scrutiny, no matter how superficial, is too much at this stage of the game. We can't afford to raise any eyebrows on this project. We're talking millions in laundered cash! Hundreds of millions, conceivably. In this case, the only acceptable investigation is no investigation."

"I thought we had friends in the legislature and the senate."

"Fool!" Emerson Collins raged. "We're talking about part-time legislatures in this state. That kind of protection only goes so far. No one is going to be willing to cover up a drug-laundering operation coupled with fraudulent contracts and slack quality control, not to mention altered and adulterated blueprints about which they know nothing. We have enough trouble just getting these nuclear plants through the Atomic Energy Commission, the Nuclear Regulatory Commission, Congress, the Senate, and the EPA. It takes us decades just to get to where we can pour the first yard of concrete. We invest millions before we even set foot on the property. Millions! There's not a legislator in this state who's going to stand behind us if they learn the truth." Emerson Collins walked around his desk, his hands clasped behind his back, and watched the rain streak the large office windows. The weather matched his mood perfectly.

"What about the contingency plans?" Young asked.

Collins shook his head. "I'd rather not use them at this point. Stuart is certainly a problem, but I think he's a problem you can solve, Mr. Young," Collins confessed, coming away from the window. "Find the man, Mr. Young. Find him within forty-eight hours. In that time frame, we can devise a reasonable story that will keep everyone off our backs. Remember, if we get this power plant on line, we all stand to be millionaires many times over. Enough to live in luxury wherever we choose."

Young shifted once again but said nothing. Collins sat heavily, the expensive leather chair feeling cold for the moment. He looked up at Young. With a gut feeling of doom, he asked, "Something else?"

Young coughed. "Yes, sir. My head of security from Clayton just informed me that one of his guards is missing. They've combed the immediate area and haven't found him."

"Is he significant?" Emerson Collins asked. Significant, in Collins vocabulary had nothing to do with the worth of a human life. It referred to monetary value only.

"I don't think so," Young replied. "The man probably just went to town without telling anyone."

"Fine," Collins said. "Now find Stuart."

"Mr. Collins?"

"What, Young?"

"About Stuart. Dead or alive?"

"I'd like to say we need him alive. It would be better, but in the end, it will make little difference."

"Yes, sir," Young acknowledged.

Young left the office. The man in the green Mercedes was already on the trail of Allen Stuart, so he figured he was ahead of the game. But he'd not told Emerson Collins the whole story. He had held back on some of the things his security head in Clayton had told him. He'd not told Collins about Carlton Graham's car leaving the main gate with two strange men in the front. He had not told Collins he had unsuccessfully tried to locate the OSHA inspector for the last hour. He had not told the head of CCI that he suspected David Michaels might have breached the security defenses of the project site, and he had held back telling him that Michaels could possibly have the harness and rope that his brother had worn the day he died.

Emerson Collins was reluctant to put his contingency plans in operation. Wayne Young had no such qualms as he picked up the phone and dialed.

CHAPTER
SEVENTEEN

1

When Morton Powell awoke, he felt like he had never slept; his head ached, his neck was stiff, and he had a sour taste in his mouth. The room was dark; the clock was the only indication that dawn had broken. He rose and walked into the common room of the suite. David Michaels was standing at a window; rivulets of rain streaked the glass. For a moment Powell thought the navy chaplain was talking to himself. Then embarrassed, he realized David Michaels was praying. The FBI agent did not believe in God, but he admired David Michaels's faith. Powell turned to go, but he was too late as he saw Michaels start to turn around.

David turned when he heard the approaching footsteps. "Morning," he greeted Powell.

Powell gestured toward David with a wave of his hand and said, "I thought you had to be on your knees or something to pray." David searched for a note of sarcasm in the agent's voice, but there was none.

"Sometimes that's how I pray, although I have to admit I'm a little behind in that area. This was just a small prayer. Spur of the moment, you might say."

"I didn't know there was such a thing. I mean . . . I . . . thought all prayers were already written out and you memorized them."

"You grew up what . . . Catholic or Anglican?" David asked.

"My mother was Catholic. My dad was NFL," Powell said lightly.

David smiled. The FBI agent had a bit of the irreverent in him, but it was due mostly to confusion rather than animosity. "That religion has a hold on quite a few people I know. NFL, I mean."

"How'd you know Catholic?" Powell asked, confusion showing on his tired features.

"Pretty good chance when you mentioned memorized prayers. I'm an evangelical chaplain. We have some written prayers, but for the most part, we make ours up as we go along. Customized to fit the situation, you might say."

"On the spur of the moment," Powell chided good-naturedly.

"Yeah, just like you and I talking to each other. That's what prayer really is, talking to God. Anyone can do it."

"I'll take your word for it. We've never really been on speaking terms. Besides, we've got other priorities this morning."

"Such as?" David asked, detecting the uneasiness Powell felt discussing religious matters.

"First thing is food. My eggs and bacon are gone. You look like you've been up for a while," Powell commented after noticing David's freshly pressed clothes, combed hair, and shaved face. "Why don't you call room service and get us some breakfast while I find a toothbrush and take a shower."

David nodded and moved to the phone. He picked it up and dialed the room service number as Morton Powell went to shower. Holding his hand over the phone while waiting for room service to answer, he yelled to Powell, "Toothbrushes are in the cabinet above the sink. Wrapped in plastic. They may be the most expensive toothbrushes either of us will ever use."

After a breakfast of eggs, biscuits, gravy, bacon, and coffee, David was beginning to feel better. He had fallen asleep the night before, thoughts of Cindy's green eyes and warm embrace drifting into his dreams. Just a few hours later, he'd been awakened. He was still not certain what had roused him in the dark.

He'd found nothing when he'd turned on the lights, but he'd had the sensation that something or someone had been in the room. Sweat was dripping from his forehead and the bedclothes were soaked when he had awakened.

Whatever he and Morton Powell were battling, it was more than flesh and blood. The men were only the symbols, chess pieces of living tissue. David trembled at the realization. Evil had a fetid smell about it.

Morton Powell, seated across the table from David, looked up at that moment, then scanned the room.

"What is it?" David asked.

"I thought I smelled something," Powell answered. "Something spoiled, maybe."

"You may have," David remarked.

"Like what?" the agent asked, looking up.

David shrugged. "Demons. Dark angels. Ghosts?" said David, only half jokingly.

Morton Powell laughed. "Okay, time to get started. If this thing's got you talking about ghosts and goblins, we better get it over with fast."

David smiled, acquiescing for the moment. "What's the plan for the day?"

Powell handed David a list of items he'd scribbled on a piece of hotel stationary. "First, we go shopping."

David reviewed the list. "We can get most of it at Radio Shack or any department store. Take a few hours to round it all up, though. Most of this stuff is basic. Is this it?" David asked dubiously.

"Basically. If I think of anything else, we can just add it as we go along. We've got some time to kill until this afternoon."

"I thought your office was here in Little Rock," said David. "Don't you already have some of this stuff?"

"Some of it, but I don't even want my office to know I'm in town," the agent replied.

"Then we're going in this afternoon, for sure?"

"Just like we planned. With the workers leaving, the guards will be at their busiest. We can just walk in carrying the items on the list. I guarantee it. All you have to do is pretend you belong. The most effective disguises come from the body language and attitude you adopt, not the clothes you put on."

David rose from the chair and walked to the window. The TV was on, and a morning weather show was predicting rain for the next twenty-four hours. A huge low-pressure system had settled over the lower Mississippi Valley and showed no signs of moving in the near future.

David gazed across at the building that was the object of their conversation. For some reason, it appeared more ominous in the morning mist and rain, as if it were a monster, its head raised in defiance. The building's gray bulk seemed to possess a character all its own, a soul as black as the night sky. The rain and dark clouds seemed to have the Collins Building at their epicenter.

David harbored no illusion about what he and Morton Powell were about to do; it was illegal. It violated every canon he espoused, everything he believed in. It was not like him. At least, to this point in his life, he had not thought it was like him. But that was before his only brother had been murdered.

Murdered! David was jolted when he realized that he now thought so easily in terms of murder and not just death. He was being pulled in two directions at once. No, he corrected himself, three . . . four . . . he'd lost count. He had Jean and the boys, Rev. Shackleford and the First Community Church, his father, Jimmy's murder and murderer, and, he admitted to himself, Cindy Tolbert to think about. Thrown into the mix was the tug of the military life to which he had become accustomed. It was not a comfortable existence, but it was predictable. David was not certain he could settle for predictable any longer. He had made the military his career because he had thought he could change some things from within. But the task had been formidable, nearly impossible, he admitted to himself. The military religious system was atuned first to the needs of the military, not the spiritual needs of its members, a self-perpetuating order on which no single human being could have an effect.

Maybe he needed a change, not only physically, but mentally and spiritually as well. The military bureaucracy had worn him down. If he'd succeeded in anything, it was in his own acceptance of the impossible, at least as far as his own powers were concerned. First Community Church might offer him the opportunity he'd sought so long ago when he'd emerged from the jungles of Southeast Asia. Maybe he could make a difference, at least in a few lives.

Right now he needed to focus; he needed to concentrate on one thing. That one thing was the successful assault on the CCI building that afternoon. He would banish the raging debate within him for the time being. Later he would have time for all the things he needed to decide—if he lived through this afternoon and tonight.

2

It looked as if it would rain till the end of the world. The dark skies over Little Rock lightened only slightly with the advent of morning. The blue-gray clouds hung so low that they obscured the tops of the downtown buildings.

Tom Frazier was standing in the doorway of the Capital Hotel drinking coffee from a Styrofoam cup. He'd lost count of the number of cups he had consumed over the last few hours. Half a dozen, he suspected, if the tightness in his lower abdomen was any indication. His unmarked car was parked exactly where he had left it last night, much to the consternation of the hotel valet who could have used the space.

The Clayton County sheriff turned from the window and rubbed his red eyes. He scanned the lobby of the old hotel. The love and care that had gone into its restoration was evident in the columns, the railings, the stained glass, and even in the carpets and furniture. A walk up the staircase was a trip back in time—back to the days when men who entered the hotel carried Colt pistols in worn, leather holsters and trail dust clung to battered hats and denim jeans. Tom Frazier had more than once thought he had been born in the wrong time. He would have been a grand cowboy, he knew. He rubbed his eyes once more and turned back to the gloom and rain just outside the plateglass window.

As he watched, a parking valet delivered Morton Powell's car to the front entrance. Frazier came alive. He moved to the doors of the Capital, waiting to see which direction Michaels and Powell would go.

David Michaels and Morton Powell came out of the Excelsior. The FBI agent went around to the driver's side and slid behind the wheel while Michaels got in on the passenger's side.

Work traffic was just beginning to clog Cantrell Road. The bridge traffic from North Little Rock was backing up across the Arkansas River. Tom Frazier was in his car when Michaels and Powell headed west on Cantrell. Frazier had parked his car headed toward the east the night before. He would have to make at least a one-block loop to follow Michaels and Powell.

Had he thought about it the night before, he would have parked east of the Excelsior on the north side of the street. From there he could have gone either direction, but fatigue had taken its toll on the Clayton County sheriff, and he had overlooked that detail. Now, with the capital city traffic congestion, he was on the verge of losing the FBI agent and the navy chaplain.

Frazier steered around the block and came back out on Cantrell. He looked to his left—west—trying to pick out the nondescript government car.

He had no guarantee that the two men would return to the hotel, and Frazier needed to stay with Powell and Michaels. He needed to know their every move. More and more, he had the feeling that lives depended on it. Certainly the lives of Michaels and Powell. Perhaps even his.

3

The final approach into Adams Field on the outskirts of Little Rock, Arkansas, took the small, twin-engined commuter plane directly over the Arkansas River. T. J. Kirby looked out the window as the river slid beneath the plane like a dark silver ribbon. Two tugs pushing barges navigated the waterway as the plane flew over them. Kirby guessed they were transporting rice or soybeans to New Orleans. Then, in an instant, Kirby was looking at the wide, white markings that designated the runway threshold. The plane touched down and threw spray into the air as the propellers whipped at the water accumulated on the runway. Kirby felt the pilot push the propellers through the feather position and into their reverse prop position, the twins engines acting as brakes. The pilot lightly touched the toe brakes above the rudder pedals, and the plane slowed and turned right off the runway at the second set of blue lights marking the taxiway.

Finally, Kirby thought. He was exhausted from the extended layover due to weather and was exasperated by the delay. He could have driven the 120 miles from Memphis to Little Rock in less time.

The plane came to a halt on the tarmac. Rain was still falling. Kirby could see the lights burning in the terminal. The plane's door was opened, and a flight attendant carried several umbrellas on board and handed one to each passenger upon exiting. As T. J. Kirby took his umbrella, the attendant said, "Good to have you home, Mr. Kirby."

Kirby glanced at the attendant and said, "Thank you. It's good to be home."

"There's a message for you at our counter in the main terminal, sir."

Kirby stopped on the top step of the deboarding ladder. "How long ago did it come?" he asked, pointedly.

"I'm not sure, sir. You would have to ask the ticket agent at the counter."

"Thank you," Kirby grunted as he exited. One of the things he didn't like about commuter flights was their lack of airphones. He had wanted to slip into Little Rock unnoticed. In order to do so, he had to sacrifice convenience. It was against policy for the chief of staff to be out of contact with the president, but Kirby felt it necessary. The waiting message could have come from only one source—the president.

Kirby hurried through the terminal to the ticket counter. The ticket agent recognized him and handed him the message. Much to Kirby's relief, no reporters or news cameras were awaiting him. At least he had arrived unnoticed to the majority of the world.

Kirby opened the message and, as he read it, his stomach twisted into tight, painful knots.

The note was not from the president. The message was in code, but Kirby understood exactly what it said. The worst possible scenario was unfolding. Kirby hurried to the baggage claim, retrieved his one bag, and stepped out into the street. He hailed a taxi and tossed his bags into the rear seat.

"The Excelsior Hotel," Kirby ordered, settling back in the seat. Kirby could feel control slipping away.

4

The sun was just breaking through the overcast sky as Allen Stuart turned into the American Airlines terminal at the Dallas–Fort Worth Airport and found a parking space on the upper level just outside one of the main doors. The decision to drive to DFW had been wise, but the long night had left him fatigued. The long hours on the interstate and the darkness had rendered him zombie-like, and he shook his head, breathing deeply in an effort to dispel the feeling. The attempt was largely unsuccessful.

Two DC-10s roared by simultaneously, taking off from the parallel runways of the Texas airport. The noise shocked the North Central Electric Cooperative general manager from his dull state as he watched the big jets climb their way into the overcast morning sky.

Stuart got out of his car, not bothering to lock it, and headed for the ticket counters inside the terminal. His gaze moved from one person to the other, trying to determine if Wayne Young had operatives planted in the DFW terminal. He looked for men who did not fit the pattern of the travelers moving through the terminal building. Men who would be conspicuous in their inactivity. Men who only pretended to read the magazines and papers they held before them. Men who worked for Young and would do whatever it took to return him to Little Rock, or, failing that, kill him with as little regard as they would give to stepping on a bug.

He saw none.

Allen Stuart breathed a sigh of relief as he approached the ticket agent. Among so many people, not even the long arms of CCI would dare to touch him.

"Geneva," Stuart said when he finally arrived at the ticket counter and the agent asked his destination.

"There will be a layover in Atlanta," the agent said, as he processed the ticket.

"How long?" Stuart asked, not caring but playing the game of the concerned traveler.

"Three hours, sir."

"No problem," Stuart remarked, handing the man his charge card.

"May I see your passport and your visa?" the agent requested.

Allen Stuart opened his briefcase and handed the small, blue pass-port folder to the agent. "I'll need to purchase a tourist card," he said. It was then he realized he had very little cash, only what he carried in his wallet. He had sacrificed ten thousand dollars in cash in his escape from CCI. "Is there an ATM machine nearby?"

"Just through those doors, sir," the agent indicated and returned the passport along with the ticket. "You can purchase the tourist card in-flight. You will have to clear Swiss customs in Geneva. Have a good flight, sir."

Stuart took the ticket and walked from the ticketing area, through the metal detectors, and into the more secure departure area. He scanned the area, but with hundreds of people around him, it was impossible to detect someone who might be looking for him. He moved to the cash machine, inserted his card, and withdrew the limit. With the cash in his pocket, he felt better. He had two hours till departure. Strolling to his gate, Stuart selected a seat with his back to the large windows overlooking the runway and closed his eyes.

For once, things were going his way.

5

Tom Frazier pounded his open palms against the steering wheel in frustration. He had Powell's car in view only briefly when he had come back out onto Cantrell Road. Then in the morning traffic congestion, a few miles west, he had lost them as they turned off Cantrell and onto Reservoir Road. He had driven down Reservoir, turned right on Rodney Parham, and scouted the west area of Little Rock looking for the car. He had guessed wrong; there was no sign of Powell and Michaels. His only hope now was that they would return to the Excelsior. He would have to wait, and waiting was not his favorite pastime.

He drove back to the Capital Hotel, this time booking a room on the front side of the hotel looking out on Cantrell. He could see the front of the Excelsior from his window. *Better to be comfortable,* he reasoned. *It could be a long wait.*

6

Wayne Young looked around his office, taking in the amenities, which had been his after accepting the job as head of security for Collins Construction. The perks had entered into his decision when he finally accepted the position, but the one overriding factor had been the money. It was not just satisfactory, it was prodigious. Almost obscene. For the first time in his life he was receiving a salary that numbered into six digits.

He had known deep inside that he was not being paid the enormous amount simply to be an administrative head of a worldwide security force. The things he did for Collins were things that could, for a man in a lesser position, result in imprisonment. At first his conscience had pricked at him. But as he went along, it became easier and easier to relegate the protesting conscience to the darker reaches of his mind.

Young could do anything now with little or no compunction. That included betraying the company and the man who had elevated him to his current position—Collins Construction International and Emerson Collins.

The man in the green Mercedes had called minutes before, inform-
ing him that Allen Stuart was nowhere to be found—at least not in the
state of Arkansas and not in western Tennessee or Mississippi. For the
rest of the border states, he could not say. He had fewer contacts going
west and north. It was possible that Stuart fled to any one of the
remaining border states. It was, quite frankly, too large an area to
cover on such short notice.

Young had fumed and cursed the man for letting Allen Stuart slip
though the dragnet. The man reminded Wayne Young that it was he,
Wayne Young, head of security for CCI, who had let Stuart get away in
the first place. Young had relented then, accepting the man's report and
setting in motion his own contingency plans. With Allen Stuart on the
loose, life could become extremely complicated very shortly.

Millions of dollars floated around CCI every day, and Wayne Young
had found his own way to tap into the cash flow of the gigantic company. He was set for life. All he had to do was get out of his current
situation alive. That included taking care of David Michaels. Young
was not a man to leave loose ends, and Commander David Michaels
was a loose end that could unravel Young's nest.

Carlton Graham was missing. One guard from the security force in
Clayton had not reported back to work. It was a safe assumption that
Michaels was involved. How, Young did not know. Why was easy to
guess. Graham knew about CCI's setup. It was something the security
head had warned Emerson Collins about at the time. Too many people
knew about CCI's mode of operation. They knew at least enough to
think it worthwhile to divulge the information to the right people.
Young knew that was exactly what Graham had done. He had no
proof, but he did not need it. This was not a court of law; this was survival of the fittest.

Young knew enough to know that if Michaels had any hope
of bringing down the corporate giant, the navy commander would
need more than the physical evidence that could be acquired at the

generating construction site. He would need records, documents, and much more. And the only way to get those would be to penetrate the CCI headquarters building.

Young knew that was impossible. With the security systems in place and guards posted at strategic points, Michaels didn't have a prayer of piercing the defenses. But Wayne Young knew the man had to try.

And he, Wayne Young, would be waiting—waiting to eliminate the only man who could prevent his ultimate triumph.

7

The man in the green Mercedes felt a sense of elation when he informed Wayne Young of Allen Stuart's escape from the clutches of CCI's corporate tentacles. He sat back, enjoying the embellishments of the large sedan still parked in the short-term lot of Adam's Field, Little Rock's airport. The weather was rainy and miserable, in a word, perfect. Young, he knew, had his own hidden agenda, just as Allen Stuart, Emerson Collins, and every other person involved in the CCI scam did. Everyone except him. His agenda went far beyond any that could be manifest in this lifetime or on this physical earth.

Things were going well. His immediate enemy was represented by the man named David Michaels. A showdown was in the offing, he knew, but he could wait.

A couple strolled past and admired the green Mercedes. They wondered how the man behind the steering wheel could sit in the car and not notice the rancid smell emanating from it.

8

Waiting was not something Cindy Tolbert enjoyed. As she and Jean Michaels sipped the hot tea Jean had prepared, she thought about her relationship with David. Maybe she was premature in even assuming a relationship, and all that was happening was no more than wishful thinking on her part. Certainly David had said nothing that could, by any stretch of the imagination, be construed as encouraging her in her feelings. But she could still feel his arms around her, first at the church, then later, just before he had left for Little Rock. *That* had not been her imagination. And the feelings overflowing from within her were not in her imagination either.

"Tea's getting cold," Jean said.

Cindy glanced at the half-filled cup, swirled the contents, and looked up. "You're right. I'm in love with him," she admitted slowly.

Jean placed a gentle hand on Cindy's shoulder.

"It shows. But I need to warn you about David," Jean said.

Cindy looked hesitantly at her friend. "What do you mean?" she asked slowly, not sure she wanted an answer to her question.

"It's just that David has been a loner all his life. His service in the military is a perfect example. David's been in a long time and he's used to the life it offers. He's accustomed to being single and mobile, free to travel all over the world. I don't know if Clayton still holds the allure it might once have."

"You don't know if he could be happy with a country girl in a small town, in other words."

"Any small town and any country girl, not just you, Cindy. I don't want to see either of you hurt. He's my brother-in-law, and you're my best friend. Both of you mean a lot to me." Jean hesitated, then said, "Just go slowly. That's about the only advice I can give you."

"And pray," Cindy added with a gentle smile.

"Yes, and pray. From what I'm hearing, I think most of my counsel is too late. Are you sure you're in love and not just remembering that high school senior with the appointment to the Naval Academy?"

Cindy Tolbert nodded. "I may have been confused at first, but talking with you has helped me to focus on my feelings. It's not the same thing I felt for Robert, but's there's no doubt about what I feel. I do love David Michaels."

"Then we have a lot of praying to do," said Jean. "And the sooner we start, the better."

Cindy smiled again at her friend as they both sank to their knees.

9

The lights in Tom Frazier's room were out, eliminating the possibility that someone from the street would see the county sheriff at his stakeout position. Frazier caught himself dozing in the comfortable climate and elegant appointments of a fifth-floor bridal suite. He stood and walked away from the window from which he could see the front of the Excelsior Hotel. Then he went to the bathroom and splashed cold water on his face. When he looked in the mirror, he winced at the sight of irritated eyes and the disheveled mop of dark hair that greeted him. The stubble of his dark beard was beginning to appear. Sleep was uppermost on his mind now. He would need some if he was going to function at his best. But he also needed to reacquire a positive contact on David Michaels and Morton Powell.

He returned to the window. An airport taxi pulled under the protected portico of the hotel across the street, and Frazier almost disregarded the vehicle as unimportant as he watched the passenger get out. But there was something familiar about the shape of the man's head, his build, and his demeanor. Frazier concentrated on the man. He lifted the Zeiss binoculars to his irritated eyes and focused on the man. Frazier involuntarily inhaled as the man across the street looked up for a split second, seemingly in his direction.

T. J. Kirby, chief of staff to the president of the United States, filled the twin lenses of the binoculars! His contact had been correct.

Suddenly Frazier's need for sleep vanished. His exhaustion had been dispelled by the presence of T. J. Kirby. His senses were alive and tingling, as if he had been shocked by a jolt of electricity. Frazier knew a connection existed between the stocky chief of staff and all that was happening with David Michaels, Morton Powell, and Collins Construction International.

10

It was almost noon when David Michaels checked his watch again. He twisted to glance at the back of the car, which was filled with an odd assortment of items: two sets of monogrammed navy blue coveralls; a plastic bag of electronic components from Radio Shack, including a rather expensive electronic testing meter; used boots from the Salvation Army store; a black, plastic tool kit with an assortment of screwdrivers and pliers; ropes and other climbing equipment from a local outdoor specialty shop; an external computer drive with ten one-gigabyte disks; parallel and series port cable connectors; and an expensive aluminum suitcase.

David was fairly sure what most of the equipment would be used for, but when Morton Powell bought the external computer drive and disks, he was stumped.

The drive was the type that could be connected to virtually any computer system in the world, if you had the correct cables. Powell had purchased several cables from a computer supply store. The disks were formatted to store computer-generated information and had the capability of storing more than five million pages of data. David knew enough about computers to know that they could not waltz into CCI, hook an external drive to the computer system, and record information at will—not without a computer expert to override the safety features sure to be installed on the system.

"Have we got everything?" Morton Powell asked David.

David consulted the list he held, mentally placing checks by each item they had purchased. "Everything," David answered.

"Let's get back to the hotel and organize this stuff. We've got plans to firm up. We may have time to catch a few winks too. We can use all the rest we can get," Powell admitted as he wended his way through early afternoon traffic.

"Sounds good to me," David agreed, not telling the FBI agent that there was no way in the world he would be able to sleep with the amount of adrenaline coursing through his system.

11

Tom Frazier was about to make a phone call to admit he had lost David Michaels and Morton Powell when he saw the agent's car pull up in front of the Excelsior. David Michaels and Morton Powell got out, said something to the attendant, and waited until the liveried man brought a wheeled luggage carrier to them.

Frazier watched. His curiosity escalated as the two men loaded an assortment of equipment onto the dolly and rolled it inside.

T. J. Kirby and now David Michaels and Morton Powell all beneath the same roof. All the elements were coming together at amazing speed.

Like a nuclear reaction, the elements would combine very soon. An awaiting cataclysm.

CHAPTER EIGHTEEN

1

Electronic and mechanical paraphernalia littered the floor of the presidential suite as David gingerly worked his way through the aggregation and into the kitchen area.

"How are we going to carry all this stuff?" David asked.

"It just looks like a lot," Morton Powell answered, without looking up from the pad he was writing on. "It will all go in the suitcase we bought."

"Government bought," David corrected.

"We bought—tax dollars, you know," Powell affirmed, smiling.

The metal suitcase lay open on the floor beside Powell. The agent began loading the electronic supplies into the empty space, followed by the external computer drive with the box of computer disks, and then the tool box.

"This better work," David remarked, "or we'll be hung out to dry."

"Tell me about it. With the stuff in this suitcase," he motioned, "we could end up serving time for industrial espionage, if we don't get shot first," Powell told David jokingly.

"It's not a joking matter," David retorted.

"Lighten up, David," Powell encouraged. "That won't happen. Plenty of people are aware of what I'm doing, in theory, at least."

"What does 'at least' mean?"

"It means the agency knows I'm working on the CCI conspiracy. They just don't know the details. We're covered, provided we can get in and out of the CCI building without getting shot."

"Lighten up, he says," David snorted. "Getting shot sounds like a permanent disability to me."

"Trust me," Powell said.

2

Whenever Tom Frazier felt the nearness of imminent action he had a nervous habit of checking the chamber of his Glock 17 to be sure there was no bullet in it. He would then check the clip loaded into the handle and the other clips attached to his belt. This was one of those times. Frazier had the feeling that everything he had worked toward in the last eight years was about to come to fruition. He would miss being Clayton County sheriff, but that had been part of the strategy. Even though his election to the office of sheriff had been manipulated for good reason, that did not appease the guilt he felt about deceiving the good folk of Clayton County. Of course they would never know, and in the next election, he was convinced, Janice Morgan would not only be the new sheriff, but the first woman to fill the post. And Frazier would move on to another place and another assignment.

He was keeping vigil by the window of his Capital Hotel wedding suite, amused that he was surrounded by an elegance intended to be enjoyed by newlywed couples. He would have to bring his wife to the Capital after this assignment. *She deserves it for putting up with my erratic hours,* Frazier told himself.

Though he checked the foot traffic going in and out of the Excelsior, he was certain that Powell and Michaels would not make a move until late afternoon. It made sense. Trouble was, if it made sense to him, then it made sense to everyone involved, and that could mean trouble.

3

The phone rang in T. J. Kirby's room. Kirby answered it. He knew that only three men in the world knew his exact location: President Donald Farmington Adams; Wayne Young, security head for Collins Construction International; and Emerson Collins, the brains behind the largest moneymaking conspiracy ever devised. Kirby was waiting on a call from Collins.

"Kirby here," he answered.

"This afternoon. Five o'clock," Wayne Young said before breaking the connection. "Quitting time here at CCI."

Kirby gaped at the phone for a moment before slamming it back into its cradle. He was one of the most powerful men in the world, and he was waiting for an appointment with Emerson Collins. Kirby found his way to the wet bar against the far wall and poured himself a drink. Maybe the narcotic effect of the alcohol would soothe the turmoil raging within him.

4

As he hung up the phone, Wayne Young swallowed. If T. J. Kirby was here in Little Rock for an appointment with Emerson Collins; then his own position was even more precarious than he had thought; the collusion in which he was a major player was rapidly unraveling at the seams.

Young made his decision. He would be available when Kirby met with Collins this afternoon; then with any luck at all, he would board a plane heading for Guatemala City. He had been to the Central American city before and found *el pais de la primavera eternidad*—the land of eternal spring—as the large sign in its airport decried, to his liking. He would have enough money to live like a king for the rest of his days. The Guatemalan women were beautiful, the living was cheap, and the weather was perfect. Young hated heat, and the city nestled among the mountains of the continental divide provided cool weather year-round.

Hours now. No more. After the Kirby-Collins meeting, he would be on his way with more than a million dollars. It could have been more, he knew, but it would have to do. Better to spend the million in the bag than long for more from a jail cell.

Young snickered at the thought of jail and particularly the picture of Emerson Collins and T. J. Kirby behind bars. He discovered he liked the idea.

5

"When you die and go to heaven," the saying goes, "you will have to change planes in Atlanta." Allen Stuart would have believed it if he believed in heaven. He considered himself too enlightened, too educated, too practical to give credence to a folk tale perpetuated by organized religion.

Allen Stuart felt more relaxed as the miles between himself and CCI increased. His chances of detection decreased in direct proportion to the number of miles he traveled. Two more flights would put him in Geneva, Switzerland. He would be free—free and rich.

He opened the briefcase to check the papers that represented what he considered to be the total worth of his life. They were still there, the account forms that showed the shares of the overseas mutual fund worth more than a half million dollars, a mutual fund heavily invested in CCI overseas stock. It would take only hours to transfer the money to a numbered account, withdraw the total, and disappear into his own version of heaven. He was certain that heaven—an afterlife—did not exist. He would create his own heaven when and where he decided. The money would see to it. For a split second he thought of his wife still back in Clayton, Arkansas. The thought was amusing. She had liked the place almost immediately, and now, thought Stuart, she could have it all to herself.

He closed the case, rose from the uncomfortably padded chair, and walked down the concourse to his international departure gate.

Only hours, he knew. He relished the thought of what he would buy with the money, and it did not include a wife who nagged about his gambling losses.

6

The blue coveralls matched perfectly. An embroidered sleeve patch designated the wearers as members of the CCI Maintenance Department, Electronics Division. David Michaels and Morton Powell looked the role they were about to play, a role whose success might well determine if the two men lived or died this night.

"Check the case again," Powell ordered, not wanting to leave its contents to chance.

David opened the metal suitcase and went through the list of items. "All here," he told Powell.

Powell checked the time. "It's time," he said. "The last shift will be getting off in about twenty minutes. That gives us enough time to walk over to the CCI building and watch the hordes get off work. If I see anything that's even the slightest bit suspicious, we terminate the operation tonight. We can try again tomorrow."

"I'll never make it tomorrow," David said. "My nerves would never take it."

"I thought you were the recon marine, the ex-SEAL."

"That's different. With marines, at least, I know what to expect. Here, I have no idea. Tends to be a little unnerving."

"Yeah, I guess it does," the agent agreed. "Don't worry. They don't know we have any intentions of inviting ourselves into their lair. It will go smoothly."

David reached down and lifted the suitcase with the electronics and external computer drive in it. "I'll carry this. It'll give me something to do with my hands."

"It'll also give you something to throw, should it come down to it," Powell joked. "Not that you need it after what you did to that guard back in Clayton."

"I sometimes act without thinking. Instinct."

"Good. I like your instincts. Don't surpress them. Let's go. Fifteen minutes before the swarm hits the street from CCI."

7

The taxi T. J. Kirby had ordered was waiting for him when he came out the front of the Excelsior Hotel. It was only a few blocks to the CCI building, but he was not taking any chances. His face was not as well-known as that of the president, and he could have walked the few blocks. But even a chance recognition could set the political hacks on his trail, and he did not need that at the present time.

"CCI building," Kirby told the driver.

The man turned around to look at his fare. "That's only a few blocks from here, sir."

"I know where it is," Kirby snapped impatiently. "Take me to the basement parking entrance."

The driver shook his head. *Takes all kinds,* he thought, as he put the car in gear and pulled away from the hotel. But this guy looked familiar for some reason. He reset the electronic meter and pulled into the afternoon traffic. It would be a minimum fare. Just his luck.

In less than five minutes, the taxi entered the basement parking garage of the CCI building. Kirby got out and handed the driver a twenty-dollar bill. "Keep it," he told the man as he turned and headed into the building.

The driver stared at the bill and thought how quickly fortunes turned.

8

"Pretend that you know what you're doing and let me do the talk-ing," Morton Powell suggested as he and David Michaels approached the CCI building.

"I've been doing that all my life," David quipped, trying to control the churning that was building in the pit of his stomach. "Pretending to know what I'm doing, that is." He wished he were back in Clayton, maybe enjoying a cup of coffee with Cindy Tolbert. He smiled at the thought, wondering if he could really relish the small-town life offered there. Life in Clayton? With Cindy Tolbert? It would be worth a try.

Powell checked his watch. Five P.M. He could see crowds of people leaving the multistoried brick CCI complex up the street. By the time they reached the building's doors, the afternoon exodus would be in full swing. That meant two things to Powell: confusion and opportunity.

Building security personnel, even good ones, tended to be lax during periods of increased activity. It was simply a matter of magnitude—too much to do in too short a time. Too many people to watch, too few to do the watching.

Confusion. Opportunity.

As Powell and Michaels neared their objective, the flow of bodies from the CCI building increased. It seemed like an unending wave. Powell and David walked into the surge of bodies leaving the building and through the open doors. Powell was ready with a story line should they be stopped by one of the guards stationed near the exit. It proved unnecessary.

Their entrance did not attract even a cursory glance from a bored guard. He, too, was anticipating off-duty hours as soon as the employee exodus ended.

Powell and David walked to the bank of elevators lining the far wall and directly into one that had just been vacated by employees. They pushed the basement button. The doors closed smoothly, and the elevator moved deeper into the bowels of the building.

"That was easier than I thought it would be," Powell commented.

"Almost too easy," David added.

Morton Powell wagged a finger in David's direction. "Never tempt fate," he advised. "We'll take what we can get. This could be tricky from here on in."

"Which raises the question you have yet to answer. I assume some of this electronic gear is to deal with the alarm system?"

The elevator slid silently to a halt as Powell answered, "Some of it, yes."

David followed the FBI agent out of the elevator and into the jumble of piping and wiring of the building's operating maze. Air conditioning ducts, wiring conduits, and ancient high-pressure steam plumbing ran through the basement in every direction.

David was overwhelmed by the complexity before him. He had wanted to break into the CCI building to find anything that would prove his brother's murder, but he realized he was out of his league. He was trained to deal with military problems and preach the Word of God. He was as comfortable living in a field tent or a ship's cabin as he was directing worship services under the shade of trees or within the confines of a military base chapel. But he realized he knew nothing about the subterfuge and stealth needed to penetrate the likes of the CCI building, much less to come away with the information he sought.

Morton Powell, on the other hand, seemed at home in the basement of the old building. He had certainly been right about getting in the building. David hoped he would be right about the rest. The alarm system sounded ominous enough. They would have to overcome that before proceeding.

David followed Powell deeper into the basement complex. The agent was searching for something, David realized. Then, almost on cue, Powell halted.

"Right here," Powell said, directing David to put the suitcase down. The agent opened the case and took out the black, plastic case that contained the assortment of tools. He opened the tool box, selected a screwdriver, and turned to what looked like a large, metal trash bin. David followed the metal ducting and realized he was looking at the ventilation system Graham had told them about back in Clayton— one of the only places in the building that was not wired into the security system—the vulnerable underbelly of the CCI building.

Opportunity.

Powell removed the cover. It was nothing but empty space as far as David could determine.

"Get in," Powell ordered.

"There?"

"Yes, there," the agent directed. "We'll hide here until tonight. Then we'll have free access to the alarm system without the chance of being surprised by a bunch of maintenance men."

David crawled into the space. He was surprised at its size. He had no trouble fitting his large frame into the space. Powell crawled in behind him, reattaching the cover from the inside with the same screws he had removed earlier.

David started to say something, and Powell held his finger to his lips, making a circular motion with his right hand. David instantly understood. The duct made a good hiding place, but it was also a fairly good intercom system reaching throughout the building. Even now David could hear jumbled words from the floors above as CCI employees joked and talked as they left the building.

Powell held up five fingers and pointed to his watch. David nodded, the message clear. They would be in the duct for five hours.

David prayed silently, hoping at the same time that Morton Powell knew what he was doing. Sequestered literally in the bowels of the CCI building, David felt helpless. He looked at Powell. He could barely see the man's face in the darkness that had closed in after Powell had screwed the duct closed. Darkness had never bothered him much, but now he felt something he had never felt before. He remembered preaching on evil and its effect on the human spirit. Those sermons had been abstract applications of spiritual truths, but what he felt now was an evil that transcended the academic and theological boundaries with which he was familiar. It was as if the building itself was composed of an ethereal matter of pure malevolence. David shivered at the thought. Until a few hours ago the battle he was waging had been one of substance, existing only in the physical realm. Now, as he sensed the oppressive weight of evil settle on him, he knew that evil was not just an academic concept, but a living entity—a substance as real as any on earth, a substance that could kill as surely as any bullet.

9

"Don't tell me I shouldn't have come," T. J. Kirby warned Emerson Collins, as he leaned over the expanse of Collins's desktop and shook his index finger in the financier's face. "Something is happening. I don't know what it is, but I suspect someone is trying to hide it, and I'm here to find out what it is."

"Calm down, T. J.," Emerson Collins said consolingly. "No one is hiding anything from anyone. We have had some setbacks recently, but they are minor situations which we are in the process of rectifying this very minute." Collins looked to Wayne Young for support. The security head took the cue.

"That's true, Mr. Kirby. I've got everything under control," Wayne Young lied. He still had not told Emerson Collins about the missing OSHA inspector.

"Adams has been on the phone to Arkansas for the last few days. What's that all about?" Kirby asked.

Emerson Collins looked at Kirby and replied, "You're chief of staff. You're supposed to be telling us, remember?"

Kirby collapsed in the chair that fronted Collins's desk. "I know that, but the man is playing it close to the vest. He hasn't told me a thing. Only one subject in Arkansas would garner so much of his time. That's CCI and the Nuclear Three and Four generating plant project," Kirby explained. "So tell me, how is that project going?"

Emerson Collins leaned back in his chair and gestured expansively with both hands. "It's the best scheme we've ever come up with. We'll all be millionaires many times over, including you," Collins said, pointing at Kirby.

"That money won't do any good if we're all wanted on fugitive flight warrants," Kirby advised.

Collins laughed. "With that kind of money, we can go anywhere in the world we want. No one can touch us."

T. J. Kirby jumped from his chair, both fists on Collins's desk. "I don't want to go anywhere," he hissed. "The idea was to launder millions of the Cali cartel's money using a multibillion-dollar project to do it. Our share alone is in the millions. International contacts are imperative. CCI is one of the few companies in the world that can launder the millions generated by the cocaine trade. I set up the deal with Cali, and you run the operation stateside. But you had to get greedy by cutting corners on the construction, something we both know you've had lots of experience at. Altering plans and blueprints. Millions from the cartels were not enough for you. You had to have more," Kirby accused. He was getting angry, his neck shading into a deep crimson. He did not like being out of control, but Collins was not only greedy, he was stupid. "So you cut the corners and some dumb rock-climbing concrete inspector discovers it and reports it to OSHA."

Collins smiled. "*Our* OSHA inspector, I should point out."

Wayne Young was uncomfortable witnessing the exchange between the two political and financial strongmen. His thoughts went to his own escape and to the money he had already accumulated. He wanted out of the room, to be on his way, but he knew he had to stay until a more opportune moment.

"Yeah," Kirby acknowledged. "He *was* our OSHA inspector. But did it ever occur to you that some of the cutbacks you're making can be detected in other ways?"

Collins came alert. "What are you talking about, Kirby?"

"For one, accounting. A good cost accountant or auditor could put the skids on this thing in minutes. And that Jimmy Michaels kid is not the only inspector. Reports go to the AEC, the NRC, the IRS, and more. Any of the reports taken individually might not add up to much, but if some bright government brainchild decides to collate the material, what do you think would show up? The point is, Emerson," Kirby sighed, "the strategy now has numerous flaws that didn't exist until greed took over."

"Relax, T. J.," Emerson Collins crooned. "When this is over and we're all millionaires, you'll find you like it."

T. J. Kirby sat back. It was clear that Emerson Collins's mind was focused only on the money. But for Kirby, the power that went with his office was as important to him as the money he would receive from CCI. Kirby also knew he was beating his head against the wall to try to rationalize with Emerson Collins where money was concerned.

"I want to talk with that OSHA inspector," Kirby said.

Wayne Young felt as if an iron poker had been thrust into his intestines. He had no idea where Graham was, and from all indications, it was entirely likely that David Michaels had the man cloistered in some out-of-the-way place. Whatever the problem, Carlton Graham could not be produced. Young would have to stall. He only needed a few hours to extricate himself from the mounting problems plaguing the operation.

"I can have Graham here in a few hours," Young assured Kirby. "He'll have to come from Clayton, though. That's a two-hour drive if I can locate him quickly. It's after hours and he may not be easy to reach."

"I'd advise you to find him, Mr. Young," Kirby said. "If you have to drive up there and get him yourself, I want him here before midnight."

Young recognized the unimpeachable voice of authority when he heard it. "I'll have him here," Young assured Kirby. The security man rose and left the room, knowing his own personal timetable for escape had just been pushed up by several hours.

CHAPTER
NINETEEN

1

The screws holding the metal panel came out easily; David Michaels and Morton Powell crawled from their hiding space. The space that had been adequate when they entered had quickly become uncomfortable. The roar of the moving air in the ventilation system had gone unnoticed upon entering the space, but after hours in the cramped enclosure, the noise had intensified until at the end it was almost deafening. Both men had been sitting with their knees folded beneath their chins, and both were stiff.

David stretched, enjoying the relief that came from the gentle exercise. Morton Powell retrieved the suitcase full of equipment and popped the latches, examining the contents with care. He closed the case, replaced the ventilation access panel, and snugged all the screws tight.

"We can talk here," Powell told David. "But keep it quiet. The machinery noise will drown out our voices."

David was hesitant. "What about the alarm system? Won't we set it off if we move around?"

"Not down here. There's no outside access to this space, and some maintenance men probably use this area even during the night. They would be setting off the alarms every minute," Powell explained, as he moved toward the north basement wall.

"You mean we might run into guards tonight?" David asked incredulously.

"Might," Powell replied offhandedly. "But don't worry about it. I took care to make these blue suits match the maintenance crew uniforms. We can talk our way out of any problem if we do run into guards."

David Michaels stared at the retreating back of the FBI agent and marveled at his composure. He jogged quickly to catch up.

Morton Powell searched the area and finally found what he was looking for. He strode to the gray box that looked like any large circuit breaker box found in an ordinary home, only larger. He placed the suitcase on the concrete floor and opened it. He removed a screwdriver, the electronic test meter, and a paper bag filled with multicolored, cylindrical objects with wires attached to each end.

"What's this?" David asked, indicating the gray box attached to the basement wall.

"Alarm system," Powell answered, pointing to the well-known initials displayed in the upper right corner of the box. He began removing the screws that held the outer gray panel in place.

David felt a surge of panic in the back of his throat. "Won't you set it off?"

Powell smiled. "Not from here. That's the reason we hid down here. Assuming the alarm system control box would be in the basement was a calculated risk, but a good one," he said, continuing to remove screws. "Generally, in these large buildings, the alarm system is located with the rest of the operational equipment. The good thing about that is, usually the maintenance and operations areas are not included in the surveillance system. Can't be. Maintenance men coming and going would set it off. That's the weakness I was planning on here. Sure enough, here's the box, and this area is excluded from alarm coverage. We can work on this box without worrying about setting it off. Unless, of course, I make a mistake and cross the wrong two wires."

"And what are the chances of that happening?"

"Better than even," Powell said, continuing to concentrate on the box. "Don't worry, my hobby is electronics. Built a TV from scratch once," he said proudly, removing the panel and placing it on the floor. "This will be a cakewalk."

"I thought this kind of system would have a battery backup."

"It does," Powell nodded. "But that's designed to work when the outside power is disconnected. I'm not going to disconnect either power source. I'm going to pull the system fuses on the solid state circuit boards. That will disengage the entire system without shutting off the power. Everything will appear normal, but the system won't function."

"Why don't burglars do the same thing in a house system?" David asked.

"Simple," Powell explained. "They don't know where the control box is. Those alarms are usually set with a lag time to allow the homeowner to disengage the system using a control panel mounted on the wall. That control panel uses a numbered code. If the code isn't punched in within the time period, the alarm is set off. Same for a burglar. He doesn't know the code. That gives him about a minute to find the box, remove the cover, and pull the fuses. Not much of a chance of that happening. Same principle here, except we found the box before even attempting to enter one of the monitored areas."

Powell picked up the meter, connected the black and red probes to the device, and began testing the circuit board. "Nothing too exotic here," he said. "Those fuses right there," he told David as he pointed out white ceramic fuses that looked like simple car fuses, "are the ones I will pull. All three control the same circuit. They're designed so that if one fails, the other takes over. With three fuses, the system can sustain two failures and stay on-line. Triple redundancy, just like the space shuttle." The agent removed three short, plastic devices from the bag and attached them to the three fuses. "Fuse pullers," he explained as he worked. Then he began testing the rest of the circuits. "Just as I figured," he said after a moment. "Hand me the bag," he requested.

David picked up the bag with the multicolored objects and handed it to him.

"This system's got a resistance indicator too."

"What's that?"

"It's an electronic circuit that monitors the resistance throughout the system and warns if it changes. Like when you try to use a jumper wire to short across the system thinking you are maintaining the circuit. Technically, the circuit is maintained, but the resistance changes, and this circuit warns of that."

"You mean," David began, "that the shows I've seen on TV where the crook uses a wire to maintain the alarm and still enter the house is a bunch of bunk?"

Powell smiled. "For the most part, yes. As soon as the wires are attached to the circuit, the alarm is activated. I'm going to use those resistors, the little colored things, to build a circuit that hopefully will duplicate the circuit's own resistance, so that when I pull the fuses, it won't recognize the intrusion."

"Then there's a chance we might still set off the alarm?"

"A chance," Powell conceded, "but not likely. There's a factor built into every system that allows for some variance. Besides, I'm good at what I do."

David watched the FBI agent work with the small resistors and other electronic components they had purchased earlier that morning. He had no idea what the man was doing, so he began looking around the huge, subterranean basement. With the maze of pipes overhead and the bundles of electrical conduit in every direction, the room reminded him of the navy ships he had served on. The only difference, as far as he could tell, was the height of the ceiling. Aboard ship, the ceiling—*overhead* in navy parlance—was no more than seven feet. The norm was less. He could recall numerous times when he had been scrambling to his general quarters station and banged his head into the overhead plumbing and wiring maze. He still had a small scar just beneath his hairline that had required seven stitches after he had banged into the metal ring surrounding a watertight door on the second deck of the USS Guadalcanal, LPH 7.

The basement of the CCI building was different. Here the ceiling soared almost two stories high. Still, the room was a jumble of related wiring, plumbing, steam pipes, and conduit.

"Just about there," Morton Powell announced.

David looked to see Powell connecting a jerry-rig of resistors and capacitors to the wiring harness inside the alarm system. "Okay," Powell said turning to David. "I'll need a hand on this. There are three fuses. We need to extract them at the same time. I've only got two hands, so you'll take the fuse on the left; I'll take the middle and the one on the right. The little plastic thing I attached earlier is a fuse puller, so you can grab it without getting an electrical shock. Just the plastic part, though," the agent warned. "Anything else and I'll be performing CPR on you. Got it?"

"Got it," David acknowledged nervously. He grasped the plastic fuse puller.

"I'll count to three and say 'pull.' On 'pull' we both jerk at the same time. Okay," he said, grasping the two fuse extractors and making certain David Michaels was ready. "One . . . two . . . three . . . pull!"

Their hands moved in unison; the fuses came out together. David discovered he'd been holding his breath, and he let it out as he held the tiny ceramic part.

"You'd make a great burglar," Powell said, turning to David.

"That's it?"

"That's it. If the alarm was going to sound, it would already be blaring. With any kind of luck, we can get to a computer terminal, get the information we need, and be out of here in less than an hour."

"Let's get this over with then," David urged.

"One thing more," Powell warned. "There's someone on the twentieth floor. We need to stay off that floor, if possible."

"How do you know that?"

Morton Powell pointed to a lighted control panel inside the alarm box. "See that row of lights?" he said as he pointed at a double line of lights that were extinguished when they pulled the fuses. "They indicate areas that were excluded from the alarm grid because people were on the floor. When I opened this up, the light on the twentieth floor was on. The only reason for that would be if someone was up there working. It's the executive floor, so there's a good chance that at least one of the Collins brothers is working late. That would be Emerson. My sources tell me that Jameson is on vacation. Maybe others too. We can't tell. We just keep it quiet, do what we came to do, and get out." Powell closed the metal suitcase, picked it up, and headed for the stairwell door.

David followed the man, impressed so far with the agent's knowledge of electronics. If not for the feeling of overwhelming evil flowing from the very stones of the building, David would be heartened by the success.

David prayed silently.

2

Cindy Tolbert jerked awake. Something was happening; she could feel it. She had stayed at the church until a number of older prayer warriors had begun showing up to take up the intercessory prayers for David. Then she had returned home to get a few hours of sleep.

The air in the room seemed heavy, almost oppressive. Her reflections flew to David. She had confessed to Jean that she was in love with him. The admission had seemed to free her very soul. It had been easier to reveal her feelings to a second party than it had been to confront them in her own mind.

Did her suppressed thoughts of David awaken her? No. That was not it, not entirely. Something else, something sinister, evil, had awakened her. Cindy climbed from her bed and knelt beside it, her hands clasped together. Prayer was the answer. She began to pray, and almost instantly the words that flowed out of her were in the form of petitions to God to spare the life of David Michaels.

He was in danger, she knew, and she also knew she could not lose him again.

3

As the rain ceased on the streets of Little Rock, Arkansas, Tom Frazier fought to stay awake. He had seen David Michaels and the FBI agent, Morton Powell, enter the CCI building wearing blue uniforms. That was over five hours ago. The employees had gone, and the building was dark, except for the top floor. There was still activity on that floor and the Clayton County sheriff thought he knew what it was about.

T. J. Kirby was in town. The man's sudden travel plans had come as a shock. Frazier had been warned, but even his contact could not guess the nature of Kirby's business. With Kirby in town, the odds were good that the lights of the executive suites of the CCI building were burning because of ongoing meetings between the president's chief of staff and Emerson Collins. The implications of such a meeting were not lost on Frazier. David Michaels and Morton Powell could be going to their death unknowingly, and there was nothing Tom Frazier could do about it, short of storming the CCI building. That was out of the question. His orders were to let the two men go as far as they could in the hope that their intrusion into the affairs of CCI would break the stalemate that had arisen between the Justice Department and the multinational corporation. The government needed information and was not opposed to sacrificing two or more men to get it.

Frazier reclined in his car and watched as the stars appeared in the sky for the first time in three days.

He hoped it was an omen.

4

The same stars just appearing over the Arkansas capital had been in view for several hours from Allen Stuart's airplane window. The SwissAir flight would land in Frankfurt, Germany, and continue on to Geneva, Switzerland.

Stuart sipped at his third drink as he looked around the first-class cabin of the L-1011 wide-body. He had not slept since his harried escape from the CCI building, and the alcohol was working faster than he would have liked.

The movie was just beginning on the screen in front of Stuart's seat. It was a recent thriller movie that used violence as a drawing card, and the general manager of North Central Electric Coop had not seen it. He put the drink down and turned his attention to the movie. He slipped the headphones on and dialed in the correct channel for the movie sound. In less than three minutes, Allen Stuart was asleep.

5

Morton Powell promised himself he would get in shape as soon as he finished with this case. He and David Michaels were on the landing of the thirteenth floor. They had worked their way up the stairs, stopping at each floor to quickly search the level for either the accounting department or the engineering department.

Powell was sweating and red-faced. David was neither.

"You're at least five years older than me and you haven't even broken a sweat," Powell complained. "You lug this suitcase up the rest of the stairs."

"Clean living," David said taking the case. "That and a five-mile run every morning along with an hour and a half of calisthenics."

"I know. A jock," Powell muttered.

"Recon marine," David corrected, "for now." He wondered why he'd included the "for now" in the statement.

"A recon marine is just a jock with an attitude," Powell argued, as he pushed open the door to the fourteenth floor.

"Aren't you afraid we'll run into guards on these floors?"

"Nope. Security designers put all their eggs in one basket. The alarm system was it. Men patrolling the areas would have set off the alarm just like we would have if we hadn't disabled it. Segregated guard posts are probably set up on certain floors, isolated from the security system, but for the most part, we're alone."

They were on the fourteenth floor, and the corridor ran off to their left and right. It was a duplicate of the first thirteen floors they had checked.

"You go that way, I'll go this way," Powell ordered.

David moved down the corridor. He could still feel the evil within the building, but the effects were dissipating as he prayed. The presence remained in the background, waiting like a stalking animal about to pounce. He passed a door then backed up—Accounting Dept. it read.

This was what Powell was looking for, David knew. He hurried back down the carpeted hallway, catching Powell just before the agent was about to round a corner.

"Accounting is up the hall," he whispered.

"Bingo. Show me."

The two men hurried back the way David had come and stopped in front of the accounting department door. Powell tried the door. It was locked. The agent pulled out what looked like a credit card with no markings on it.

"Magic," Powell said, inserting the plastic card between the door and the door frame. When the card contacted the door's locking mechanism, he pushed down hard and the door swung open. "Find me a computer terminal with a 'scussi' connection," Powell told the surprised chaplain.

"What's a 'scussi' connection?"

"S . . . C . . . S . . . I," Powell spelled. "Stands for 'small computer systems interface.' It'll be a plug on the back of the CPU, provided there's a CPU up here. They could be using a networked system, but in CCI's case, I'm going to bet there's too much volatile information in the accounting records to be on a network system. If it is a network, the processing unit will be located somewhere else in the building. But I'm depending on the accounting department using an isolated system. A system-wide LAN would mean others would have access to the information, and I don't think that's what Collins wants."

"LAN?" asked David.

"Local Area Network. Ties various CPUs together for multiple use."

David started in one area while Powell looked in offices at the end of a long corridor. The navy chaplain entered the office of the senior bookkeeper. It was utilitarian, furnished with durable, not fashionable furniture. What Powell was looking for sat on a metal computer table.

David went to the door. Powell was in the hallway moving toward the office. David motioned the agent to follow him.

"That's it," Powell declared happily. He opened the metal suitcase once again and removed the external drive, the formatted disks, and the cables from the computer supply store. Powell examined the rear of the unit, selected a cable, and connected it first to the computer and then to the external drive. "We can store any information we find on the disks. Better than printing it out or having to write it down, especially if we need as much information as I think we might. If we need hard copy, we can print it out at my office."

"You're a computer whiz too?" David said.

"One of the best," Powell boasted.

"And an accountant, I suppose?"

"CPA certificate and a law degree. Lot's of FBI agents are accountants. I got more education than shows," Powell joked as he typed on the computer's keyboard. "Of course, the education may not be worth a hill of beans if I can't defeat the security system."

"Security system? You didn't say anything about that."

Powell smiled. "Didn't want to upset you too much. But, yeah, there's got to be some sort of security system. Might be as simple as a password or multiple passwords at different access levels." Powell began typing while he talked. "I'm going to assume that since this is an accounting department computer, it's going to have at least three varying levels: at least an operator level, a comptroller level, and the highest would be an auditor level."

"You're going to have to break three levels of security?" asked David.

"Hopefully not. Most accounting programs allow for a single password to access the three levels from the auditor level. If I can break that code, I can access all the files I need. The highest security level should access all the lower ones. This type system is used to keep nosy accounting clerks from changing data, dates, even fiscal year-ends, all of which would compromise the integrity of the systems and the data. An operator can only access entry-level data. An auditor can access the highest levels, where changes in the system can be made."

"You make it sound easy."

"Not easy, but predictable. Most accountants are notorious for their lack of imagination. At least, that's the latest word. What I need is some information on the guy who runs this department. Look around for anything. Pictures of family, notes, maybe even the password written down somewhere."

"What if the password changes?"

"Better yet. The chances of it being written down somewhere are greater than ever. Everyone forgets rotating passwords."

David began shuffling through material. The office was Spartan when it came to personal touches, and he came up with nothing. All the while, he could hear Powell tapping away at the keyboard. Once or twice a low curse escaped the agent, and David smiled to himself. He continued searching as Powell typed.

"That's it!" Powell exclaimed after less than three minutes.

David joined the FBI agent at the console. The security screen that had been displayed earlier had given way to a main menu. Powell had cracked the code.

"I told you most that most accountants lack imagination. The password was a series of numbers: Seven-one-one-one-six." Powell looked at David as if the number sequence was the most logical one in existence.

"Come on, Powell. How the devil did you come up with that? I mean, seven-one-one-one-six is not the first number sequence that pops into my mind."

"Easy. All us accountants types adhere to a set of guidelines we call generally accepted accounting principles: GAAPs for short."

"And the numbers correspond to the number of the letters within the alphabet."

"You got it. G is seven, A is one, and P is sixteen, or, in this case, one and six. Now to work."

David Michaels had never gotten used to the computer age. He marveled at the speed with which the FBI agent manipulated the

machine. Screen after screen appeared, was examined, and then ban-
ished to an electronic purgatory. He watched the screen until he was
no longer certain what he was looking at.

Then, with no warning, Powell exclaimed, "Got it!"

David leaned over his shoulder, eyeing the screen. "What's it?"

"The cost accounting figures and estimates for the Nuclear Three
and Four project in Clayton. I need that," he said as he typed and a
"saving file" message appeared on the screen as the external drive
hummed on command.

In seconds Powell was scrolling through accounting data so complex David Michaels could not understand the names of the accounts.
Powell stopped and saved information periodically. The drive was
humming and saving damning information at the stroke of a key.
Powell changed disks and continued.

David listened, hoping he would hear nothing to indicate they had
been discovered. He had stopped praying, and now he realized the evil
he had identified earlier had returned. It was not as strong, but it was
there, nonetheless.

"Finished," Powell said.

"You got all you need?"

"From the cursory examination, I'd say I've got enough to put
CCI out of business and the principals in prison for the better part of a
hundred years."

"Then let's get out of here," David urged. "There's something
strange going on. I've got a feeling we don't have much time."

"Save your feelings for a second. I saw something a few files back
I want to check on. I hope it's not what I suspect, but we'll know in a
few minutes," Powell assured David.

"Hurry."

Powell punched in the commands and the screen read: OVERSEAS
ACCOUNTING AND CONTRACTS. He then called up the contract
portion of the file. It was listed by countries with the dates used as

cross-references. The agent reviewed the list, selected a country, and waited for the information to appear. When it did, Morton Powell felt his blood run cold.

"Michaels. Look at this," Powell whispered with a note of terror in his voice.

David reviewed the information on the screen and looked at Powell. "Is that possible?" he asked in horror.

"Not only possible," Powell said, revulsion sweeping over him. "It happened! And CCI was responsible!"

6

The intercom buzzed seemingly for the millionth time. Wayne Young slapped at the device, knowing Emerson Collins was on the other end.

"Yes, sir?" Young seethed, keeping his voice under control with effort.

"Where's that OSHA inspector, Graham?"

"He told me he was on his way. He could have been held up by the rain, Mr. Emerson," Young stalled, knowing the rain had ceased an hour ago. He had still not been able to contact Carlton Graham, and for Young it was a bad sign. His intuition told him the CCI empire was about to collapse around its shaky foundation. Wayne Young planned on being well clear when that happened. "I'll hustle him to your office as soon as he arrives," Young said, continuing the charade. He tapped the intercom to shut it off just as a new sound caught his attention.

Young felt faint as the sound echoed through his office. It was the one sound he never thought he would hear.

The high-pitched staccato sound filled the security head with dread. He walked to a panel next to his desk and ran his fingers down the double row of indicator lights. His finger stopped at the light indicating the accounting department. It glowed incessantly and was accompanied by the shrill shriek of the warning buzzer.

Someone had just accessed one of the accounting department's secure files without the proper clearance! Theoretically that was impossible. Multiple passwords and file blocks should have insured system integrity. It would take a computer genius to override the passwords and security systems necessary to access the files, but here was the visible proof in front of him.

Young dialed the security office located down the hall from his office. Two guards were on duty. Supposedly they were redundant. The alarm system should have detected any intrusion, called the police, and locked the building all at the same time. Something obviously had happened to the system. That made Young and the two guards the total defense for the building.

"Meet me on the fourteenth floor. Accounting department," Young ordered when the guard answered the phone.

"The alarm system . . .?"

". . . is off," Young screamed as he slammed the phone down. He pulled a Walther PPK from his desk drawer and headed for the accounting department. He could see the guards just entering the elevator as he rounded a corner. The door was shut by the time he got there. He pushed the call button and waited. It seemed an eternity before the elevator arrived. Young stepped in and pushed fourteen. He hoped the guards had enough sense to wait on him. Whoever had entered the accounting department had bypassed the alarm system and decoded the internal security codes of the computer system. A person that smart was smart enough to take out two guards with little trouble.

The bell rang, and Young stepped out into the fourteenth floor corridor. The guards were nowhere in sight.

7

"Try April 26, 1986," David Michaels instructed.

Morton Powell typed the date and pushed "enter."

"There it is," David said, pointing to one particular line displayed on the screen.

"It's not possible," Morton Powell continued to mutter. "These people have murdered *thousands* of innocent people. *Thousands!*"

David Michaels felt tears burn his cheeks. He had never expected to find such horrors contained in the computer system of Collins Construction International. The obscenity overwhelmed him. For once in his life he wanted to kill—to kill the organization that was CCI, to kill the people who controlled it, the men who had sacrificed lives for money.

Rage replaced the fear that had been his constant companion earlier. David pounded the desk before him and ignored the noise and the pain. He wanted to kill the evil that was Collins Construction International.

8

The odor was overpowering now, a stench from the very bowels of hell. The man in the green Mercedes was sweating. The prayers from First Community Church in Clayton were being added to by others in the community. The man cradled his head in his hands, pressing to relieve the pressure of the obscene prayers that tortured him.

It was almost over. He could still win. It would be close, but he could feel success within his grasp as he fumed and spit and cursed the prayer warriors in Clayton.

David Michaels could still die.

CHAPTER
TWENTY

1

The information on the computer screen was so demonic that David Michaels and Morton Powell sat stunned. So profound was their concentration, that they did not hear the two CCI guards enter the accounting department and make their way toward the open office door of the senior bookkeeper.

"It's beyond comprehension," David Michaels said, recovering first, the horror in his voice expressed not only in his words, but in his low tenor, as well.

"But it makes sense," Powell added, "in a perverted manner."

"Collins Construction International was doing business with the Soviet Union even before the breakup of the Soviet Republic. How is that possible? I thought you had to have State Department clearance, not to mention approval from the Nuclear Regulatory Commission, the Atomic Energy Commission, and the Senate Subcommittee on Nuclear Technology. There are checks and counterchecks. Safeguards. Restrictions."

"Anything is possible with the right connections, remember? Boundaries are only what man makes of them. Governments have and do alter such demarcations at will."

"You're insinuating that Donald Adams is involved in this, and I refuse to believe the president of the United States is part of this monstrosity," David argued.

"If not him, then someone with just as much clout. Enough clout to intimidate congressional committees, bypass the NRC, AEC, the Senate, and Customs, and allow the shipment of nuclear components to communist countries via secondary routes. The real problem is getting the restricted equipment out of the country. Now who do you know that has that kind of authority?"

"Offhand, no one. Particularly not the president. He operates under intense scrutiny. Every move is observed, cataloged, and reported. But that doesn't mean others don't exist. We're looking at the evidence before us," David conceded. "I don't understand how this is possible."

Powell smiled. "I know it's a common conception that such components can't be shipped without proper clearances, and up to a point, that's true. But no law, regulation, or agency can police the nuclear industry completely—especially when politics enters the picture. Laws and regulations can be bypassed or at least suspended for certain transactions. One of the greatest failures in our society occurs when the regulating agencies follow the laws and the people who write those laws do not. But I never expected anything like this," Powell confessed.

"Collins Construction International operated in the Soviet Union and built the Chernobyl nuclear reactor knowing it would fail! When it failed, it killed hundreds, maybe thousands, of innocent people whose only sin was believing what their government told them. Heaven knows how many will still die from the radiation. And CCI built the reactor knowing the design was defective, knowing that eventually the graphite-designed reactor core would fail! And the company even used substandard material to construct a defectively designed reactor! Those people living around the reactor never had a chance. An entire section of the earth has been contaminated for thousands of years. People were killed and maimed—all in the name of profit," David Michaels said.

"The combination of defective design and inferior materials practically guaranteed a common-mode failure," Powell said. He typed another command, and the screen again filled with data. "Look at this. CCI sold nuclear reactor technology to mainland China through several of its overseas subsidiaries. The components were shipped through France. The same RBMK-type reactor that exploded at Chernobyl. And the company used the same accounting methods to hide that deal too. Several subsidiaries were used to ultimately launder the nuclear components—a kind of reverse laundering. We're dealing with an evil so diabolical, it goes beyond human comprehension," Powell whispered.

"What's this common-mode failure you just mentioned?" David asked.

Powell swiveled in his seat. "Nuclear jargon used to explain a single event that can cause simultaneous, multiple malfunctions in a nuclear reactor. Supposedly there's sufficient redundancy built into the system. Unfortunately, we've found most common-mode failures when the failure occurred at a point previously thought to be immune. The Chernobyl explosion was caused by a feedwater problem. The technicians on duty should have been able to handle the situation, but rather than scramming the pile, they opened more feedwater valves and ended up dumping water directly on the reactor core. That's what caused the explosion; the superheated steam was formed by their mistake."

"But that wasn't CCI's fault," Michaels interjected.

"No, it wasn't. But the feedwater problem wouldn't have happened in a properly designed reactor. And even if it had, a properly designed core would have shut down automatically. And if by some strange set of circumstances the water was dumped on the core, the containment building should have mitigated the damage. It was a chain reaction that started when CCI cheated on the construction."

"I see what you're saying. CCI could have gotten away with it if the original problem had never showed up."

"Exactly."

"Enter March 28, 1979," Michaels said.

Powell turned back to the computer and entered the date. The data scrolled across the screen and stopped on the entry.

"I don't believe it!"

"Believe it," Powell said. "Collins Construction Company was the subcontractor on the Three Mile Island project. Their contract called for the construction of the containment building and outer cooling jacket only. Do you know what failed at Three Mile?" Powell asked.

"No, but I have a feeling you do."

"I do. A relief valve directly associated with the outer cooling jacket. Part of CCI's contract!"

David felt a strange emptiness in the pit of his stomach.

"It was a feedwater problem at Three Mile Island too. This time a maintenance crew had been trying to clear a clogged feedwater pipe and accidentally closed off the water flow to the reactor."

"Then it still had coolant?"

"Only in a technical sense of the word. The cooling water has to be kept moving, like the water in your car. The car radiator is like the cooling towers, and the engine is like the reactor core. When the flow stops, the car overheats. The same is true with a nuclear reactor. And at Three Mile Island we're talking about a light water reactor. That means it uses regular water as its coolant. It's imperative for the water to keep circulating. When the crew shut down the wrong valves, the water next to the core overheated in a matter of seconds. It popped a relief valve just like the one on a pressure cooker. Unlike a pressure cooker, however, the relief valve on a nuclear reactor is supposed to shut automatically and signal for more feedwater from alternate systems. That's what failed in Pennsylvania. And it's directly tied to CCI."

"Don't move!" a voice ordered.

David Michaels and the FBI agent froze. David slowly turned to see two uniformed CCI security men holding pistols trained on them. The two guards moved through the door widely separated, each in a crouch, holding automatic pistols in the classic two-handed grip.

"Hands behind your head and interlace your fingers," the smaller of the guards ordered. "You at the computer, stand up and interlace your fingers."

Morton Powell considered going for his Beretta, but knew he would never make it. These two men were trained. More mercenaries. He stood and did as he was told.

"To the wall," the guard directed. The second security officer remained at a distance as the smaller one directed them to the wall. "Hands behind your backs and lean your heads against the wall. Spread your legs."

With the weapons leveled at them, David Michaels and Morton Powell had no option but to obey.

One security man frisked Michaels and Powell while the other one stood at the ready. The guard removed the Beretta Powell carried inside the blue coveralls. The man cuffed David Michaels while his head still rested against the wall. Next he cuffed Powell and moved away from the two men.

"All right. Over here!"

Both men turned to face the two security guards and the pistols they carried.

"Mercenaries," Morton Powell realized in an instant.

"Very good, friend," the smaller guard acknowledged.

"Very good, indeed," a voice boomed from the corridor. Wayne Young entered the office, the Walther PPK displayed in his right hand. He stood between the two guards, the master overseeing his kingdom.

"You would be Wayne Young," Morton Powell began.

Young laughed. "I'm impressed. And flattered. How do you know who I am?"

"From the file I have on you and everyone here at CCI," Powell continued. From the looks of the men holding them at gunpoint, they had little to lose by explaining the seriousness of what they were about to do. Mercenaries were no more than soldiers for hire, but even some of them did not like breaking the laws of their homeland. "I'm FBI Special Agent Morton Powell. You two men are not involved in this," he addressed the two guards. "You can walk away right now. If this goes any further, you'll be put away just like your boss."

Wayne Young smiled. "You don't understand, Mr. . . Powell is it? Mr. Powell, what we have here at CCI is a sort of profit-sharing. While it doesn't extend to every employee here at CCI, it does include the entire security staff. I'm sure you can see the rationale behind that, Mr. Powell. These men are loyal. Not to me and not to Collins Construction, but to the dollar. And the dollar here at CCI is much greater than the dollar you could produce from any of your government agencies."

"Loyalty based on greed is not much loyalty," David Michaels said.

"On the contrary. It's the only kind of loyalty you can truly count on. You must be the chaplain. You've been causing some problems in Clayton. Now I see it extends to Little Rock as well. I must say I'm surprised at a man of God breaking the law."

"These are extenuating circumstances," Michaels countered.

"Your brother's death, of course. A terrible accident, but that's all it was, an accident. You would have lived longer if you could have accepted that," Young said.

"We have the safety harness and rope Jimmy was using. I think we can find some honest inspectors who might be interested in it."

Young's grin disappeared and then quickly returned. "What can you tell from a bit of leather and a rope? That it was tampered with? Maybe. But who did it? And why? I think you would have trouble proving intent. That is, if you ever get the chance."

Powell spoke up, "I think you've already shown intent from what I've seen in this computer system."

"What is it you think you know?"

"Chernobyl, Three Mile Island, nuclear technology sold to the Chinese. Who knows what else CCI is involved in. I'm sure we can find more," Powell said.

"Well, to tell the truth, this company really took off after the Pennsylvania project. That was when we learned we could build nuclear power plants cheaply."

"You're talking about Three Mile Island like it was nothing more than a fish pond," Michaels accused.

"That's where CCI learned just how profitable this line of work can be. We've done well. But that's beside the point. We're going upstairs. I think you should meet some people, and I'm sure they would like to meet you." Wayne Young turned to the two guards. "Let's get them upstairs to Mr. Collins's office."

The guards separated and motioned with their weapons. David Michaels and Morton Powell moved though the door and out of the accounting department, headed for the top floor of the CCI building and the master demon who'd orchestrated the creation of the rogue construction company.

2

It was not something Morton Powell liked to think about, but death was a possibility in his line of work. He had been exposed to Michaels too long. He had watched the chaplain in action and had seen a different side of religion. For Michaels, his beliefs were an integral part of who he was. That much was evident. And those beliefs had not stopped the man from acting to save their lives when it had been necessary.

For Powell, the abstract concepts of religion and the manner in which such beliefs actually played a part in the real world were coming together. Maybe, if he got out of the CCI building in one piece, he would sit down and talk with the navy chaplain.

Provided, of course, they got out.

3

There was something familiar about the man sitting with his back to the door.

David and Powell had been escorted to the office of Emerson Collins by the security guards and Wayne Young. The walk had been a transition from the barren, vinyl tile floors of the lower levels to the deep carpeted luxury of the executive floor. The smaller guard prodded David in the back with his pistol once during the walk, a reminder of who was in charge.

As they moved through the corridors of the CCI building, David noticed that the evil he had been sensing was becoming more pronounced, stronger. The evil grew with every inch they ascended in the elevator. He had glanced at Powell once and noted the discomfort reflected in the agent's face. David knew Powell was feeling the same press of evil, the same satanic presence. Powell had glanced at David, and David had raised an eyebrow in response. The agent shook his head and turned away.

The office of Emerson Collins was impressive. The polished wood, thick carpet, leather furniture, and array of floor-to-ceiling windows with a view of the Arkansas River made a lavish display. David would have been moved by the opulence had it not been for the overwhelming presence of evil that filled the room with the odor of dead and dying flesh.

Emerson Collins was seated behind his desk when David and Powell entered the office. Another man sat in the chair directly across from Collins; only his head was visible to the two men.

"What's this all about?" Emerson Collins asked, rising from his chair.

"Two trespassers, Mr. Collins. Not just any two, though. We have David Michaels, Jimmy Michaels's brother, and Special Agent Morton Powell of the FBI."

"Gentlemen, come in. Please," the head of CCI gestured. "I have someone you might like to meet."

T. J. Kirby rose from his chair and turned to David Michaels and Morton Powell. The chief of staff smiled at the two manacled men. David Michaels felt his pulse race as he stared disbelievingly at Kirby.

"I was right," Powell said with a feeling of vindication. "Somebody is always behind this kind of activity. The only thing I was wrong about was the position of the power," he continued. "I thought that maybe the president was the one responsible for the influence peddling to foreign powers. Right building, wrong person."

"The president knows nothing about what's going on," Kirby said. "This operation is sort of an in-house organization, you might say. Adams was nothing more than a front man when CCI moved to Arkansas. I was the one responsible. It was my foresight that brought CCI to Arkansas."

Morton Powell could not believe what he was hearing. T. J. Kirby was admitting to the conspiracy and evil that was CCI, clearing the president in the process. The reverse side of the confession, the agent realized, was that the men in the office exhibited no fear. Confidence was paramount in Kirby's expression. These men feared no one. Their confession was Michaels's and his death sentence, Powell knew.

"What you've done is abhorrent," David interjected.

"Abhorrent? That depends on who you're talking to, doesn't it, Commander?" Kirby asked. "You see, Commander, I do know about you. Probably more than you think."

"It makes no difference who you're talking to," David replied. "Murder is murder. It makes no difference if it's done with a gun or faulty construction procedures. It's all the same. As a matter of fact, the crimes you've committed are more shocking, more diabolical than the man with the gun. You're mass murderers with a profit motive."

Emerson Collins moved from behind his desk, coming to stand beside T. J. Kirby. David could feel the evil issuing forth from the two men, as if they themselves were demons from the underworld. They were men without conscience, adhering to their own warped sense of morals. They had destroyed lives without qualm, here in the U.S. and in foreign lands. And now David could feel the evil power that drove the men. The confrontation was reduced to its simplest terms—good versus evil.

4

The L-1011 touched down in Frankfurt, Germany, braking smoothly and turning onto the taxiway.

Allen Stuart felt victory closer and closer with each mile he put between himself and CCI. He had no doubt that he had escaped the realm of absolute power and into the peripheries of lesser power. He was feeling safer as he went. A few more hours and he would be walking the streets of Geneva, Switzerland, gazing into the deep beauty of Lake Geneva and luxuriating in the European city's extravagances.

Half a million dollars of CCI overseas stock would see to that.

5

"Take them downstairs," Emerson Collins ordered. "We'll have to get rid of them so no one will ever find them. Agreed?" he asked, turning to T. J. Kirby.

"Agreed," Kirby affirmed. "Make sure their bodies will never be found. We can't afford even the slightest hint of wrongdoing on CCI's part. We may be able to salvage our position with them out of the way."

Wayne Young moved forward, "We can dispose of the bodies in Clayton. We're about to pour the concrete around the bases of the cooling towers."

Kirby laughed. "I think that would be a fitting tribute for the trouble they've caused us. Do it," he said, not bothering to consult Collins.

"Yes, sir, Mr. Kirby," Young acknowledged, knowing that the chief of staff had effectively taken control of the situation. "Take them downstairs," Young ordered the two security guards. "And be careful with the FBI man. If he gets out of hand, shoot him and carry him down."

The two guards nudged David and Powell with the pistol barrels. "You heard the man," the smaller guard said. "Move."

David Michaels caught the glance of Morton Powell. It was all in the agent's eyes. They would never leave the CCI building alive unless they acted.

David recognized one bright spot. Young was concerned about Morton Powell because he was the trained law-enforcement officer. The guards would be concentrating on the agent, content to let David tag along. To them, David was just a chaplain, a preacher, and preachers were not as dangerous as FBI agents. David would wait for an opportunity to show them how wrong they were.

The four men moved into the elevator, and the larger guard pushed the button for the basement. David watched the larger man. He had pocketed the keys to the handcuffs. The smaller, pockmarked man was in charge, though.

David once again caught Powell's attention. He nodded toward the smaller guard. Morton Powell understood.

So did the smaller man. "If you're thinking about trying anything, you should know we're both experts in self-defense and we're both excellent shots with handguns. Of course, at this range we couldn't miss if we tried. It's up to you. Go for it if you think you can," the man sneered.

The man was bragging, confident in his abilities and those of his partner. That confidence would be their downfall, David knew.

The navy chaplain quickly glanced at the FBI agent. David could see resignation in Powell's demeanor. He knew he had to make a move now or they'd both be killed in less than two minutes when the elevator reached the basement level.

David coughed. Both guards turned toward the sound. In a flash, David threw his body against the larger man who stood near the elevator control panel, his right leg pushing off the back wall of the elevator transferring as much force as possible to the larger man.

The guard was caught between the elevator panel and David Michaels's body. At the same instant, Morton Powell kicked out with his left foot. The kick caught the smaller guard just below the right kneecap, and Powell was awarded with a snapping sound. The explosion of his pistol filled the small enclosure. The man went down screaming, his hands clutching at his injured leg.

The larger guard, his face bleeding from the impact with the panel, turned and raised his pistol. David pushed off the back wall once again, getting inside the perimeter of the man's reach. His body slammed into the mercenary with enough force to make David Michaels grimace in pain. David could feel his left shoulder digging up under the larger man's breast bone, finding the tender area of the solar plexus. He drove up and in with his shoulder.

The man grunted, the wind forcibly expelled from his lungs. His chest erupted in fiery agony. David backed off and struck again, lowering his shoulder once again. This time he contacted the man directly over the heart, driving hard like a fullback penetrating the center of his own line.

The big man's eyes glazed over, his lips moving in a failed attempt at speech. But no words came; that ability was gone with the expulsion of air from his lungs. The man collapsed.

David heard a thud behind him. He turned to see Morton Powell's kick land on the side of the head of the smaller, downed guard. The man's eyes instantly rolled into the top of his head as he crumpled back against the wall of the elevator.

"Get the keys," Powell wheezed.

David searched the bigger guard's pockets, found the keys, and removed his cuffs. He moved to free Powell. Before he could get to the man, the FBI agent collapsed on the floor of the elevator. David knelt beside the man, searching his face.

Morton Powell managed one word. "Shot," he said.

David had assumed the small guard's shot had gone astray. Now, as he examined the FBI agent, his hand came away with blood on it. He checked Powell's chest. Foamy red blood oozed from a hole in the agent's left side. David reached around the man, seeking an exit wound. He didn't find one.

Morton Powell coughed; flecks of blood stained his lips. David ripped at the man's clothing, exposing the wound. Blood mixed with air bubbled from the wound! Pneumothorax! Sucking chest wound! David had seen many wounds like this in combat and had been trained to deal with just such situations. He needed something to seal the hole before the lung had a chance to collapse.

A small, red cross was displayed next to the elevator control panel. David opened the small door. Inside he found the emergency telephone and a small first-aid kit. He opened the kit, relieved to find cotton balls and adhesive tape. He rushed back to Powell. The agent was a pasty white. Shock was imminent. Death would follow.

David quickly cleansed the wound with the cotton so the tape would stick and covered the hole with a small piece of the white tape. He then reinforced the covering with more tape and sealed off the bubbling blood coming from Powell's chest. The treatment would keep the lung from collapsing for the time being, but the FBI man needed a chest tube and the attention of a trauma team as soon as possible. He had no way to determine how much blood was trapped in the agent's chest.

David positioned Powell so his feet would rest on the body of the smaller, downed guard. In seconds, with the blood rushing back to Powell's head and upper torso, his color came back.

David retrieved the handcuffs he'd removed and secured the two guards just as the elevator door slid open on the basement level.

David pushed the hold button to keep the elevator doors open and checked warily for another guard. He helped Morton Powell out of the elevator and out into the basement parking garage. Then he raced back to the elevator. The smaller guard was conscious; low moans came from the man. The larger man was still out cold. He couldn't do anything with either of them.

The smaller man looked at David through the red haze of pain. "You're more than a preacher," he accused.

He raised the guard's pistol he had retrieved earlier and shoved it under the man's nose. "If I were you, I wouldn't count on any sympathy from me. You're part of the organization that killed my brother," David spat.

The guard closed his eyes, fighting the pain in his knee. He had known grizzled mercenaries less intimidating than this navy chaplain.

"Keep your friend here if you know what's good for both of you."

The guard looked at the still unconscious form of the larger man. "I don't think he's going anywhere soon. You probably killed him."

"He's all right," David replied. "Just knocked the wind out of him. Both of you stay here." David rose and raced for the garage.

Morton Powell was where David had left him. His color was better, but there were still spots of fresh blood on his lips. He was bleeding internally, David knew. He needed an ambulance and blood volume expanders if he was to live.

Then, as if from the depths of the earth, Morton Powell spoke. "The drive," he said, struggling to raise himself on one elbow. "We need the drive."

The external computer drive, along with the disks with all the information had been abandoned when the guards had found them. Chances were, the guards thought it another piece of CCI's computer equipment, meaning it was still in the accounting office. David would have to get the disks and the evidence they contained.

He would have to return to the fourteenth floor!

6

The SwissAir L-1011 was following the Rhine Valley route into Switzerland. It had taken off from Frankfurt, Germany, and was flying in undisturbed air on a southwesterly course that would take the giant aircraft directly over Lake Geneva.

Allen Stuart was completing the immigration papers required by the Swiss government and humming a tune under his breath. He had finally relaxed completely. The departure from Germany marked the final leg of his flight to freedom.

With the papers completed, Stuart reached for the airphone snugged into the rear of the seat in front of him. He inserted his American Express card and dialed. After the fifth ring, he decided the party with whom he wanted to speak was, for the time being, out of the office. It made no difference. Allen Stuart knew he could complete his transaction at any time.

7

The two CCI guards were still crumpled in the elevator when David returned for the second time. He checked their bindings. Satisfied they were still secure, he punched the "up" button.

The feeling of evil persisted. CCI was a corporation out of control. Or, to be more precise, a corporation controlled by an evil so diabolical, it defied description.

David stepped into the elevator when the doors slid open and pushed the button for the fourteenth floor. He had the eerie feeling he was being consumed by a beast from hell and the elevator was its mouth.

The elevator rose. David could taste the fear; it was a brackish taste he couldn't seem to shake. His palms were sweating, and his brow was damp. He'd been trained to ignore fear. But here in the heart of the CCI empire, the training no longer helped.

The door opened onto the fourteenth floor. David pulled the large red "stop" button to lock the elevator in place. He ran for the accounting department and the external drive and disks containing the information about the aberration that was Collins Construction International.

The office door of the head bookkeeper was still open, just as they had left it when they had been captured by the two guards and Wayne Young. David moved around the desk to the computer terminal. He unplugged the drive, collected the various disks, and bundled the whole works under his arm.

So far so good. All he had to do was make it to the elevator and back down to the basement garage ahead of Wayne Young. David had no illusions about the head of CCI security. The man meant to kill them and make them a permanent part of the Nuclear Three and Four project in Clayton, Arkansas.

David engaged the elevator's power button and punched the basement button; the elevator dropped. In less than a minute, he was stepping from the elevator at the basement level.

As he stepped from the elevator, he came face-to-face with the Walther PPK of Wayne Young!

8

"I see I underestimated you, Commander," Young said.

"It happens," David Michaels responded coldly.

"You did quite a job on my two men over there. I don't think I'll give you a chance to do the same to me," the security chief motioned with the automatic toward the garage. "And don't think that FBI friend of yours is going to interfere. I've already taken care of him."

David's anger flared. "What did you do?"

"Nothing drastic. Not yet. He's in the trunk of one of the security cars. I figured you both might like to go together," he smirked. "Put these on," Young ordered, throwing a pair of handcuffs to the chaplain.

David fastened the handcuffs around his wrists, his hands in front of his body. Wayne Young made no move to reposition the cuffs with Michaels's hands in back. The security man had underestimated him again.

"Out," Young directed.

David walked out into the garage area.

"That one over there," Wayne Young pointed to a CCI security car.

David moved toward the car. Just as he drew near the vehicle, he hit the ground and rolled toward the front of the car. He heard Young fire the Walther and recognized the sound of a glancing bullet as it struck the concrete near his head. He rolled in front of the car and quickly sought the protective cover of the car parked next to where Morton Powell was trapped.

Wayne Young had not thought the chaplain capable of moving so quickly. His one shot had been a vain attempt to kill the troublesome preacher. Now the navy commander was hiding among the security cars that filled this area of the parking garage. But he was alone and handcuffed. Young methodically moved in and out of the parked cars, searching for Michaels. This time, when he found him, he would make sure the man would cause no more trouble.

David moved in a modified crouch position and worked his way toward the far end of the garage. He planned to draw Young to the far end, double back among the cars, and escape out the basement entrance near Powell's trapped position. If he could get out of the building, he might be able to hail a passing patrolman.

For some reason, David felt confident, almost as if he was empowered by an external force. He moved deeper into the parking garage, using the security cars for protection. He could hear Young's footsteps following, echoing off the concrete surroundings. It was working.

Young moved deeper into the garage, following David Michaels. When he heard the running footsteps, he knew he had been suckered. He turned in time to see the tall figure of David Michaels as the naval officer sprinted for the open entrance door.

Young leveled the Walther at David and squeezed the trigger. Three quick shots kicked up concrete dust just behind Michaels's running feet.

David heard the shots and felt the small rocks sting his ankles as he ran. The shots were close but not close enough. And then he was out of the CCI basement garage and running down the street. The street was wet, but the rain had ceased. David splashed through puddles as he fled, his shackled hands preventing an all-out sprint. He turned once to look back and saw the big shape of Wayne Young emerge from the basement garage, backlighted in the darkness by the garage lights. With him was the larger guard David had attacked earlier in the elevator. He was free and recovered from the battering he had taken, eager, no doubt, to exact revenge on David.

David ran, his cuffed hands slowing his progress on the rain-slicked streets. He rounded a corner and turned toward the Excelsior Hotel only two blocks away. He renewed his effort. He was not breathing hard. He thanked God for his marine training as he ran. He was sure he could outrun the two larger men, but he knew he would never outrun the bullets that would come in a desperate attempt to stop him.

David came out onto Cantrell Road, but he was blocks from where he thought he would be. He was close to the I-30 bridge and just above Little Rock's Riverview Park.

A bullet ricocheted off the wall to his left. A second one followed the first and hit almost the same place. David sprinted for the Riverview Park area. If he could make it to the river, he could escape. Even with his hands secured in the handcuffs, David knew he could survive in the whirling, cold waters of the Arkansas River.

He had been a U.S. Navy SEAL once. One phase of SEAL training involved drownproofing. He had spent over an hour in a water tank, his hands tied behind his back, his feet bound with cord. It was an exercise in self-control, but it proved to every would-be SEAL that water was an ally, a sanctuary, not the enemy.

David Michaels could save his life and maybe that of Morton Powell, if he could make the river.

His footsteps reverberated off the surrounding buildings as he ran. He could hear the pursuing footfalls of Young and the larger guard. Another shot resounded through the streets. David redoubled his effort.

Riverview Park was just ahead. He could see the river flowing on its way to meet the Mississippi downstream. It was up slightly, and David wondered fleetingly if he really could survive in the treacherous swirling waters of the Arkansas River.

He glanced over his shoulder. Young and the guard had fallen back. The security head was red-faced and puffing, gasping for air. The guard was not much better off, but he was the closer of the two and represented the more immediate danger.

David sprinted for the park gate just below the I-30 bridge. He was almost there when he became aware of a nearby presence.

9

Morton Powell awakened in the trunk of the car where Wayne Young had left him. He had believed all his life that the only good in the world was the good man produced. And should man choose not to produce that good, chaos would reign.

Now, as he lay in the darkness of the cramped trunk, his chest on fire from the guard's bullet, he felt a presence that transcended any he had ever known. He had heard about and read the stories of near-death experiences—of the white light and the peaceful feeling. He had discounted the stories as the fantasies and ravings of religious fanatics, the illusions of oxygen-deprived brains.

Something was with him in the damp coldness of the trunk. It was not the evil presence he had experienced earlier on the top floor of the CCI building. It was an all-encompassing, all-compassionate presence. He thumped his head against the floor of the trunk to be sure he was awake. He was. This was not a dream.

In that instant of love and warmth that transcended any he had ever known, Morton Powell, special agent for the FBI, knew that a God existed and that Jesus was his Son. He knew the stories. They had filled his memory from childhood. They had always been nothing more than fables, worn for the telling over the years.

In a split second, an unbeliever became a believer. It was that belief that saved David Michaels's life.

10

He had experienced it before—Vietnam, Saudi Arabia, and in the CCI building—but never like this. David Michaels recognized the smell of evil, and as he pulled up short in front of a green Mercedes, he knew instantly that it was evil in all its malignant malevolence standing before him.

A man leaned against the sedan, arms folded, a smile on his misshapen features. David recognized the incarnation of pure evil, the face of a demon exposed.

"This is as far as you go, Chaplain," the man hissed. Lightening crackled above the two men, splitting the sky.

"I don't think so," David answered, his heart pounding, his pulse racing in spite of his conditioning. David recognized the initial signs of terror.

The man moved toward David; David did not move. The demon hesitated.

"He who hesitates is lost," David smiled, knowing the battle now raged in front of him. Time was suspended, irrelevant to the events being played out on the Little Rock street.

David quickly surveyed his surroundings. He was in the middle of a city street. Brick walls of silent buildings lined both sides of the street. In front of him, the man leaned against the green Mercedes. To his rear, somewhere, Young and the guard were pursuing him.

"Won't do you any good, preacher," the man said. "Ain't no place to run."

"I have no intention of running," David shot back, the terror still with him, but somehow diminished.

The man's mouth twisted into a distorted slash. "You're dead, Chaplain," he hissed.

Another bolt of lightening leapt from the ever-darkening clouds, striking the flag mast of a nearby building. "That is only a fraction of the power at my disposal, Chaplain." The word "chaplain" came out as a curse.

The thunder struck David with the power of a sledgehammer; the impact drove him to his knees. He had never experienced such force before, not even from enemy shelling.

David rose, forcing his weakened legs to support him; he stared into the man's yellow eyes. Never in his life had he experienced such pure evil . . . He felt the hair stand up on the back of his neck. Except for the thunder and lightening, there were no other sounds around him. He instinctively knew he could not break eye contact with this being. David knew he faced the ultimate test of his faith in this encounter. Logic and reason had nothing to offer here. Would he choose to stand in the power of God or would he crumble in the face of evil? Here, there was no room for doubt.

"I suspect Mr. Young did not know who he was dealing with when he hired you," David said.

The man laughed. "Young is a fool. He has no concept of evil, not real evil. He will learn in time."

"Young did not pit you against me, did he?"

"I am impressed, Chaplain. But then that is why you were chosen. You are too intuitive for your own good. Young had nothing to do with this encounter, despite what he might think. This showdown has been long in coming. You are a threat to us. Fanatics we can deal with. They may mislead a few misguided souls now and then, but their actions are so unreasonable that intelligent people easily dismiss their rantings. But you, you struggle through your doubts and find true faith. You have not seen and yet you still believe. We must stop people like you, people who understand what faith really means, people who can persuade those who have the power to change the world. God has plans for you, plans beyond your wildest dreams. And we cannot allow those plans to be accomplished. I have been given the power to dispose of you," the man smiled.

"Your power is nothing," David responded, his eyes challenging the man.

A shrill laugh erupted from the man. "Nothing! Nothing, you say?" He moved toward David slowly, his hand waving toward the sky. Lightening again slashed across the heavens.

David resisted the urge to flee, knowing such a breach of faith would cost him his life. He uttered a silent prayer.

"Nothing, Chaplain? Mine is the power of the ages, of the eons," the man screamed. "It is much more than nothing. It is the power of the depths, of history, of eternity! You, you have no power. Watch and see." Suddenly lightning flashed and thunder rolled, but this thunder shook the earth as well. Once again, David was knocked to his knees. "There is my power. Show me yours."

In an instant, David knew the lie for what it was. He climbed to his feet. "I repeat, your power is nothing. It comes from the depths, that is true. But you have no control over me. You may control a portion of this physical world, but that is nothing. You are nothing more than a hireling, and a poor one at that. I have no power to show you. The only power I claim is the only one I need—the power of Jesus' name. In that name, I stand," David said. A roar exploded from the deepest regions of the man's being; a horrific odor enveloped David at the same time.

David felt a wave of nausea sweep over him; he fought the urge to retch. Fear enveloped him like a blanket. As the spiritual conflict intensified, David grew aware of allies he couldn't see. Prayers were being offered on his behalf, forming a protective barrier around him.

"You will die, Chaplain," the man screeched, moving closer, his putrid breath coming at David in waves. "It will be a most horrible death. The men who pursue you will see to it. I will see to it."

David sensed an unseen power infuse him with courage and truth, as if an inner light had been switched on. He smiled at the man; the simple gesture enraged the demon. "Death is not defeat," David said softly. "That is, and always has been, your greatest mistake. Your lies are transparent to any who care to examine them. Truth will always defeat you, and truth is to be had only for the asking. Jesus is the truth."

At the name of Jesus, the man's hands flew to his ears; a piercing scream cut the air.

For David, the sound was strangely comforting.

"You have existed even before the dawn of humanity," David continued, pressing the confrontation. "Too bad you have never understood the art of humanity. You are defeated, demon. You have been since Calvary. Go back to your leader, if you dare, and tell him he has lost again."

The demon's countenance changed before David's eyes. From the form of a man, he was transformed into a figure no more than two feet tall, its misshapen features resembling the face of a melting wax figure, its limbs bent and twisted at odd angles. Only the eyes remained the same, a putrid, bilious yellow.

David understood in an instant. He had recognized the evil for what it was—not the strong, vigorous figure of the man who had driven the Mercedes, but a small, insignificant form that haunted the darker reaches of man's memory, given strength only when man chose to ignore the Light of the World.

The creature's grotesque grin was swallowed by a set of misshapened teeth in a guttural hiss. He had expected David Michaels to flee, to run for his life. But the navy chaplain had stood his ground in complete confidence. The creature's strength was gone. At that moment, that moment of faith, he had been defeated. His power, the power of doubt and fear, was gone. The prayers issuing forth from First Community Church and the homes in Clayton pierced the demon's putrid flesh like flaming arrows. The pain was unbearable.

Lightening illuminated the streets again; the thunder rattled the windows of surrounding buildings. But this time it was different. The power was gone; time had been restored.

Young and the guard were on top of him now, their pistols pointed at David's chest. David saw the self-satisfied smirk crease Wayne Young's face as the security head tightened his finger on the trigger. David could see the man's finger whiten with the pressure.

"Drop it!" a voice shouted from behind the two men.

Both whirled in unison at the sound of the shouted command. Their pistols were up, each prepared to shoot. Two shots split the air, reverberating off the brick and concrete walls surrounding them. Wayne Young was thrown backwards by an unseen force. The guard was spun around like a child's top, a 9 mm slug breaking his right arm.

Both men were down. Wayne Young was dead. The bullet had struck him dead center, penetrating his heart and killing him instantly. The big guard's arm was shattered, twisted beneath him at a sickening angle.

David Michaels was stunned. He had not seen the man who shouted; he had only heard the command and then the shots. As Sheriff Tom Frazier ran to the two downed men, David felt a sudden surge of relief.

"Frazier! How'd you get here? What's going on?"

"All in good time, David." the sheriff said, holstering his weapon and reaching for his wallet. "Take a look at this and you might begin to understand," Frazier continued, bending over to examine the two men he had shot.

David took the wallet and examined the plastic-encased identification card. It identified Tom Frazier as an agent working out of the office of the president of the United States. Tom Frazier was a federal agent, a very special federal agent working on a very special federal case.

David Michaels turned back to where the green Mercedes and its demon-owner had stood only seconds earlier. Both had disappeared, as had the nauseating odor.

David knew he would have to face the evil again, perhaps much sooner than he would like.

EPILOGUE

1

The view from Morton Powell's hospital room in Little Rock's Baptist Memorial Hospital faced west. David Michaels could see the busy Interstate-430 bypass that bordered Little Rock in that direction, the same roadway the two men had taken into the city what seemed like eons ago. Cars and trucks traveled the highway, oblivious to the struggle between good and evil that had just occurred in the Arkansas capital city.

"What's to see out there that's so interesting?" Powell asked.

"People," David answered. "Most of whom don't know that good and evil even exist. To most, they're just abstract concepts. No absolutes. It's a dangerous thought pattern to get into," the chaplain added as he turned to the man in the bed.

An IV ran into Powell's right arm, a portable heart monitor recorded his life force, and a chest tube extended from his left side. *Not bad,* David thought, *only three days out of surgery.*

"You have to give people the benefit of the doubt, David," Powell said. "After all, if I can become a believer, anyone can."

"That's just the point," David argued. "Anyone can. It's not magic. There's no hocus-pocus to it. You just do it."

"That's the hard part," Powell interjected. "It sounds so simple that it's hard to believe salvation is that easy, that accessible."

"It *is* simple," corrected David. "As for easy, you'll probably learn that being a Christian in today's world is one of the toughest things you will ever do. But it's worth every minute of it," he added.

"I know," Morton Powell admitted, grimacing as a bolt of pain shot through his body. Breathing was difficult. He settled back in the bed and asked, "What about Tom Frazier?"

"He was more than a sheriff. Actually, he was working for the Office of the President all along. He's been on this case for more than eight years. He told me the Nuclear Regulatory Commission and the Atomic Energy Commission got interested in Collins after Three Mile Island. Instead of sending out their own investigators, who at that point were somewhat suspect, they petitioned the president for his involvement. Frazier was assigned the task of documenting the charges against Collins. Eight years ago, when it became evident that CCI would get the contract to build Arkansas' Nuclear Three and Four, the government rigged the election to have Frazier win. As it turned out, that was not necessary because Tom was from the area and the people knew and trusted him. He actually won fair and square."

"And he kept up with the activity in Clayton. A cop operating undercover as another cop. There's a certain irony to that, don't you think?"

"I hadn't thought about that angle," David conceded. He walked back to the window and gazed over the rolling hills of western Little Rock. "The Office of the President, the NRC, the AEC, and the FBI have been on this a long time." David turned back to Powell. "Your own fellow agents didn't even tell you about it. They were working through the OCTF, using that as their cover. You naturally assumed CCI had some organized crime connection. It didn't, but the agents investigating CCI had reached a stalemate, so they assigned you. Seems you have a reputation as a maverick. You went to work, and I just happened to appear on the scene at an opportune time. The decision was to let you and me run loose and see what we could shake up."

"We shook up plenty," Powell coughed and gritted his teeth.

"That we did," David agreed.

"What about Emerson and Kirby?"

"Both arrested. The president knew Kirby was involved all along. He needed evidence, though. The computer disks from the CCI computer network gave enough information to hang most of the CCI management."

"They can't be used as evidence. I got that information illegally," Powell reminded David.

"Technically, *I* got it. All you did was record it. The computer drive never left the building in your possession. I had to go back to retrieve it. Seems there's enough legal difference there to make it admissible. A law enforcement officer didn't steal the information, a citizen provided it. They'll hang."

The wide door opened, and Tom Frazier entered the room. "How are the heroes today?" he joked.

"I'm great," David answered. "Mort's a little out of it. Says he doesn't like being shot, even in the line of duty."

"I can identify with that," Frazier grinned.

"By the way, thanks again for saving my life," David said.

"Same here." Powell recoiled at a new stab of pain.

"My job. The president would have had my head if I'd let you two get injured any worse than you already are. If you ever need a job, let me know. We could use some men like you in the Office of the President. By the way, CCI was into laundering drug money from the Cali cartel in Colombia. That's what necessitated Kirby's initial involvement. We shut down a dual operation when we stopped Kirby and Emerson Collins."

"Evil has a way of multiplying under the right circumstances," David mused and then joked, "I guess we should feel important, being in the company of a man who speaks directly to the president," David chided.

"Not really. I worked for OOP long before Don Adams was elected. Not too many people even know our department exists. That's the way we like it, by the way. I have to admit that it's been nice, knowing the president on a personal basis. We played ball together. When he was elected, he kept me on in my present status. Actually, as an investigator for OOP, I'm supposedly out of control of the incoming president, but who's going to stay on the job if the man wants you out? I got lucky."

"Your luck rubbed off on us, thankfully," David added.

"What about you, David? When are you going back to Pendleton?"

"I think I'll hang around for a while. A little church up in Clayton can use me, I think."

"Not to mention a certain county clerk," Frazier smiled.

"Is it that obvious?"

"It's all over your face. And hers. She told me to tell you she'll be waiting when you get back to Clayton."

"You going to stay on as sheriff?"

"Nope. My job's over up there. I'm leaving a lot to clean up, though. I think I know a perfect candidate for the job."

"Janice Morgan."

"She'll be the first female sheriff in Arkansas," Tom Frazier said. "Might start a trend."

"What about the Nuclear Three and Four? A lot of money has been sunk into that place."

"Seems Jameson Collins never was part of this conspiracy. He was more like the pretty face. Emerson was the brains behind CCI—the evil part of CCI, that is. With Emerson gone, Jameson is taking over, under the watchful eye of government regulators. He's pledged to build the reactor to specifications, even if he has to tear it all down and begin again," Frazier explained. "He's also reviewing every overseas project for viability and conformance. If any laws have been broken, Jameson says the project will be scrapped. He's already placed a hold on component shipments."

Frazier turned to leave. "I will see you both again. In the meantime, take care." Frazier turned to David, "As far as knowing someone who talks to the president, I consider myself privileged to know a man who talks to God the way you do."

"Amen," Morton Powell said and smiled weakly.

"Take care, Tom," David said as the man disappeared out the door. He turned back to Morton Powell. "I'd better be going. The nurse told me to stay only a few minutes. I'm pushing it."

"Do me a favor, David. Pray with me before you leave."

David knelt beside the bed as Morton Powell prayed. It was not an elegant prayer, but it was sincere. When Powell said "amen," David rose and with a last look at the man in the bed, walked out of the room. Tomorrow was Sunday, and he had some thinking to do. He had accepted an invitation from Rev. Shackleford to preach the morning sermon at First Community Church, and in less than three hours, he had an appointment to meet with the preacher in the pastor's study at the church. He also needed to talk to a certain county clerk.

2

The pastor's study at First Community Church seemed smaller than most, but to David, it did not have the same claustrophobic bent as others he'd been in. For some reason, it felt more like a den one might find in one of the older homes that dominated the area around the church.

"You've been through quite an experience," the old pastor said, his elbow resting on the desk, his fingers peaked under his chin.

"That's somewhat of an understatement," David acknowledged. "I had no idea what I was getting into when I started looking into Jimmy's death."

The old man leaned back in his chair. The springs squeaked a gentle rebuke. "Now I've got something else for you to think about. I'm within a few months of retiring. This church needs some fresh blood, fresh views. You would be perfect. What would you think about taking over the pulpit of First Community? Before you answer, let me say a few things." The old pastor rose from the chair and walked to the framed photos hanging on the study's wall. They were all pictures of the church at varying stages of growth. "This is not a large church as churches go. But the congregation is dedicated and motivated. That's more than can be said for many larger congregations. There's a spirit of love and cooperation here that you can't find everywhere, especially in the military."

With those last words, Shackleford turned to David. "I think it just might be the place for you after all that's happened. I know it would be the place for you if we were to ask your father. He would never say it, but I think he hopes you will stay for a while. Jimmy's death was a tragedy. It will take a lot of love and understanding for the family to overcome it. And by family, I include you."

"I know what you say is true, but I'm not so sure my military experience will translate to a local church. The service is a different world. It has its own rules, its own way of doing things. I might do more damage than good."

"You're still a preacher, and once a preacher, always a preacher."

David shook his head. "I've been fighting that battle since I've been in the military. A chaplain and a civilian preacher are not even close to the same animal."

The old preacher smiled, a wide, open-faced grin. "I've heard that argument before. I'm not sure who first used it—probably some chaplain who was afraid to face the 'civilian populace,' as you call it, or some preacher trying to stay out of the military. You see, the argument could go both ways. It doesn't matter. I've known both, and the only difference between the two is a matter of semantics. We all fight the same battles, spiritually speaking, that is. You would be good for this church."

David rose from his chair and walked to the wall where Rev. Shackleford stood. He scanned the photos on the wall. The old man's words had the ring of truth, truth that he himself had begun to see. After all, the argument had been boiling in his mind these last days, had it not? Wasn't it time for a change, to accept the defeats and victories he had won during his military career and try to do what he could here in Clayton? The offer was tempting.

"You're preaching the Sunday morning service," the old man stated. "Let that be your test. If you feel God speaking to you through that message, then you do what he tells you, not what this old man or anyone else advises. This is between you and God. How's that?"

David thought about it for a moment, then nodded. "That's fair enough. We'll both see what God has to say about this."

"Good! Good! Now that it's settled, let's have some coffee. I think the drugstore is still open. You been there since you been back?"

David laughed. "Once. I still owe some of the boys down there a cup of coffee. Let's go pay up."

The two men walked from the church. Outside, the storm system, which had plagued the state for the last week, was quickly being blown away by the clear air of a new cold front. Blue sky and sunshine replaced the rain clouds, and the two men walked along, neither talking, both enjoying the creation of God.

3

Allen Stuart strolled along the walk bordering Lake Geneva. His plane had landed late, and he had spent the night in a hotel near the *Banque Internationale de Commerce,* where he was now headed to make the half-million-dollar transfer from CCI overseas stock to cash. Plus interest, he reminded himself.

The facade of the bank was impressive in its early Baroque architecture. For Stuart, the bank's appearance represented the stability he associated with the Swiss banking system.

Stuart pushed through the doors and went directly to the offices lining the far left wall. He located the office that handled money transfers between countries and knocked.

"Kommen zie!" a voice ordered in German.

Stuart entered the impressive office. "I'm Allen Stuart, and I need to initiate an overseas funds transfer," he indicated.

The man motioned Stuart to a chair. "What type of funds transfer are we speaking of?"

Allen Stuart handed the man the portfolio he carried. "I need these stocks converted to cash and the cash wire-transferred to the bank at the bottom of that paper."

The man took the papers and perused them quickly, looking up only once. "Excuse me one moment, sir. I need to confer with my manager."

Stuart felt a twinge of uneasiness creep up his spine, but brushed it aside. *A half million dollars will ease the uncertainty,* he thought.

The man returned; he was followed by a short, balding man of about sixty. The short man was holding the paper that represented the

EPILOGUE

rest of Allen Stuart's life in comfort and leisure.

"*Herr* Stuart," the man began. "I am Ulrich Fritchard, the manager of this bank. It is my duty to inform you of a most unfortunate set of circumstances directly connected to your fund account."

Allen Stuart shot out of his chair. "What circumstances?" he demanded.

"Unfortunately, we are unable to convert your overseas holding to cash at this time. I regret the circumstances that precipitate such a stance."

"What do you mean, *unable*?" Allen Stuart demanded, his voice rising with ever syllable.

"As of last night, the president of the United States, your president, froze all assets of Collins Construction International. That carries over to this stock fund. We have to honor the request according to international agreement. I'm sorry."

"That's impossible!" Stuart screamed.

Bank customers throughout the building looked up, startled by the outburst of the American in the far office.

"On the contrary. It is not only possible, but it has happened. I must ask you to leave, sir. We are not accustomed to having customers raise their voices in our bank."

"I'll do more than raise my voice," Stuart began. Before he could finish, he was in the arms of two burly guards who lifted him off the floor and ejected him from the building. He turned to reenter the bank and was stopped by the two men who had remained outside with orders to see to it that the brash American did not return.

Stuart stared at the two men for a long moment, then turned and left.

The next morning, the Geneva papers carried the story of an American who had committed suicide the night before. The only identification on the body was a bank book from an Argentine bank, showing a zero balance.

4

"You're staying, then," Cindy Tolbert said.

"I've thought about what you said. About what Rev. Shackleford said. It's time I give up one life for another," David explained, not certain at this point how to continue, how to tell Cindy Tolbert that he had fallen in love with her, wanted to be with her, to see her every day. He said nothing about his agreement with the old pastor about letting God decide his fate during the Sunday morning service. Already he had felt God's hand in the process. The sermon, he was certain, would only confirm what he now knew, what he felt in his heart.

"Does your decision have anything to do with me?" Cindy asked.

David smiled at the question. He was only just beginning to understand the meaning of "woman's intuition."

"It has everything to do with you," he confessed. "More you than anything else in this town." The two were seated in the living room of James Michaels's home. David rose from his chair and walked over to where Cindy sat on the sofa. He sat down beside her, allowing his arm to ease around her shoulders. "I'm not going to say you're the only factor in this decision. That would be a lie. I think Dad, Jean, and the boys need me around. We've got a lot of grief to work through. I'll miss Jimmy, but at least I'll be close to the people he loved. But I'll also be close to you, and that means a lot to me."

She looked into David's face. "You're sure about this? I don't want you to realize a few months from now that you did the wrong thing and then start blaming me. I'm in love with you, David Michaels. I guess I always have been, in one way or another. But I don't want that to deprive you of what you really want."

David looked down into the green eyes, understanding what love was all about. "I'm just now beginning to realize what I really want. I suspect, when I examine my earlier motives for continuing in the military, I'll find them lacking. Despite what has happened in these last days, I am happier now than I've been in all my years of service."

Cindy snuggled into the curve of David's embrace. For her, it felt like home.

"I love you, Cindy Tolbert," David whispered, his embrace tightening, his spirit soaring. He had never in all his life felt so alive and loved.

5

The Sunday morning following his visit with Morton Powell and his conversation with Rev. Shackleford, David Michaels preached his first sermon at First Community Church of Clayton. His text was Ephesians 6:10–18.

The next week, in an all-church business meeting, David Michaels was unanimously selected as the next pastor to succeed Rev. Glen Shackleford.

Two weeks later, David Michaels drove out the main gate of Camp Pendleton, California, for the last time.

...More Spine-Tingling
Fiction Thrillers

Murder On The Titanic
Jim Walker

An unsolvable murder. An impenetrable briefcase. An unsinkable ship. A mystery not to be missed! Stumbling upon a robbery, a bewildered aristocrat is compelled by the dying victim to deliver a secret message to the American War Department. He is given only two things: a briefcase and a first-class ticket aboard the Titanic. That's just the beginning of Morgan Fairfield's remarkable adventure in this dazzling mystery full of startling surprises and labyrinthine twists. Using the Titanic's historic voyage and tragedy as a backdrop, the story follows the fictional hero as he tries to stay alive and protect his valuable cargo – a proposed peace treaty.

0-8054-6279-1

Guilt By Association
Michael Farris

When a pro-life group begins a peaceful protest against an abortion clinic, they find themselves at war with the clinic's owners in their small college town. The protesters carefully avoid illegal or extreme behavior, but the clinic's owners hire an infiltrator to escalate the conflict. The clinic burns to the ground in a tragic fire. Suzie O'Dell, a college student on the clinic's board, is charged with the crime. In the face of daunting evidence to the contrary, the pro-life group hires Peter Barron to fight the charges in Federal Court.

0-8054-0155-5

Anonymous Tip
Michael Farris

Anonymous Tip will keep you on the edge of your seat as Gwen Landis and four-year-old Casey fight a system driven by jealousy, ambition, and a drift toward ever-greater intrusion in the lives and hearts of families. With God on their side, Gwen and Casey learn to draw on faith they never knew they had to battle a faceless, nameless accuser whose words could separate them forever.

0-8054-6293-7

Circumstantial Evidence
James Scott Bell

Tracy Shepherd is a young widow with two small children, working as a deputy district attorney in Los Angeles. When she gets her first murder case – the gangland killing of a Hollywood producer – she wonders if she's up to the task. But soon she feels something just isn't right. The evidence seems weak, witnesses are afraid to talk, and she begins receiving anonymous threats. Someone is out to get her. But who? And why? In the murky world of the criminal justice system, a world that challenges her Christian faith and threatens her very life, Tracy Shepherd must somehow survive. And see that justice is done.

0-8054-6359-3

Available at fine bookstores everywhere